THE ADVENTURES OF PETER
THE BRAZEN, VOLUME 5

George F. Worts

Tarantula Tower: The Adventures of
Scarlet and Bradshaw, Volume 4

BY THEODORE ROSCOE

Henry Plays a Hunch: The Complete
Tales of Sheriff Henry, Volume 5

W.C. TUTTLE

King of the Dead: The Saga of Monella, Volume 3

FRANK AUBREY

The Monster of the Lagoon: The Complete
Adventures of Singapore Sammy, Volume 3

GEORGE F. WORTS

The Fourteen Points

ARTHUR B. REEVE

War Dragons: The Complete Adventures of
Cordie, Soldier of Fortune, Volume 4

W. WIRT

Shark Trail: The Complete Adventures
of Bellow Bill Williams, Volume 3

RALPH R. PERRY

Minions of the Shadow

WILLIAM GRAY BEYER

Rats of the Harbor: The Complete
Cases of Dirk and Baker

RAY CUMMINGS

CAVE OF THE BLUE SCORPION

THE COMPLETE ADVENTURES OF PETER THE BRAZEN, VOLUME 5

LORING BRENT

ILLUSTRATED BY

SAMUEL CAHAN
DOUGLAS HILLIKER
JOHN R. NEILL

COVER BY

PAUL STAHR

STEEGER BOOKS • 2021

PUBLISHING HISTORY

"Vampire" originally appeared in the April 25 & May 2, 1931 issues of *Argosy* magazine (Vol. 220, Nos. 4 & 5). Copyright © 1931 by The Frank A. Munsey Company. Copyright renewed © 1958 and assigned to Steeger Properties, LLC. All rights reserved.

"Chinese for Racket" originally appeared in the May 30 & June 6, 1931 issues of *Argosy* magazine (Vol. 221, Nos. 3 & 4). Copyright © 1931 by The Frank A. Munsey Company. Copyright renewed © 1958 and assigned to Steeger Properties, LLC. All rights reserved.

"Cave of the Blue Scorpion" originally appeared in the November 21, 1931 issue of *Argosy* magazine (Vol. 225, No. 4). Copyright © 1931 by The Frank A. Munsey Company. Copyright renewed © 1959 and assigned to Steeger Properties, LLC. All rights reserved.

"About the Author" originally appeared in the January 25, 1930 issue of *Argosy* magazine (Vol. 209, No. 5). Copyright © 1930 by The Frank A. Munsey Company. Copyright renewed © 1957 and assigned to Steeger Properties, LLC. All rights reserved.

Visit argosymagazine.com for more books like this.

TABLE OF CONTENTS

VAMPIRE

*Groans heard through the fog on the Hongkong
water front lead Peter Moore, known to all
the East as Peter the Brazen, into the most
gruesome adventure of his colorful career*

CHAPTER I

THE WOMAN OF HORROR

THAT SHOCKING EXPERIENCE in the fog on the Hong-kong water front was an episode left dangling, so to speak, in mid-air—with the power of sending iced winds down Peter Moore's spine for hours afterward. It was an Oriental mystery without beginning, end, or solution. Or so it seemed at the time.

The tall American was swinging down the bund, having just left the musty offices of a coastwise steamship company with a ticket to Shanghai stowed away in his pocket.

Dusk and fog had fallen upon the "Pearl of Asia." The tepid water of the Pei-Kiang, which drains the heart of Southern China, had encountered chill air currents, and the warm river vapors were magically transformed into billowing yellow visibility.

There is something almost tangible about a Hongkong fog—tangible and menacing. Some fogs are gray. A Hongkong fog is yellow. Eerie shapes seem to swirl and writhe about in it, as evil genii might swirl and writhe in the smoke bubbling up from an Oriental sorcerer's incense-pot. The winds sliding off the hill-tops do this.

To his left, as Peter Moore struck down the bund toward his hotel, golden blurs and patches of light showed feebly where granite office buildings were. These solid evidences of modern civilization were offset by the crooked ugly spars of shipping on his right—fishing junks and sampans where some of China's teeming millions live and die—like rats.

The odor of Oriental evening cookery was in the dank air—
the sour smells of rice and weeds and fish stewing on char-
coal braziers. And from some hulk afar came the muffled,
measured beating of a witch doctor's medicine drum, as sinister, as blood-stirring as the tom-tom of an African tribe. It got
under your skin, that noise. And into your blood.

In spite of himself, Peter Moore kept time to it. *Tumpa-dum-
dum! Tumpa-dum-dum!*

A slim dark figure materialized startlingly from the fog and
collided with him. He caught a brief glimpse of a Eurasian girl's
tragic white face, with its enormous staring black eyes, a red slash
for a mouth. She sprang back from him with a long-drawn hiss
and vanished into the fog.

Tumpa-dum-dum! Tumpa-dum-dum! The fog was thicker
now. Vague shapes slithered past. It was a night for strange and
sinister affairs to be afoot.

Strange, how the fog cheated your senses. The mournful whistle of a tramp freighter seemed to be suspended in the air a
dozen feet above his head. An odor of spices was so intense that
a hand containing them might have been drawn an inch under
his nose. Next thing it was opium.

Through a rift in the mist he saw a heavy door swing open.
Beyond was another door of finely wrought iron. And beyond
this fantastic grille was a room of scarlet, as bright as the heart of
the half-set sun. Gilt embroidery glowed on cushions and walls
of vivid scarlet satin. A half-naked black woman was sprawled
on scarlet satin cushions eagerly drawing at a white opium pipe.
It might have been silver or even platinum.

Peter saw the powder-blue smoke squirt in twin jets from her
black nostrils; caught the momentary gleam of pearl-white teeth
in a red and savage grin, then the door went shut with a thud like
that of a heavy teak scuttle-hatch cover being dropped in place.

One saw such things in daytime Hongkong and thought
nothing of it. Dusk and the fog lent them vividness and mystery.

WATER GURGLED at Peter's feet. He had the sense of being

He reached over the retaining wall

lost. Then a terrifying sound came across the water. A voice in agony:

"Oh, my God! Oh, my God!" Over and over.

Peter Moore stopped sharply. It chanced that the moaning voice had stopped him at a spot almost under a street light, but the glow from that source was of little assistance. The strong rays penetrated a few feet and were greedily devoured by the fog.

Layers of fog like countless layers of straw-colored chiffon drifted about on the surface of the water at his feet. He knew that he was somewhere near the jetty, because no sampans were moored inshore here.

He bent down and tried to see through the swirling vapors until his eyes ached. The voice was gurgling and moaning still. It was distinguished by a weird whistling, as of breath being sucked through a parched throat—a slim ghost of sound destined to haunt the American throughout that night.

Some one out there was struggling toward shore, fighting for very life. In prickling suspense, Peter waited. There was nothing he could do. The thin whistling, the labored groaning came closer. Now it was attended by a feeble splashing. The sobbing of a man in the depths of agony followed.

Peter's heart was trip-hammering high in his chest. He felt chill moisture ooze out on his forehead and the palms of his hands. Those sounds, coming from an unseen spot in the fog, were terrifying. The position from which the sounds seemed to come would change! First, they would come from the right, then from the left.

Then suddenly he saw something moving toward him in the water, only an arm's-length away—a feebly moving hand, then a head from which blood was welling and flowing down.

Peter reached down from the stone retaining wall and grasped the hand. The weird whistling of indrawn breath occurred; then the sobbing, agonized voice, "Oh—God!"

Peter said sharply: "Give me your other hand."

The other hand came out of the dirty yellow water, fumbled for his. Both these hands which he grasped were as cold, as clammy as seaweed.

Dimly in the fog he saw the man's face as he pulled him up to a sitting position on the retaining wall; the slender face of a man of thirty, twisted with torture.

He was naked to the waist. The entire top of his head was like a pool of blood, which overflowed and ran down his neck to his shoulder's. There, mingling with sea water, it ran down in thin diluted streams. And blood flowed from a deep puncture, such as might have been made with a skewer, in his left wrist. Blood pulsed from the small round hole there.

The man was breathing in short, whistling gasps. His eyes were glazed with terror and pain.

"Don't let them get me!" he whimpered. "They're after me! I know they started after me!"

"Who?" Peter gasped.

"That—that woman and that yellow devil! She had eyes just like a snake's—and not a hair on her head! They held me down and pumped my blood into her! She had teeth like a rat's—and there wasn't a hair on her head! They scalped me! Look at me! They took knives and scalped me! Give me a drink!"

"I'll get you some brandy, and call the police and a doctor," Peter said.

"Don't go! Wait! If you leave me, they'll get me! Look at my head! They held me down and pumped my blood into her arm through a rubber tube. And while they were pumping my blood into her, they took these knives and held me so I couldn't move and scalped me. They—"

"Who are they?" Peter savagely demanded. "Where are they?"

The pain-sick eyes rolled.

"That woman without any hair on her head—and that yellow devil! He said it was an experiment. He said he was going to scalp me to see if it could be done, because he was going to graft somebody's scalp on her head—"

"Don't you know who they are?" Peter cried. "Don't you know whether it was a sampan or a junk?" It was all too horribly Oriental to have occurred elsewhere but aboard a sampan or a junk.

The tortured man did not answer. He had fainted. Peter paused only long enough to bind a handkerchief about that pulsing hole in the unknown's wrist.

THEN HE started off at a run toward a grog shop a half block away. He collided with a man, knocked him aside, and ran on. As he ran, the sound of the devil-drum kept time with him. *Tumpa-dum-dum! Tumpa-dum-dum!* Through this measured drumming he heard a different sound—the muffled exhaust of a powerful motor boat.

Peter found the grog shop. He tossed a bill down on the counter and barked, "Give me a pint of good brandy. Send for the police and a doctor at once. A man has been almost murdered. You'll find us under the street light nearest the small boat jetty. Hurry!"

The bartender stuttered, "Y-yes, sir!" and Peter ran out, The fog was closing down in earnest now. Ships at anchor were creating a din with their whistles. The beating of the drum had stopped or was drowned out.

Peter's face was dripping with sweat when he returned to the street light Under that street light he stopped and stared about him in bewilderment.

The unknown victim of Oriental torturers was gone!

Peter shouted. His voice was like that of a man in a dream. The episode, from beginning to end, was already beginning to have the fantastic quality of a nightmare.

He ran on down the retaining wall to the next street light, thinking he might have made a mistake. The tortured victim of "a woman with eyes like a snake's and not a hair on her head," was nowhere to be seen.

He ran back to the other light; he struck matches, and found splotches of blood, pools of blood mingling with the mud.

While he stood, shivering with apprehension, he heard again the muttering of the motor boat's exhaust. He cried, "Motor boat, ahoy! Ahoy, there!"

There was no answer for a moment; then he heard the unmistakable sound of the man's whistling breath. For a moment he believed that the poor devil had leaped into the water to kill himself.

Then Peter heard a low, hissing voice, followed by the man's whistling, "Help! Oh, God! No! No!" This frantic entreaty was followed by a gurgling sob, then a strangling sound, low on the water.

Peter shouted, "Ahoy, there! Damn you, ahoy!"

Silence was broken by the sprightly purring of the motor boat's exhaust. This grew rapidly fainter, until it merged with the harbor hubbub.

It was Peter's guess, impossible to verify, that the scalped man had been overtaken by his torturers, snatched back into the water, drowned.

He started for the sampan jetty with the intention of hiring a sampan and making a search. The obvious futility of such an attempt halted him.

PETER LEANED against the lamp post, suddenly weak with fury and sickness. There was nothing he could do. Hongkong harbor, aswarm with mysteries, had simply tossed up at his feet the human victim of some fiendish Oriental plan, and snatched him back into the yellow fog whence he came. A story of blood-chilling horror, without beginning or end, was told. That was all.

The brandy bottle slipped out of Peter's limp fingers to the stone pavement and smashed.

He accused himself of cruel stupidity for not staying with the poor devil until his shouts brought help. Why had he abandoned him to this further horrible fate?

There was nothing to do now. Police would arrive in a moment. They would listen to him skeptically; raise their eyebrows, and exchange glances. They would point out to him the futility of attempting to find an unknown boat among those thousands of unknown boats with which Hongkong harbor is cluttered—or they would see a sinister connection between him and that blood at his feet.

Peter did not want to be questioned by the police. They could accomplish nothing. No one could do anything for that poor sobbing devil now. A grim incident of a fogbound Hongkong evening was closed.

But it wasn't closed for Peter. As he started on toward his hotel, cold, weak, trembling, Peter heard again the whistled babblings of the tortured man and tried to piece sense out of them.

He had been the victim, it would seem, of a modern kind of Oriental vampire; a horrible, hairless woman with snakelike eyes who had employed him for a blood transfusion. But why had the unfortunate man's scalp been sliced off? He had said, "They were scalping me to see if it could be done, because he was going to graft somebody else's scalp on her naked head." It sounded too horrible to be true.

Was all this part of some hideous old Oriental ceremony of

which Peter had never heard? He would probably never know. He was certain now on one point; he wanted to get it all out of his mind as quickly as possible.

Peter would have been sicker still if he could have foreseen the fantastic part this snake-eyed, hairless vampire was to play in his own affairs.

CHAPTER II

STRANGE INVITATIONS

THE WARMTH AND brightness of the Oriental Hotel lobby was a welcome relief from the clammy fog and the experience he had just undergone. An American tourist party had just come in from a Canton River boat. Young men and girls were chattering gayly over their experiences. A pretty debutante glanced at Peter, and her glance became a stare of candid curiosity.

Peter went on to the desk. The clerk looked at him and said, "Mr. Moore, are you ill? You are terribly pale."

"I'll shake it off," Peter said. "Is there any mail for me?"

He was hoping there would be a letter or a cablegram from Susan O'Gilvie. Susan was in Manila; had gone to the Philippines about two weeks previously, looking for thrills. He had missed her. And he certainly needed some one like her now. Susan was sunny, bright, always gay.

When Susan was away from him, he was convinced he was in love with her. It was when she was with him and manifesting her insatiable love for dangerous thrills and mad adventure that he realized what a mistake any sane man would make to marry Susan. But Peter wasn't sane now. He was sick and furious and full of hatred for China.

The clerk handed him three missives—a cablegram, an unstamped envelope with his name written across it with a flourish, and a chit. Peter opened the cablegram first. It bore a Schenectady, New York, date line, and read:

Advise urgency in Fong Toy deal. Am advised other interests are hot on trail.

It was signed Corliss. Bill Corliss was Peter Moore's immediate superior in the radio research division of the General Electric Company. And Fong Toy was a brilliant young Chinese scientist who had perfected in his Hongkong laboratories a device for eliminating static from radio reception.

Fong Toy had so far proved inaccessible to Peter. The young Chinese was shy, or calculating. Peter did not have to be told by Bill Corliss that Japanese, English and German radio concerns were also on Fong Toy's trail. Failing or succeeding to see Fong Toy this evening, Peter was sailing for Shanghai to-morrow to consult bankers there who were said to be Fong Toy's backers.

This mission to negotiate with Fong Toy had been entrusted to Peter because of his wide knowledge of China and the Chinese. He was authorized to offer Fong Toy a million dollars plus a generous royalty.

Opening the chit, he read:

Mr. Peter Moore,
Oriental Hotel.
SIR:

Dr. Fong Toy has authorized me to say that a meeting between you and himself may be arranged this evening if you so desire. You will kindly be prepared to present your credentials. As Dr. Fong Toy works only at night, the most convenient time for this preliminary conference would be twelve o'clock midnight, when Dr. Fong Toy ceases work for a half hour for supper. I will call for you a few minutes before midnight.

Trusting that this rather informal arrangement meets with your approval, I remain,

Yr. obdt. servant.
WAN SANG,
Secretary to Dr. Fong Toy.

Peter smiled faintly. It was so typical of young China trying to be brisk and modern and businesslike. He folded up the chit and opened the unstamped envelope. In a hasty scrawl was written,

His Royal Highness
Chong Foo Shommon,
The Sultan of Sakala,
Requests the Honor of Your Presence
At an Informal Ball to be Given
To-night in the Grand Ballroom of
The Oriental Hotel, Nine o'clock.

PETER LOOKED up from the strange invitation and found the clerk smiling at him.

"I'll have to explain that, Mr. Moore," the clerk said. "We got a radio from the Sultan's yacht this afternoon, ordering us to issue five hundred invitations to the five hundred most important people in Hongkong. We didn't have time to get them printed, so we've all been busy writing them out, addressing them and delivering them. The Sultan of Sakala is a strange and eccentric young chap."

"I know of him," Peter said. "When the Sultan throws a party, he believes in throwing a party!"

The clerk laughed. "The Sultan hasn't landed from his yacht yet. He'll be along any minute. The fog is probably holding him up. Did you ever see that yacht? It's called the Sapphire."

"I don't believe I ever did."

"He had it built in England, and I understand it cost upward of a million pounds. Some yacht! It's as large as some ocean liners and has every convenience, including a swimming pool. They say his own suite alone has nine large rooms! Will you go to the party?"

"I imagine I'll look in," Peter said.

He did not have entirely pleasant recollections of the Sultan of Sakala. Although he had never met him, Peter's personal opinion was that Chong Foo Shommon was an exceedingly dangerous and unscrupulous young man. But he would go to the party. He needed the liveliness of a big party to make him forget what he had just seen on the water front.

Peter went into the bar. It was crowded with Hongkong business men who had dropped in for cocktails before going home, and there was a sprinkling of ship's officers, tourists and westernized Orientals. Peter looked about for some one to drink with, but saw no familiar faces. He found a place at the bar and ordered Scotch.

The bartender introduced him to the first of an evening-long series of mysterious surprises. Peter had known him years before, when Mike—no one ever knew him by another name—had been a bar steward in the Transpacific Service, on the old Vandalia.

Mike placed the Scotch before him and said: "Mr. Moore, take a good look at that guy standin' halfway down the bar, there."

Peter looked; frowned. The bar was crowded.

"Which one?"

"Tall, slender, blue-eyed, blond; blue suit. See him?"

Peter looked again and said, "Yes. What about him, Mike?"

"Don't you see the resemblance, Mr. Moore?"

"No," Peter said after a further perusal of the stranger's features. "Who is he?"

"He's Jeffery Douglas, the young Chicago lawyer who's been cleanin' up on them beer racketeers. He's travelin' in the Far East for his health. They say if he hadn't left Chicago, they would have made lead dumplin's out o' him. Don't you see the resemblance? It almost took my breath away!"

Peter laughed and answered, "I'm stumped, Mike. Whom does he resemble?"

"You! You might be twins! Take a good look."

Peter did. It is always hard for a man to see himself in another man whom his friends say is his double. Peter smiled and said: "Well, maybe you're right, Mike. He's about my height and build."

"Shucks!" Mike exclaimed. "He's got your eyes, nose and hair. He's a spittin' image of you!"

A few minutes later, the Chicago lawyer caught Peter's eye and stared at him. He smiled and Peter smiled in return. The two men who were evidently with Jeffery Douglas turned and stared at Peter, then laughed.

Peter would have liked to talk to Jeffery Douglas. He was interested, as all Americans are, in racketeering; but the lawyer and his two companions walked out a moment later.

THE SECOND surprise took the form of a pair of eyes in a thin, dark face. Peter saw these in the bar mirror. The owner of the eyes was obviously an Oriental. Peter's guess was Tonkinese. His face lacked the thickness at the cheeks of the Northern Chinese.

Peter glanced at the eyes reflected in the mirror, and glanced again. Certainly, the eyes were measuring him. There was nothing of friendliness about them. They were small, black and glittering with purpose. They made Peter feel a little uncomfortable. Why was this fellow, whoever he was, staring at him with such hostility—such calculating hostility?

When Peter glanced again, the eyes were gone. A feeling of definite uneasiness caused Peter to look rather carefully about the bar, but the Tonkinese—or Cambodian—was no longer in evidence.

Peter finished his highball. He was replacing the empty glass on the bar when he suddenly felt a cold draft on the back of his neck. He glanced around. Close to the end of the bar at which he stood was a frosted glass window.

Some one had stealthily raised the window. Peter could see out into a service alley; saw fog rolling along it in a pale-yellow cloud. Then he saw a thin brown hand flutter in the half darkness.

Fascinated, he stared. He heard Mike say, "Goin' to have another, Mr. Moore?"

Before he could answer, the thin brown hand reappeared. It seemed to be attached to no arm, but to be magically floating about in the fog. The surprise now rushed on to its climax. A pair of eyes close-set in a thin, brown face stared at him. The mysterious hand was now in possession of a knife—a curved, short knife with a bone handle such as Malay sailors use. The hand was holding the dagger, not by the handle, but by the gleaming blade.

It happened so suddenly that Peter had hardly time to think. The hand, holding the knife withdrew in a queer, quick gesture. In that instant, Peter dropped flat to the floor; heard a sharp, splintering thump less than a foot above his head, and sprang up to leap at the window.

He did not have to look to know that that knife was buried in the wood where he had been standing. He knew that if he had not dropped when he did, that knife would have found its swift way into his back.

Peter scrambled over the sill; looked right, then left. Nothing but fog.

He climbed back into the room and met the questioning eyes of Mike in a suddenly paper-white face. Peter closed the window and Mike said, weakly: "Get you?"

"No."

The bartender leaned over the bar and looked down at the knife. It was one of the strange features of the incident that no other man in the room was aware of what had taken place. The cheerful soft roar of conversation and laughter went on as before.

Peter grasped the haft of the intended assassin's weapon and yanked it out of the wood; tossed it down with a clatter before Mike.

"There's a souvenir for you," he said.

Mike looked fearfully at the knife, then his dazed eyes returned to Peter's face.

"I heard," he said, "you were out here on business, Mr. Moore. I didn't know you were up to trouble."

"I didn't either," Peter said.

Mike drew a long, tremulous breath. "Say!" he gasped. "That

guy certainly meant that knife for you. What's the big idea, anyway, Mr. Moore?"

"That," Peter answered, "is what I'm curious to know. I need another drink, Mike."

"I'll tell the cock-eyed world you do!"

CHAPTER III

A HARD-BOILED RADIO MAN

NOW OCCURRED THE next surprise. Peter was reaching for the drink when his arm was roughly seized and he was spun about to face a pale young man in the crisp white uniform of a ship's officer. Jagged symbols of lightning were embroidered in gold on the uniform collar; so that Peter knew that the young man was the wireless operator on some ship.

The young man was glaring at him with eyes blurred with drink. His breath was sour with alcohol and his manner was very belligerent.

Gripping Peter by the elbow, he said: "You're the guy I'm looking for. You're Peter Moore, aren't you?"

Peter, wondering if there was some connection between the intoxicated young stranger and the knife, nodded.

"Well, I'm Chester Blunt," stated the uniformed young man. "I'm the senior wireless operator on the Vandalia. You used to punch brass on her five or six years ago, didn't you?"

"Yes." Peter wondered why Chester Blunt was so belligerent.

"Listen," he said. "I've heard about you for years. I'm sick of your name, get me? All I've heard ever since I started poundin' brass on the China run was what a clever guy this Peter Moore is, and how good this Peter Moore is with a key. 'Yeah?' says I. 'Well, I'm gonna meet this guy Moore and give him an earful.' They kept tellin' me about all the excitin' adventures you used to have. Say! I've been on this run for two years, and I haven't seen anythin' I couldn't see back home in little old

N' York. What's more, I'll bet you I'm a better operator than you ever were. I'll bet you I have more nerve than you ever had!"

Was this merely a drunk's belligerent speech, or was it concealing another surprise?

Peter said calmly: "Where's the argument?"

Operator Blunt shook his fist under Peter's nose. "There isn't any argument," he snapped. "I'm just tellin' you—thassall!"

The young man thereupon turned about with great dignity— and sat down heavily on the floor!

Peter thoughtfully helped him to his feet, helped him across the room to a chair, and sat him down. Then he looked about the bar, prepared for almost anything.

Nothing happened. When he was quite sure that no further surprises were preparing to spring at him, Peter left the bar and proceeded to his room.

He hoped there would be no more disagreeable experiences this evening. That water front episode had shaken him; made him feel physically sick. And the unaccountable attack upon him in the bar by the Tonkinese had left his nerves shakier still.

What was it all about? In his previous visits to the Far East, when he was meddling in various sinister Oriental affairs, such a surprise attack could have been expected. But he was a serious-minded business man now, quite content to let sleeping dogs lie.

He put down the suspicion that one of these old dogs had awakened, fearing that he meant trouble. Thinking it over, as he prepared to bathe and dress, he suddenly recalled the Chicago lawyer. He must have been taken for Jeffery Douglas. An old Chicago feud had been carried over here!

But, Peter reasoned, a Chicago gunman, if he had wanted to put Jeffery Douglas on the spot would not have employed a Tonkinese knife thrower. He would have come to Hongkong with a sub-machine gun.

The only other possible explanation was entirely too far-fetched. Chong Foo Shommon, the Sultan of Sakala, was

Tonkinese. Peter had once crossed Chong's path; had thwarted an elaborate little scheme of Chong's. But that was in the past. And why should Chong want him out of the way now?

PETER LAID out his dress suit on the bed and went into the bathroom to bathe and shave. While he was lathering his face, he believed he heard the click that a key might have made in a lock. A moment later, he was almost certain he heard some one moving about in his bedroom.

But his nerves were jumpy, and he put it down to imagination. He could not, however, put down to imagination a sudden resounding crash in the bedroom, as if a heavy piece of furniture had been overturned.

Peter went charging into the bedroom, only in time to see a thin, brown-skinned, black-haired man reach for the light switch and plunge the room into instant blackness.

He did this with his left hand. With his right, he reached into a side pocket of his coat.

Peter rushed at him, barked his shins on a chair and sprawled to the floor just as two blue-red spurts of flame flicked out to the accompaniment of explosions.

He lay where he had fallen and awaited developments. At least fifteen seconds passed, with Peter lying there in the darkness.

Light from the bathroom seeped in and Peter's eyes gradually adjusted themselves to the faint glow in the murk, until he was certain he made out the slim shadow of his unknown antagonist against the wall and near the switch.

It was an exceedingly ticklish situation. Peter's gun, a thirty-eight caliber Colt's super-automatic, was reposing in a drawer in his wardrobe trunk—across the room. The invader had only to switch on the light, take careful aim and kill him.

Peter's only chance lay in a swift surprise attack while his unknown enemy hesitated. Slowly, cautiously, Peter wriggled toward him. He heard the man's quick, heavy breathing.

When he was less than a dozen feet away, Peter sprang up and leaped. He struck the unknown's gun as it went off. But before he could seize the man or secure the gun, the fellow writhed away like a snake, threw open the door and slammed it after him.

Peter switched on the light, dashed into the bathroom where he had left his dressing gown, and rushed back to the door. When he opened it and looked out, the corridor was empty.

A door across the way opened. A starry-eyed blond girl in filmy orchid negligee stared at him. Her eyes widened.

"I heard some shots," she said. "What's happening—another Chinese revolution?"

"A burglar broke into my room," Peter explained, "and took a couple of pot shots at me."

"Did he hit you?" she cried.

"No."

"Did he get away?"

"Yes."

The girl slammed the door. A broad-shouldered, gray-haired man in blue came up the corridor. He said:

"I'm the house detective. Somebody phoned down they heard some shots around here. What do you know about it?"

"Nothing," Peter replied; "except that they were fired at me."

The house detective followed him into the room, where he and Peter made several discoveries. Two bullets were embedded in the floor; one was lodged in the ceiling. But these did not affect Peter half so much as the discovery that the contents of all the bureau drawers were strewn on the floor and that his automatic pistol was gone from the wardrobe trunk.

Peter said nothing of this loss to the house detective. He knew that the house detective could do nothing about it, anyway. And it certainly had not been a burglar.

WHEN THE house detective was gone, Peter lit a cigarette and tried to do some constructive thinking. He was not quite certain that the man who fired the shots and the man who had thrown the knife were one and the same; but they had looked sufficiently alike to provide grounds for the assumption. Both had been dark-skinned Orientals. Both had certainly been after his life.

Just as certainly, the man who had entered this room had not mistaken Peter for Jeffery Douglas, the Chicago lawyer. One could therefore assume that the knife had been meant for Peter, not for the man he so closely resembled.

It was beginning to appear that Peter, whether he wished to be or not, was being drawn into the web of some mysterious, Oriental plan. That assumption could no longer be questioned. But who stood back of it?

If Susan O'Gilvie were in Hongkong instead of Manila, he would have suspected that she was up to some of her mischief. Ever since he had put foot in China she had somehow managed to keep him most of the time in hot water. But Susan was not in Hongkong; she was safely out of the way in Manila.

What next?

Peter shot the bolt on his door, saw that his windows were locked, and finished shaving. Despite the recent exciting incidents which had occurred, his mind went back to that poor devil he had fished out of the water. He could not get the pain-tortured eyes out of his mind.

For the twentieth time he wished that Susan O'Gilvie were here. Susan was a great little pal. He wished he could sit down with Susan and chatter about absolutely nothing by the hour, and forget China.

When Peter was dressed he went down and had dinner in the grill room and shortly after nine went up to the grand ballroom. The ballroom and the large bar adjoining were already full of people prepared to enjoy the Sultan's impromptu party.

Peter drifted about and felt more lonesome than ever. Never in his life had he seen so many pretty girls, but he knew none of them. For each girl there seemed to be five men. A large and excellent orchestra was playing popular fox trots.

He heard a man say, "The Sultan's just come!"

Peter thought, "What of it? I do not want to dance with

the Sultan." He felt blue. He went into the bar and had several drinks of straight whisky.

Then he went back to the ballroom and watched the dancing. He could not get that poor devil's whistling voice, his agonized eyes, out of his head. Now occurred the next surprise of the evening.

A voice beside him exclaimed:

"Why! Peter! I thought you were in Shanghai!"

"Well, I'll be—" Peter gasped. "Well, for cry—"

"In person!" Susan laughed. "Not an animated cartoon!"

CHAPTER IV

NERVES

IT WAS CERTAIN that never in his life had Peter been so glad to see anyone. Charming, beautiful, romantic, fun-loving Susan! Her hair, he saw, was done in a clever new way—drawn back from her face and into a little bun at the back of her head. It was naturally curly and full of bright lights.

Her small face was rosy. Her eyes were brighter and bigger than stars—and much riskier. He was delighted to see her, and he wondered why she seemed so startled, even embarrassed, at seeing him. She seemed much more startled than glad.

"How come, Susan?" he asked when the shock had worn off. "Why aren't you in Manila?"

"Oh, Hongkong called," Susan replied airily. "Have you seen Fong Toy yet?"

"I expect to see him to-night… Who brought you?"

"A lame brain from the American consulate. He wants me to marry him and live in Prairie Center, Kansas."

Peter glanced at the ten thousand dollar string of pearls Susan wore around her lovely neck and tried to picture her living in Prairie Center, Kansas. Then he saw that there was a new addition to the pearl necklace—a large and beautiful *cabochon* sapphire. It had the quality of a starry midnight sky in the tropics.

"Are you marrying him?"

"Nope." She looked at him sharply. "What's the matter, old dear? You look ill."

"Oh, I'm all right."

Peter had no intention of telling her why he looked shaken. He wanted to forget that poor devil on the water front. He asked Susan about the new gem on her necklace.

"It's a singing sapphire. I think it is hollowed out, and perhaps there's a reed in it. If you rub it on silk, it sings—very faintly."

Susan was blushing and looking at Peter strangely. He thought she was joking. It did not occur to him until later that his reference to the sapphire might have embarrassed her.

The orchestra began playing. Peter gathered her in and they moved out onto the glasslike floor. Susan smiled up at him mistily and showed him the tip of her tongue. Her breath smelled like violets.

It struck Peter that Susan was different. In some mysterious way, she had changed. He wondered what had happened in Manila. A girl with her beauty, her millions, and her appetite for thrills was running a gantlet all the time. And he wondered if her presence in Hongkong was in any way accountable for any of the surprises which had been visited upon him this evening.

He said, "Susan, you aren't up to any new deviltries, are you?"

She looked at him sharply. "None that concern you," she answered.

"Then, you are up to deviltries?"

"I'm not up to anything, Peter, that remotely concerns you." She changed the subject. "Miss me?"

"Nope."

"Liar!"

Peter wondered what mischief she was up to this time. It was always the same. She was always planning little adventures which didn't involve him in the least. In the end, he was in them up to his ears.

"I'm learning," she told him. "I'm hard now, Peter."

They glided past an elderly Englishman and a dowager who stared at them through a monocle and a lorgnon respectively.

"Do you approve of my dancing?" Susan asked, and for a while they exchanged light comments. It was, Peter realized, all on the surface. Under their banter, they were sparring. He sensed that Susan was displeased because he was here instead of being in Shanghai. She had something up her sleeve. What was it? What did it have to do with the man who had thrown the knife; the man who had taken pot shots at him in his room?

SUSAN SUDDENLY exclaimed: "For crying out loud, Peter! There's your twin!"

Peter glanced behind him; saw the Chicago lawyer Mike had pointed out in the bar. Jeffery Douglas was dancing with a languid Eurasian girl.

"He's a fighting lawyer from Chicago," Peter said, "making war on beer racketeers. He's taking a trip because Chicago stopped being healthy."

"It's amazing, Peter! He even laughs the way you do. I want to meet that man. I'll bet he even has your voice!"

"I'll do something about it," Peter promised.

Then he saw Chester Blunt, the wireless man, weaving his way across the floor toward them.

"This bird," Peter said quickly, "is the wireless man on the Vandalia. He looks as if he is going to ask you for a dance. Don't desert me."

"I know him," Susan said. "His name is Chester Blunt."

"Where'd you meet him?"

"Oh, you'd be s'prised."

"I'm getting used to surprises," Peter said dryly. He knew now that it was no use to question Susan. She was up to her ears in something. Did it explain why Chester Blunt had insulted him in the bar? What in the devil was going on?

Some one thumped Peter violently on the back. The American custom of cutting in at dances had long ago reached Hongkong. But the custom was to tap a man on the back, not to knock his wind out, if you wanted to dance with his girl.

"Pardon me, Moore. May I cut in, Susan?"

"Certainly, Chester! Sorry, Pete!"

Peter watched her go away. He was completely mystified. The girl had certainly changed. He could not recall when she wouldn't have rather spent an entire evening with him to the exclusion of all other men. What had happened in Manila? Who had changed her? Chester Blunt? Susan liked her men exciting, adventurous, dangerous. She liked to play with fire. Was Chester Blunt fire?

Peter studied them. Usually when Susan met him after an absence she threw her arms around his neck; kissed him enthusiastically, no matter how many people were watching. What scheme was buzzing around in Susan's beautiful little head—a scheme having to do with wireless operators, knife throwers and Oriental gunmen?

Chester Blunt was a clever dancer. He did tricky things with his feet. Susan followed him beautifully. They seemed to be on terms of almost intimate friendship. Susan was smiling up into his face, flirting with him. Chester Blunt was looking down with impassioned, imploring eyes.

Peter wondered if he was jealous. He had been on the verge of falling for Susan ever since they had met; but hadn't quite toppled over the edge, because common sense had held him back. Susan was dynamite: she was nothing but a rich little thrill-hunter. No; he wasn't jealous, but he was curious to know what had happened in Manila—what chain of events started there had resulted in two deliberate attempts on his life?

When Susan and Chester Blunt came around, Peter waded out and tapped the operator on the shoulder.

"Pardon me, Mr. Blunt. May I, Susan?"

"Certainly, Peter! Sorry, Chester."

The operator glared at Peter. Susan was giggling.

Peter said: "Will you kindly tell me what ax you're grinding this time?"

She said sharply, "Don't be silly."

"I want to hear that sapphire sing," he said grimly. "Let's go out on a nice quiet little balcony and look at the harbor and hear the sapphire sing."

"There's a fog," Susan said. "You can't see the harbor to-night. And in your present state of mind, I am wary of dark little balconies. Let's go into the bar, instead. I need a drink."

PETER STOPPED dancing, took her firmly by the elbow and started for a door which gave upon a balcony. Susan's uneasiness seemed to increase.

"Peter, I'd rather not go out on the balcony." She looked anxiously about her.

"Why not?"

"I'd just rather not. I have reasons."

He took her by both elbows and propelled her toward the balcony.

Susan said breathlessly: "Will you promise to be good?"

"Why should I?"

"Don't be silly, Peter. Look here. You aren't really in love with me, are you?"

"I'm mighty fond of you."

"But you're not in love with me. Peter, I'm not joking. I want to know. I positively won't go out until we settle this. I don't want you to be in love with me. I mean it. Tell me you aren't in love with me."

"All right," Peter said. "I'm not in love with you."

"So that if you did kiss me, it wouldn't be anything but—but friendship!"

"Let the kisses fall where they may," Peter answered. "Why all this dog-goned mystery?"

She looked at him quickly; bit her lip, and narrowed her eyes.

They went out onto the balcony, into the fog. It seemed to twist and swirl about them. The fog reminded Peter of that poor half-dead fellow he had seen on the bund. He shivered.

Susan removed a cushion from a chair, placed it on the balustrade, sat down, and looked up at him. Her face was soft and misty in the dim light.

"Give me your handkerchief," she said huskily.

Peter took one out of his pocket, unfolded it and gave it to her.

"Put your head down."

Peter put his head down. Susan briskly rubbed the sapphire which dangled on her string of pearls and quickly held it to his ear. Pete heard a very faint, high-pitched musical note, like that of a distant violin. He took the sapphire out of her hand and held it closer.

She was looking up at him, as he cocked his head. She smiled faintly.

"**I KNOW** what's the matter with you," said Peter suddenly. "You've fallen for somebody. You're afraid of hurting me. Well, don't be foolish, Susan. You were bound to fall for somebody. I'm interested only in one thing: He's got to be fit for you."

"I don't want to discuss it, Peter."

"I do," Peter said firmly. "Did you meet him in Manila?"

"Please, Peter!"

"Who gave you that sapphire?"

"The same man who gave me this one." She held up her left hand. Peter saw another *cabochon* sapphire set in a ring on her engagement finger.

"Where did you meet Chester Blunt?"

"In Manila."

"When did you get into Hongkong?"

"Just now."

"There was no ship from Manila putting into Hongkong to-night."

"Did I say I came on a ship?"

Peter laughed. "Did you swim, Susan?"

"Nope. I came on a yacht. A party of a dozen of us came over front Manila."

"Whose yacht?"

"Didn't I say it was the Sultan's? He was simply wonderful to us."

"Whose ring are you wearing?"

"It was a present from the man I'm going to marry."

"One of the men in that party?"

"Yes!"

"Can you think of any reason," he said slowly, "why your engagement, or anything else you've been up to, should have caused any one to try to kill me?"

"Peter!" she wailed. "What happened?"

He told her briefly about the knife-thrower and the shooting episode in his bedroom.

"Peter, I can't understand it! I simply can't believe that anything I've done would cause such attacks on you. They won't happen again."

"How can you stop them?"

"Did I cause them?" she demanded hysterically. "Nothing I could have done caused them. It's one of your old enemies. It has nothing to do with me. I haven't done anything. You've got to be careful."

"Yes; I'll be careful. The point is, the Far East is full of rotters. I'd hate to see you fall for one of them. Won't you tell me who this man is you've fallen for?"

CHAPTER V

UNDER A WEIRD SPELL

SUSAN STUBBORNLY SHOOK her head. The orchestra was playing "Chant of the Jungle." Much nearer was the sound of a Chinese flute from the fog-bound city beneath them.

It wailed in the mournful dissonance peculiar to all Oriental music. Susan, listening to it, was suddenly like a girl bewitched. It was as if she had forgotten Peter's existence. She had lifted her eyes, was holding her hands, with fingers curling upward, above her knees, in the attitude of one entranced.

"I'm thirsty," she said. "They're serving free drinks in the bar." She jumped up. "Peter!" she wailed. "You're the best friend I have in the world. Tell me that nothing I do will make you hate me!"

"I couldn't hate you," Peter said.

They fought their way through the mob in the bar. Jammed in, arm to arm, Peter asked what she would have to drink.

Susan's eyes were stormy stars.

"Champagne."

"Champagne," Peter said to the bartender.

A pint bottle was opened and two goblets were filled.

"Peter, do you remember the night we met?"

Looking at this extremely dangerous new Susan, Peter remembered vividly.

"I was out on deck in a steamer chair, watching the gale," he said. "We were due in Yokohama the following morning. Suddenly you came down the deck—up to your ears in trouble."

"As usual?" Susan asked, draining her goblet.

"Did I say that?"

"Well, I was in trouble. I was on my way to Tonking, at the invitation of Chong Poo Shommon—our host to-night."

"Yes," Peter affirmed. "The Sultan of Sakala. You had met him in San Francisco on his tour of the United States, and he had tricked you into at least starting for Sakala—to take charge of his educational system. You were going to bring sweetness and light to the dumb little Tonkinese."

"And I'm convinced now," Susan said dreamily, "that I made a great mistake in letting you dissuade me. I know the Sultan better now. He isn't any of the things you said he was."

"Why go into that?" Peter asked. "It seemed advisable at the time to prevent your going there. When we reached Yokohama, I put you aboard the first American-bound ship and said good-by—"

"And I slipped ashore in the pilot's boat and followed you to Shanghai. But you were wrong about the Sultan. He is thoroughly Americanized… Another bottle, please," Susan said to the bartender."

"To celebrate your engagement," Peter agreed, "to Mr. X."

"I bumped into the Sultan in Manila," Susan said, "at a ball given by the Filipino Legislature for the Governor-General and his wife."

"Did he mention the Tonkinese educational system this time?"

Susan laughed softly. "Not once! He was very charming. I mean, he really was very charming."

"Finish your drink," Peter said. "I feel like getting tight. It's seldom I feel like celebrating anybody's engagement. This is a historic night. I have an idea I'm going to make it more historic."

"You're a wonderful man, Peter, and you've been a wonderful pal. Listen! There's going to be a little party—just the twelve of us who came over from Manila together—down at a place called the Tiger's Den. It's on Hai-Phong Road. We're all going to duck out and go down there at midnight. Will you take me?"

"I will if my date with Fong Toy falls through."

"They have a Chinese orchestra and funny cabaret stunts."

"I know the Tiger's Den. It used to be a tough joint, but they've dolled it all up for the tourists."

"I'll meet you in the lobby," Susan said, "at twelve sharp. If you're not there, I'll know you had to see Fong Toy. Come later, if we miss each other. It may be the last chance we'll have to see each other."

"Why?"

"I'm getting married to-morrow."

"To-morrow?" Peter repeated.

"Yes, Peter."

HE FELT cold dew forming on his forehead.

"Bartender," he said, "let's have another bottle of that stuff." He folded his arms and looked at Susan. He was pale and his eyes were glittering.

Susan was pale, too.

"Peter," she cried. "You promised you wouldn't get sore."

"I'm not sore. I'm only wondering why you're so mysterious. We've been through a lot together, Susan. Why won't you tell me who this man is? Ashamed to tell me?"

Her chin flew up. "How dare you say such things?"

"If you aren't ashamed, why don't you tell me?"

"Because if I told you, you'd take it upon yourself to interfere. I'm free, white and twenty-one. I can marry any man I choose."

"Sure, you can!" Peter said angrily. "Why, indeed, should I interfere?"

"You've got to promise me that when you do find out, you won't come butting in."

"I don't have to promise it! I would not dream of butting in!"

"I'm old enough to know what I want." Susan was growing hysterical. "I won't have you riding herd on me as if I were fifteen years old!"

"I heard you the first time," Peter said. "I'm through riding herd on you. I won't interfere. I won't butt in."

"And another thing—" Susan began.

She stopped and her face suddenly went pink.

There was a commotion about the bar. Peter looked around and saw a short, thickset man with a round, brown face making his way toward them. He wore a small black mustache. But that wasn't what especially distinguished him. It was his white suit and his turban. The suit was fashioned along the conventional lines of a full dress suit, but it was white. The turban was sapphire-blue. Where the intricate folds crossed in the front blazed a *cabochon* sapphire as large, it seemed to Peter, as a pear.

Other sapphires were in evidence. The studs in his shirt bosom were *cabochon* sapphires. A *cabochon* sapphire adorned the thumb of the hand which he held in front of him.

Peter thought at first that the man was wearing a fancy-dress costume. He looked at Susan. She was white now, staring at the splendid, bizarre stranger.

"Peter," she began in a small, husky voice, "I want you to meet—"

The man in the turban interrupted.

"My darling! Where have you been? I've been looking everywhere for you!"

"I'm sorry, Chong," Susan said in a tight, breathless little voice. "Peter, I want you to meet my *fiancé*. Your majesty, this is Mr. Peter Moore. I think you've heard of each other, Peter—this is His Majesty Chong Foo Shommon, Sultan of Sakala."

THE EYES of the Sultan reminded Peter of overripe blueberries. His pudgy brown hand did not move. Nor did Peter extend his hand. Susan watched him anxiously, as if she were afraid that Peter might do something rash. But Peter did nothing.

The Sultan said, "I am charmed to know you, Mr. Moore. I have heard a great deal about you."

"Thank you, your majesty."

"I have heard that you are a very troublesome and dangerous young man. I have heard, in fact, the most amazing legends about you—and the trouble you have caused in certain parts of the Far East."

"I am certain, your majesty," Peter returned, "that the reports were greatly exaggerated."

The blueberry eyes ran down the American's long, lanky frame. They returned to Peter's face.

For an instant Peter could have sworn he glimpsed smoldering red fire in them; that they were twin threats of hatred and murder. Then the moment passed.

"Mr. Moore has changed, Chong," Susan said eagerly. "He isn't in the Far East to start trouble. He's over here on a business trip. His old days of trouble hunting are past."

"I trust so," the Sultan said significantly.

Peter's eyes flicked from his round brown face, with its little toy mustache, to another brown face just behind him; another Tonkinese, but a tall and lean one, with a distinguishing star-shaped scar beside his nose. Peter had not clearly seen the face of the knife-thrower, or the face of the man who had broken into his bedroom, and he wondered now if this were the same man.

Chong Foo Shommon laughed and said, "My darling, I would like to dance. You dance so beautifully."

"All right," Susan said, "but I want to talk to Mr. Moore a moment longer. I'll meet you by the orchestra in ten minutes, dearest."

The Sultan smiled and withdrew with his bodyguard. Susan returned her eyes to Peter's face. She was suddenly pale and her eyes were glittering with determination.

"You haven't congratulated me," she said.

It was a deliberate and downright challenge. Susan did not

like the look of disgust in Peter's eyes and she was going to remove it.

Peter's smile was thin and hard.

"Have you done something," he asked dryly, "that deserves my congratulations?"

"Haven't I? Chong is one of the greatest men in the Far East. I'm terribly proud of him. You think I'm doing something rash, reckless, foolish. You're wrong."

"All right; I'm wrong."

"Then stop looking at me like that!"

"You'd better run along with your Sultan."

Susan's eyes were blazing now.

"I'm going to make you congratulate me!"

"You're tight."

"So are you. And I'm thinking straight. You're just jealous. Chong is really a great man. If he weren't a Sultan by inheritance, he would be a great scientist and surgeon."

"He's quite an authority," Peter agreed, "on Oriental methods of poisoning. He could write quite a book on the different methods he's used for poisoning his enemies."

"That's a lie!" Susan snapped. "There are more lying legends about Chong than any man in the Far East."

"Where there's smoke," Peter argued, "isn't there apt to be a little fire?"

"I don't care a damn what you say or think!" Susan declared. "I admire and respect him tremendously. Congratulate me!"

"No."

"We're going to settle this," Susan said in a furious voice. "Tell me why I shouldn't marry Chong. Because he is an Oriental? That's out. He's a king!"

"It will be thrilling," Peter said, "to be addressed as 'your majesty.' Her majesty the sultana!"

"I don't deny it. What girl wouldn't be thrilled? I don't deny

I'm looking for thrills. The thicker they come, the better I like 'em!"

"You'll get plenty," Peter said. "Get Chong to tell you some time how he murdered his brother."

"That's another lie!"

"Is it? I heard he killed him by giving him a diluted dose of cobra venom and sat there and watched him die in the most horrible agony."

"I don't believe it. You haven't given me one good reason yet why I shouldn't marry Chong. You can't tell me anything I don't know about him. And I'm in love with him—very much in love with him. I think he's perfectly fascinating."

"You win," Peter said.

"Do you congratulate me?"

"No, Susan."

"You will before I'm through!"

"Will you make," Peter asked, "his fifty-first or fifty-second wife?"

"Oh, I know all about his fifty wives. He hates the whole idea. A harem was expected of him. The Sultans of Sakala for hundreds of years have had harems. He can't upset all those old traditions in a day. He and I are going to modernize Sakala."

"You, Chong, and Anarra?" Peter asked.

WHEN SUSAN was angry, her violet eyes looked purple. They looked purple now.

"Who is Anarra?"

"Don't you know about Anarra? She's a girl Chong bought from a Siamese prince in the Lao. I understand he paid a half million *ticals* for Anarra. They say she's very beautiful; a slim, golden-skinned tigress of the jungles with the most beautiful hair in the world. They say Anarra has Chong wrapped around her little finger and that he worships her as some men worship Buddha."

Susan laughed harshly.

"You're making that up as you go along."

"How many people were in the party that Chong brought back from Manila on the Sapphire?"

"Twelve, including myself."

"Did he show you about the Sapphire?"

"Of course he did!"

"Were there any Bluebeard's rooms—forbidden places?"

"Don't be fantastic, Peter. Naturally, we didn't go into his personal suite. A girl has to draw the line somewhere."

"Are you sure Anarra wasn't aboard?"

Susan looked at him with crinkling eyes, then burst into laughter. "Not unless he kept her locked in a state-room." She sobered. "Peter, I'm going to make a confession. I have not definitely decided to marry Chong."

"Then, for God's sake, don't!"

"Wait, Peter! I told him I wouldn't give him a definite answer until to-morrow morning."

"Then, why are you wearing his ring?"

"Oh, what's a ring? I told him you were my advisor and that I would not commit myself to marrying him until I'd had a talk with you. Well, I've had a talk with you. And you haven't convinced me at all. Chong is going back to the Sapphire before midnight, and I'm going to have breakfast with him here in the morning. I'm going to give him my answer then. It's going, to be—*yes!*"

Peter said, "Very well."

Susan searched his face anxiously, "Peter, I'm asking you, very bluntly, to keep out of this."

"I haven't the slightest intention of interfering."

"But you're tight, and you're going to get tighter; and when you're tight you always look for trouble. I want you to keep away from Chong and the Sapphire."

"That's a promise," Peter said grimly.

"Now—do you feel like congratulating a girl?"

"You have my deepest condolences," Peter answered.

Susan glared at him.

"I hate you," she said slowly. "You're a prig. You won't congratulate me because you're jealous. You're sore because I'm marrying him and not you."

"If I were your brother," Peter replied, "I'd spank you and lock you in your room until you got some sense."

"You wouldn't be so mad if you weren't in love with me!"

"What of it? Run along to your damned Sultan. And will you kindly request him to call off his gunmen and knife-throwers?"

"If you do interfere, I won't be responsible for what happens."

"Good-by, Susan," Peter said.

He couldn't stand any more of this. The thought of Susan marrying a man like Chong made him sick.

Her eyes were suddenly wet. Susan must have known that he meant good-by forever. She extended one hand toward him, then snatched it back; turned and walked rapidly away on firm high heels.

CHAPTER VI

THE SULTAN'S DARKNESS

PETER, WITH HIS back to the bar, watched her go. He had thought that some of the recent adventures they had been through together had tempered, if not cured, her love for dangerous thrills. It seemed that Susan had an insatiable appetite. Certainly, she must know that Chong was one of the most dangerous men in the Far East: a man who would have been clapped behind bars long ago if it had not been for his great wealth and power.

A man spoke Peter's name, but Peter was so immersed in his thoughts he did not even hear him. He went to the arched doorway and watched the dancers. Over by the dais, where the orchestra was, he saw the Sultan, resplendent in his white dress suit and sapphire-blue turban, evidently deep in conference with two slim, sinister-looking young men who were brown-skinned and black-haired.

The two young men were listening attentively to Chong. At intervals they nodded curtly, as if in understanding. The belief grew upon Peter that Chong was plotting something; and, if Peter was not mistaken, it had something to do with himself.

He saw the two slim young Tonkinese drift off into the crowd as Susan made her way to Chong's side; saw her lift a white, unsmiling face to this man she was so foolishly determined to marry.

The orchestra started as if on signal. Peter watched Susan lift her arms, saw Chong enfold her. It made him madder than ever. He wanted to go out and do physical violence to Chong. Knowing Susan, he was certain that she had fallen under the man's sinister fascination, just as a bird falls under the fascination of a kreit adder.

If Peter were Susan's brother, he would have forcibly removed her from Chong's arms. But he was only a man who was much too fond of her for his peace of mind. He must not prevent her from making this mistake. Why? Because it was being committed in the name of love. Love! What the devil was love?

He decided that he wanted some fresh air; wanted to bring some more thought to bear on Susan's latest recklessness. He skirted the floor and went out on the balcony which he and Susan had left just a few minutes before.

The cold fog flowed past him and cleared his brain somewhat. And it carried him back again to the earlier distressing incident of the evening. It seemed to him he could hear that poor devil's groans again; his pitiful, gasping cry for help as they pushed him below the surface. And from some hulk afar off, the devilish beating of that drum. *Tumpa-dum-dum!* A woman with eyes like a snake's and not a hair on her head. Blood welling from the scalped head of her victim.

SUDDENLY PETER was aware that a blue-tinted electric bulb on the wall above him gave the effect of misty tropical moonlight. He had not noticed it before. Then he realized that the golden light from the ballroom was no longer streaming through the doorway.

He looked in and saw that the great room was in total darkness. It was as black as a cave. He supposed that this was to be a spotlight dance, to the accompaniment of dreamy music. But no spotlights flashed on. The ballroom remained in blackness. The orchestra played on a few seconds longer, then faltered to a stop.

Something was wrong. Either a fuse had burned out or some one had deliberately turned the lights off.

A babbling of voices arose in protest. Suddenly a woman sharply screamed.

The scream served to clear Peter's thoughts and to bring them into focus. If he had not been twice this evening the intended victim of Chong's assassins, he would not have been so suspicious now. But it suddenly occurred to him that the blackness would give the Sultan's knife experts an excellent opportunity to pounce on him. Under Chong's orders, one or more of them had watched him; would spring on him at any moment. And when the lights came on—who would know who had done the stabbing?

Peter felt that he had seen all he wished of Chong's attacks. He was sick of Chong's party, anyhow. He would return to his room. But he did not reënter the ballroom through the doorway by which he had left it. He proceeded to the end of the balcony and quietly slipped in through another door.

The voices of several hundred men and women were now shouting for lights. Fireflies began to dance into being about the room, as men flashed on pocket cigarette lighters and held them up.

Peter slipped along the walls toward the main corridor at the end of the large room. Just as he reached the end of the room, the lights blazed on. He slipped out and went downstairs to his room. As he neared his room, he wished that he had a pistol or some kind of weapon.

He entered his room and quickly turned on the lights. He was not surprised to find that, in his absence, his room had been entered and ransacked again. Every article of clothing he possessed was on the floor. The bureau drawers, which he had carefully repacked after the gunman had fled, had been jerked out again and dumped. The contents of his steamer trunk were strewn about.

But no one was in his suite, and the windows were still locked. He shot the bolt on the door; glanced at his watch. It was now eleven-twenty. He telephoned the night clerk and told him that when a Mr. Wan Sang called, to send him right up.

He hoped that Chong would let him alone. He had no intention of interfering with Susan's preposterous marriage. He was definitely out of her life. If he still loved her, he would have to get over it as best he could. He would confer with Dr. Fong Toy, try to persuade the young scientist to sell or lease the static eliminator to the General Electric Company, and return to the United States on the first fast ship.

HE WAS finishing repacking his trunk when a sharp rap sounded on the door. Peter glanced up and looked at the heavy wooden panel. Who, he wondered, was there? He hesitated a moment, then opened the door.

With something of relief, Peter saw that his visitor was Chester Blunt. The wireless man's hair was rumpled, his eyes were bloodshot, and his skin had the waxy pallor which some men acquire when drunk.

The wireless man tried to focus his glazed eyes on Peter.

"Listen here, you—" he thickly began.

"Blunt," Peter quietly interrupted, "I have troubles enough without taking you on. Would you mind taking your hoop and rolling it along and playing with somebody who feels playful? I do not feel playful."

"I don't feel playful," Blunt said. "I feel kind of sick. A terrible thing has just happened. A guy was just stabbed to death up in the ballroom. He was a Chicago lawyer. The Chicago beer barons had put him on a spot, and he beat it off to China. They sent a killer after him. Somebody doused the lights, and this killer stuck a knife into his heart."

Peter, looking at him, swayed slightly. The attempt to kill him in the bar downstairs had failed. The attempt to kill him in his room had failed. And the third attempt had, ironically, resulted in the death of an innocent man who had fled to China because he had feared Chicago racketeers would put him on a spot.

CHAPTER VII

MIDNIGHT

THE WIRELESS OPERATOR was staring steadily at Peter now. He seemed less drunk.

"But I didn't come down here to tell you about how Douglas was stabbed downstairs," he said. "I've come here to talk to you about Susan O'Gilvie."

"Let's not talk about her," Peter said.

"Got to talk about her," Chester Blunt insisted. "She gave me a message for you."

"When?".

"A minute before they turned the lights out."

"Were you dancing with her?"

"Yep. I cut in on Chong—you know, the Sultan. She asked me to look you up and tell you to be sure to come down to the Tiger's Den after you got through with Fong Toy, whoever he is. She says she wants to have another talk with you about something very important. She says you've got to come, and that I'm to bring you myself, by force, if you won't come willingly."

Peter looked at him thoughtfully; wondered if Chester Blunt, too, were somehow in league with Chong. Peter was in a mood now to suspect everybody.

"You run back and tell her I'll make it if I can."

"Nothing doing," said the wireless man. "The party's broken up, and she's gone to her room."

"Where is Chong?"

"He went back aboard his yacht. Susan told me to stay with you. She says maybe you will need somebody around, anyhow, in case you get into a fight."

"Have you a gun?" Peter asked hopefully.

Chester Blunt laughed. "Why in hell should I pack a gun? Say, listen, Moore. Are you trying to kid me? Maybe while I'm riding herd on you you can show me something of this mysterious, evil China Susan was talking about—the China you and she saw. That's what I want to see. Show it to me! Scare me! I wanna be scared!"

"I don't think it's possible to scare you," Peter said dryly.

"China!" the other jeered, "A Chicago killer follows a lawyer to Hongkong and stabs him. That's modern China! I want to see dragons and secret passageways—"

He paused. A man had come down the corridor and was standing behind him; a slim young Chinese, very modern in dress and manner and wearing the tortoise-rimmed glasses without which no modern young Chinese business man seems complete.

He said in a suave voice, "I beg your pardon, but which of you gentlemen is Mr. Peter Moore?"

"There he is," Blunt said; "in the flesh."

The Chinese smiled at him, then addressed himself to Peter.

"My name is Wan Sang. I am Dr. Fong Toy's secretary. The doctor has sent me here to see if you can come to his laboratory immediately. Can you come?"

Peter nodded; picked up his trench coat and hat from the bed. He and Wan Sang went down the hall, with Chester Blunt determinedly following.

ALL THREE descended to the lobby and out to the ricksha compound. Two rickshas came rolling out of the fog, side by side. Peter climbed into one, Wan Sang into the other. Not until later did Peter realize that Wan Sang gave no address, no directions

*Pater hastily
swung the parang*

to the coolies. His wits might have been sharper if his brain had not been so full of champagne, bourbon—and Susan.

Wan Sang said: "Who is this young man in uniform—a friend of yours?"

Chester Blunt, overhearing, answered: "A great admirer—that's all. Whither he goest, I goest."

The Chinese, was obviously displeased. Shoe-button eyes behind thick lenses glittered. He said to Peter:

"Does this young man intend to follow you?"

Peter answered: "Don't pay any attention to him."

"That's right!" Blunt snorted. "Ignore me. But lead the way. Lead the way into darkest China! Scare me! Give me a thrill!"

Peter grinned at Wan Sang, but the Chinese refused to see any humor in the situation.

The two rickshas started off. A third trailed them. From time to time, Wan Sang glanced back at Chester Blunt, who was crouched behind the rubber apron drawn up to his chin to protect him against the elements. His wireless cap was cocked jauntily over one ear. Wan Sang would glance at him, then at Peter. He seemed to be in something of a dilemma.

Peter did not remark this at the time, but he did later. In view of what had happened so far this evening, it was a little strange that he was not at all suspicious of Wan Sang's reliability. He had had so many dealings with Orientals that he had learned by what roundabout and deceptive methods they sometimes accomplished their results. But he was too busy thinking about Susan and Chong even to notice where the rickshas were going.

Ghostly shapes seemed to twist and writhe in the fog. It was so dense that, even under street lights, he could hardly see the naked calves of his coolie.

Suddenly the two rickshas, with the third trailing a dozen feet behind, swung into what appeared to be a hole in a stone wall; a high stone wall dripping and green with moss. It was actually an arched alleyway. Peter tried to orient himself. He suddenly realized that, despite his long familiarity with the twisting alleys, lanes and streets of Hongkong, he had not the slightest idea where in the world he was.

Ahead was dense blackness. Then a pin point of green light glowed in the fog. The light flickered on the wet wall of the arched tunnel; seemed to spill and scatter in green drops like emeralds.

Wan Sang was invisible. Peter sharply inquired: "Is this Fong Toy's laboratory?"

The Chinese did not answer. Peter called: "Blunt, are you back there?"

The answer came jovially, "Try and shake me, big boy!"

THEN A door swung open at the back of what appeared to be a large enclosed yard. It was paved with red bricks. Light glistened wetly on them. Peter drew in quick lungfuls of foggy air and smelled sandalwood incense and the unmistakable acrid scent of opium.

Where in the devil was he?

A man stood in the doorway holding up a brass lantern. He

peered into the courtyard. The flickering yellow flame played on his face and made it look like brown lacquer.

Peter, staring at him, felt his pulses leap; felt the wet chill of shock form on his forehead. He was suddenly sober and alert. The man in the doorway was, unmistakably, the one who had stood behind the Sultan when Susan had introduced Peter to him—the lean, brown man with the star-shaped scar!

It was a deliberate trap—another surprise. Chong, having been frustrated three times to-night in his attempts at having Peter out of his way, had staged this elaborate ambush. For a moment before he acted, Peter wondered how Chong had learned about his scheduled visit to Fong Toy's laboratory. But men with the power of Chong had the peculiar faculty of learning anything they wished to know. Perhaps the note itself was spurious.

Peter's coolie lowered the ricksha shafts to the ground, so that Peter could alight. Peter had no means of knowing how many men surrounded him in the darkness—from what direction a knife might come.

He shouted: "Blunt! We're trapped! Get out and run like Sam Hill!"

Peter heard the wireless man's skeptical laugh behind him, then alighted from the ricksha, but not in the usual way. He leaped out of the seat and upon the back of the coolie. They crashed to the ground, with the coolie underneath.

He had learned, in previous tight corners, that the man who acts a split second sooner than his enemy often carries into a fight an overwhelming advantage.

Peter leaped up from the stunned coolie as men poured from the doorway. He saw the gleam of a curved knife and heard the wireless man say, "Hey! What's the big idea!"

"Get out of here!" Peter barked. He grasped the ricksha shafts, turned the vehicle about so that its rear end faced the doorway, and used the ricksha as an impromptu rolling battering-ram—

sent it flying into the midst of the knot of men dashing toward him from the doorway.

A cold, wet hand clutched his throat. Peter swung wildly; heard the satisfactory sound of a sick grunt as his fist smashed into a bony jaw.

Then came the knife. It slashed his coat open from shoulder to wrist, slicing through the flesh at his elbow to the bone.

Peter struck out at this unseen assailant; missed him; struck again, lower, and landed a blow somewhere near an invisible yellow man's solar plexus.

Blunt, behind him cried: "Moore! Where are you? I'm stabbed!"

The man in the doorway still held the brass lantern aloft, shouting orders in Tonkinese. Peter dimly saw a club rise above his head. He grabbed with both hands as the club came down; felt a finger snap, but hung onto the club and wrenched it free.

He heard Blunt's sobbing breath behind him: "Where are you, Moore? For God's sake, where are you?"

Peter brought the club down on a skull, wheeled about and groped for the wireless man.

"Here!" he said. "Take this club!"

He pushed the club into the operator's hand and growled: "Down that alley!"

"They got me in the shoulder!"

PETER HEARD something go hissing past his ear; dimly saw a grimacing brown face and lashed out at it with his fist. He missed the face, but the brown man ducked and gave Peter an opening. He saw the white glimmer now of Blunt's uniform; grasped his shoulder, gave him a push and repeated, "Down that alley!" His hand came away from the operator's shoulder wet and sticky.

Blunt moaned, "I don't know where the damned alley is!"

Peter gave him another shove; ducked and struck out at

another brown face, grasped Blunt's arm and started him off at a stumbling run down the covered alleyway.

That hurtling ricksha had evidently worked havoc on the scar-faced man's plans. He was shrieking orders now.

WITH BLUNT sobbing and moaning beside him, Peter started down the dimly glowing arched hole he had come through a moment before.

The wireless man struck down two men with the club as they started. Then they broke into a run. Halfway down the dark tunnel Peter collided with a man, heard the hiss of savagely indrawn breath and blindly struck at him; hit him in the face and stomach; sent him stumbling back with a crash against the brick wall.

The two Americans started running again. They reached the sidewalk and continued to run. The fog swallowed them; lent them a cloak of invisibility, but Peter did not permit Chester Blunt to slow down until he had got his bearings.

Peter found that they were on Tung Street, above Upper Lascar Row. Reaching Bonham Strand, Peter was certain that they were, at least for the time being, secure from attack.

Under a street light they stopped and Peter examined the wireless man's wound. Like his own, it was superficial, but bleeding freely.

"I've got to sit down," Blunt gasped. "Boy! That was some scrap! So this is China! Hongkong—hello! But say, what in hell was the rumpus all about?"

Peter told him briefly. "You were wrong about that Chicago lawyer," he said. "That knife in his heart was meant for me. This little party was Chong's fourth attempt to get me out of his way."

The two young men seated themselves in a dark doorway. Chester Blunt lighted a cigarette and expelled smoke through his teeth. He was shaking with excitement.

"I thought Chong was on the level," he declared. "I thought he was a great guy."

"Where did you meet him?"

"At a party Chong threw for a gang of us at Baguio, outside Manila. That's why I missed my ship. Chong told me to come along to Hongkong and catch her on his yacht. Of course, I can't see Susan's marrying him. She's just biting off trouble for herself. But I wouldn't go butting in on her affairs. None of my business."

"**THAT'S HOW** I feel," Peter said. "Chong is a rotten yellow dog. Susan knows it. She's looking for thrills and she welcomes trouble. She thinks this is adventure. She's going into it with her eyes wide open."

"Yeah," the wireless man agreed. "And she's going to saw herself off plenty trouble. She says she's going to marry Chong to-morrow. I wonder what Anarra will think of that. Ever see Anarra?"

"No. Is she on the Sapphire?"

"Sure, she is! They say Chong is nuts about her. I got it from an American doctor who lives in Bangkok. He was a passenger on the Vandalia last trip. I heard in Manila that Anarra has the most beautiful hair in the world. Well, she hasn't any more. This doctor told me Chong had brought Anarra to him. She had had some kind of jungle fever and lost all her hair and came down with some kind of pernicious anemia, so she has to have blood transfusions all the time. I saw her. She's as bald as a billiard ball. Hey! What's the big idea?"

Peter had savagely seized his arm.

"Did you see that girl on the Sapphire?"

"Sure! I used to see her peeking through a hole in a door when Chong was trying to make love to Susan. She has snaky eyes, this Anarra."

"Didn't Susan ever see her?"

"I don't know. I don't think so. Anarra kept herself pretty well hidden."

"Did you ever mention her to Susan?"

"Nope. I was engaged in minding my own business. Why all the excitement?"

"Listen, Blunt," Peter said. "I hope you're sober enough to understand what I'm going to tell you. This evening, on the bund, I pulled a fellow out of the water who had been scalped. He was babbling about a bald-headed woman with eyes like a snake's. He mentioned a yellow devil who had held him while his blood was pumped into this hairless woman. The scalping was an experiment. I ran to get him some brandy. When I got back, he was gone. I heard them drowning him out in the fog. Do you know what this means?"

The wireless man said, "You don't think they're framing up Susan—Oh, hell, Moore; that's preposterous! You mean, Chong doesn't want to marry Susan, but wants her hair and blood—"

"—For that vampire of his," Peter finished.

Chester Blunt sprang up. His eyes seemed to be all whites. For a moment, Peter was afraid he was going to faint from sheer horror.

"I don't believe it!" the operator stammered. "And if it's true, I—I don't want to get mixed up in this. What do you want to do?"

"We'll go to the Tiger's Den," Peter said.

CHAPTER VIII

DREAM DUST

SUSAN, HOPING THAT Peter's appointment with Fong Toy would not materialize, waited for him in the Oriental Hotel lobby until almost half past twelve. Then the young man from the American consulate who had brought her to Chong's impromptu party, and two of the girls who had come over on the Sultan's yacht from Manila happened along and urged her to go with them.

"Jim Bonner said he couldn't hold a table down there much later than midnight," the young man pointed out.

"But I gave Chester a message telling Mr. Moore I'd meet him here," Susan said.

"You'd better not wait," the vice-consul argued. "He may not show up at all. And it's dangerous to run around after dark in a ricksha in this man's town."

"Leave a chit in his mail box and tell him to come on down," one of the girls suggested.

Susan agreed to do this. She wanted to have another talk with Peter. For very private reasons of her own, she was piqued by his attitude. The one thing she had wanted him to say, the one question she had wanted him to ask, he had failed to utter. She wanted to give him another chance to plead with her. Her campaign so far had miserably failed. She didn't actually love Chong. She had used him simply as a club over Peter's head— and Peter had failed to react according to her scheme.

Susan's pride was now terribly involved. If Peter didn't try in

51

the right way to dissuade her from marrying Chong, she would marry him just to spite Peter.

She seated herself at a writing desk in the lobby and scribbled a hasty note:

> DEAR OLD BUM:
>   Please don't fail me. I feel there are certain angles of this situation which we haven't yet discussed. I am going down to the Tiger's Den now with some of the crowd. If you don't show up by one-thirty, I am very apt to get mad and go home and to bed. Come on! You'll like my gang, and we will have one last dance and one last drink together, for to-morrow we die.
>   SUSAN.

This note she left with the night clerk at the desk, requesting him to give it to Peter Moore the instant he came in.

"It's very urgent," she said. Then she joined her friends.

THE MOMENT she had gone, the night clerk opened the envelope, copied the message, resealed the original one and placed it in its envelope, pasting down the flap. The copy he gave to a slim, brown-skinned young man who was sitting idly in the lobby and who, clutching the message, now hastened out of the lobby and into a waiting ricksha.

Now, the Tiger's Den in Hongkong is typical of a certain type of native cabaret which has sprung into being in the treaty ports of China as a result of the heavy influx of tourists, especially Americans. Once a third-rate hop joint and native chow house, its antique, Oriental and sinister flavor made it gradually popular as a place for tourists to see native vice at its worst—as they imagined.

Its wily proprietors saw an excellent opportunity to cash in, and cashed in. Retaining the sinister, Oriental and antique flavor, they abolished the opium-smoking stalls, hired a Chinese orchestra and presented for the tourists' enthusiastic approval the kind of chow house Americans can squander money in under the delusion that they are seeing darkest China, and then go home and boast of it.

To this spurious imitation, Susan and her friends flocked that evening to glimpse something of China in the raw. Incense burned in braziers. Lamps and candles flickered on chains from the ceiling and in sockets on the aged sandalwood walls.

The air was thick with incense smoke, cigar and cigarette smoke and the fumes of whisky, gin *bijt* and pungent Javanese arrack. If you wanted *samshu*—Chinese rice whisky—you could have it. Price, fifty cents a drink: worth fifty cents a gallon, and a headache free of charge.

The orchestra, by listening to American orchestras at the hotels, had learned how to imitate American dance music, after a fashion. It was impossible to identify what they were trying to play, but they kept a jiggly kind of time to which it was possible to dance on a floor not much larger than a steamer rug.

Susan bad seen enough of the real China with Peter to know that the Tiger's Den was a tawdry imitation, but she loved it, anyway. They had a large table beside the dance floor.

But her fun was spoiled by Peter's non-appearance. She glanced frequently at her wrist watch, tapped a high heel impatiently, and vowed that if Peter didn't show up soon she'd never speak to him again as long as she lived. She had forgotten that, after to-morrow, she would never see Peter again.

AT A little before one o'clock a waiter came to her side and asked, with a gleaming smile:

"Missy, what name hab got?"

Susan told him. He said, above the shrill din of the orchestra:

"That Masta' Moo', him talkee my, wanchee you that side chop-chop. Can do?"

Simply translated, Peter was outside and wanted to see her.

"You talkee that Masta Moore," Susan answered, "to come this side chop-chop. You talkee him my wanchee him this side. Sabbe?"

"Yes, missy. But that Masta' Moo', he talkee he no can come this side. He talkee you come that side."

It vexed Susan. She said to Jim Bonner:

"My boy friend is outside, but he's too damned shy to come in."

The waiter said anxiously: "That Masta' Moo' say, no talkee. No wanchee bhobbery. Sabbe? He say, wanchee you come that side befo' he come this side. He say, velly impoltant."

"I don't get this at all," Susan said. "It doesn't make sense."

But she arose and followed the waiter. It made still less sense when she reached the lobby and found no Peter. The waiter gave her his gleaming smile and said, "That Masta' Moo', he outside in licksha. Velly sick."

"Sick!" Susan shrieked. "Why in the devil didn't you say so in the first place?"

She hastened indignantly and anxiously out into Hai-Phong Road. The tall Mongolian doorman stood with folded arms and looked down at her with the calm inscrutability of a temple god.

"Where's Mr. Moore?" she demanded.

The Mongolian shrugged. "My no sabbe, missy."

Susan peered helplessly into the fog. Several rickshas were drawn up in the mud. Several seemed to be occupied; several, empty.

"Peter!" she cried. "Peter! Where are you?"

Listening for his answer, she heard that disturbing exotic sound Peter had heard earlier in the evening—the faraway, rhythmic thumping of a witch-drum. *Tumpa-dum-dum!* It recalled to her sharply the tom-toms of the Indo-Chinese jungles.

A man had appeared magically at her side. In the light from the doorway, she saw, to her amazement, the round, brown face of Chong Foo Shommon. He wore a black cape over his white clothing.

Her face lighted up. She cried: "Why, Chong! What in the world are you doing here? I thought you were on the Sapphire!"

He had taken her elbow firmly.

"I want to have a talk with you, Susan."

Still smiling, she said, "No, Chong. Nothing doing. I promised to have breakfast with you at ten o'clock at the hotel. And you promised not to interfere with me in any way until then."

SUSAN TRIED to shake off his hand. When she could not, she laughed. "Chong, what's the big idea? Let go my arm. You're hurting me."

"I want you to come with me. Get into this ricksha."

Susan laughed again. It was a nervous laugh. Chong had always been so amiable, jolly, considerate. She did not know him now.

"Get into this ricksha!" he repeated sternly.

"But why?" she cried.

"I want to talk to you."

"Talk to me here."

"No."

"Then you'll have to wait till breakfast time, Chong. I don't like this. Really, I don't like it a little bit. My friends are inside. I can't run out on them. And I won't. Let me go."

Still she was only surprised; not afraid.

"I said, get—into—this—ricksha!"

Susan was not accustomed to being ordered about by anybody. An American dollar princess, she had always given orders and always intended to.

"I won't!" she snapped. "Chong, what's got into you?"

"You're coming with me."

"But what for?"

"Because I tell you to."

And not until then did the beautiful little thrill-lover become actually uneasy. The look in his eyes was alarming. The expression about his mouth was strange and hard. It came to Susan suddenly that she was tired of this game she had been playing with Chong. Quite as suddenly she realized that she had been playing with fire.

"Chong," she said rapidly, "listen. It's all off. I'm not going to marry you. I don't love you. Let me go."

His grip on her arm tightened. His hand, on her bare flesh, felt sticky. She looked down at it—saw that it was dark red with drying blood.

Susan screamed briefly—a piercing little scream. Chong withdrew his other hand from a fold of the cape; opened it under her face with a curious snapping gesture.

Brownish powder floated in a puff into her face. It stung her eyes, made her want to sneeze.

Susan's last impression, before the drug sent misty blackness flooding down on her, blinding her, paralyzing all her senses, was of a remote sound—a drum or tom-tom far out over the fog-bound harbor. *Tumpa-dum-dum! Tumpa-dum-dum!*

CHAPTER IX

MISSING

PETER MOORE AND the senior wireless officer of the Vandalia proceeded at a lope down Wing Lok Street to Des Voeux Road until they reached Hai-Phong Street. The Mongolian doorman of the Tiger's Den scrutinized them, glanced with Oriental indifference at Peter's slit sleeve and the wireless man's bloody shoulder, and let them pass.

Chester Blunt, staring out over the smoke-filled, noisy room, exclaimed, "Thank God, the gang's still here!"

Peter followed his eyes and saw the large table. The orchestra was playing a Hongkong conception of "I Love You So Much." The small dance floor was crowded with swaying couples. Peter did not see Susan at the table, and presumed that she was dancing.

The wireless man took him around to the table and introduced him to Jim Bonner, who was a plump, pink-cheeked young man, with a pronounced Harvard accent.

Jim Bonner said that Susan had mentioned Peter frequently. Then: "Did you bring her back?"

"Back?" Peter repeated.

"Sure!" said Bonner. "Back! The party can't go on without Susie. Where is she?"

"Isn't she here?"

Jim Bonner stared at him, then laughed. "Susie didn't tell me you were a practical joker, Mr. Moore,"

"I'm not joking," Peter said. "Susan told me to join your party down here."

Further confusion was now added by one of the girls' discovery that Chester Blunt had been stabbed in the shoulder.

"Yeah," the operator said, "Moore and I got into a mix-up with a lot of Tonkinese cutthroats. If it hadn't been for some quick work, I never would have got us out of that jam."

Peter let that pass.

A blond girl exclaimed: "You were hurt, too, Mr. Moore!"

"It isn't anything," Peter said. And to Jim Bonner: "I'm worried about Susan. She said she'd be here. And she's absolutely dependable."

But his remarks were lost. Jim Bonner was now listening to Chester Blunt's exciting account of that ambush in this darkened alley off Tung Street.

"Moore says it's the fourth attempt Chong has made on his life to-night."

Some one cried, "That's ridiculous! Chong wouldn't—"

Peter grabbed Jim Bonner's arm and swung him roughly around. "I want to know where Susan is!"

The smile went away from the plump young man's mouth. "How do I know where she is?" he demanded. "You called for her ten minutes ago, didn't you? You told her you wanted her to come outside a moment, didn't you?"

"I did not."

"Well, I heard a waiter tell her you wanted her outside, and she went outside; and I supposed you and she had gone off somewhere. It doesn't seem to make much sense, does it?"

"Yes," Peter said. "It makes too much sense. Blunt, come on along."

"More excitement?"

TAKING HIM by the elbow, Peter hurried Blunt into the lobby. Then he tried to explain. "Chong must have called for her and sent in word that I was calling. He's taken her aboard that yacht."

"What makes you so sure?"

"Where else would he take her? Come on!"

The wireless man was reluctant. He said: "Listen, Moore; I'm not sure Chong took her aboard the Sapphire. There's dozens of places in Hongkong where he could have taken her. Maybe she framed it with that waiter and went back to the hotel. Shall we try the hotel first?"

"No," Peter said firmly. "Where's the Sapphire lying?"

"Out in the roadstead, between Honghom and North Point—over Kowloon way. But I'm sure—"

"That's where we're going!"

The operator grew more reluctant. He didn't believe Susan was on the Sapphire. "I don't think Chong means any harm to her, anyway."

"We'll find that out when we're aboard the Sapphire."

Peter urged him along Connaught Road until it joined the bund proper. His objective was the sampan jetty at the foot of Peddars Street.

Not far from the street light where Peter had pulled that groaning unfortunate out of the water, Chester Blunt stopped. He refused to go farther.

"Listen, Moore; maybe you're right and maybe you're wrong. I think you are wrong. One way or another, I don't care for any more of this."

"But it's too much for me single-handed," Peter argued.

"That isn't any skin off my back, Moore. I didn't ask for this. Count me out."

"Are you," Peter asked, "going to let that girl be torn apart by these devils?"

"I'm thinking of my own scalp. After all, she's nothing in my life."

"Where are you going?"

"Back to the Tiger's Den. You're crazy. You can't make me believe Chong is such a fiend as all that. It's preposterous."

"So long," Peter said curtly, and abruptly left him.

He hastened out onto the sampan jetty. At the outshore end he was stopped by a red-turbaned Sikh policeman, who was courteous but firm. No one but ships' officers could use the sampans to-night, sahib. The risk was too great. Pirates and harbor cutthroats were too active.

Pete discarded as utterly impractical the idea of telling the policeman about Chong and his vampire woman. Sikh policemen think slowly. This one would take Peter to Police Headquarters. Time would be lost. Unless Peter was mistaken, Chong would lose little time in putting to sea. The Sapphire might be under weigh at this very moment.

Peter obeyed an impulse. It was his only chance now. He ran down Connaught Road toward Hai-Phong Street. Through the fog he heard again the thumping of the witch drum. He all but collided with Chester Blunt, a white figure in the fog, as he swung off Connaught Road into Hai-Phong.

"Lend me that uniform," he said. "Take it off. My clothes will fit you well enough."

The wireless operator looked at him and laughed. Peter slugged him on the point of the chin. And so nicely timed was the blow that he caught the limp young man neatly in his arms as he pitched forward.

A GOLDEN temple spire extended at least five hundred feet into the air. About the base of this great *wat*—far greater than the Schwe Dagon, in Rangoon—were smaller *wats*, each containing a deity wrought of the same precious yellow metal. In the foreheads of some of these lesser Buddhas were emeralds, as green as the Java Sea; in the brows of others were sapphires, diamonds, rubies.

The air about the compound of the golden temple was perfumed with the fragrance of jasmine blossoms, with the smoke from incense burners, and it was sweet with the songs of jungle birds.

Susan O'Gilvie climbed up white marble steps to the courtyard and found, to her amazement, that it was paved with slabs of purest silver. As she waited, a butterfly of brilliant blue with wings flapping indolently, floated toward her from the misty greenness of a breadfruit tree. She heard the silvery call of a mango bird.

She had the sensation that she had been in this place before, yet she could not recall just when it had been or what the circumstances were. She was waiting here for some one. It was an appointment. Yet she could not recall the man's name.

As she tried to force it from her memory, the golden scene suddenly shifted. Magically and very mysteriously, she found herself drifting high above the earth, defying gravitation and other earthly laws.

Calm and insistent reason now penetrated these heavenly sensations, and she realized that she was being carried in the arms of some man. Who was he? Where was she going?

Her brain cleared marvelously. It became as clear as a drop of rain water. It was a crystal in which all past events stood out with cameo sharpness. This mental clarity reminded her of the one and only time she had smoked opium, when each thought that came to her was vivid and exciting; yet she could not quite recall where or when she had smoked the opium. It had been on a ship.

Her next distinct impression was that of the gurgling of water. Then she sensed that she was being lowered; that her numb body was being passed from the arms of one man to the arms of another. Her brain was crystal-clear, but her body was utterly without sensation. It was as if she were nonexistent from the neck down.

Sounds seemed to come from far off. She heard a familiar sound; identified it as the throbbing exhaust of a motor boat. Then she felt a cool damp breeze against her cheeks. Her eyes fluttered open to encounter perfect darkness, and she wondered if she had suddenly gone blind. All about her in the blackness were strange clankings and soft bellowings. It seemed to her that these bellowings came from the steel lungs of ships, but she could not focus her mind on it—or on anything.

Susan was completely detached from the reality about her. Her brain refused to put obvious twos and twos together.

At length, a radiance fell on her closed eyelids. She opened them to behold what appeared to be a long necklace made of bright lights. Above this was a similar necklace, but not so bright. Far above, two bright solitary lights rode. There were more gurglings; then the far-away muttering of men, and once again the sensation of floating in space.

The necklace came closer. She tried to lift her chin from her breastbone, but the muscles of her neck refused the command. Looking down she saw narrow white planks spaced with black lines. There was something about this pattern that suggested a ship, a yacht, to her; but she could not say for sure just what it meant.

She was vaguely aware, now, that a man was on each side of her—a dark-skinned man. Looking down again, she saw her feet dangling above the narrow white planks with their black spacings. Her feet were not touching the planks. She was floating above them, with a man on each side of her.

IN SPITE of the crystal clearness of her brain, she could not remember when she had been in this place before; yet she had been here before. She recognized a mahogany door, and knew that just beyond it there would be a grass-green carpet, with a mirror in the wall just opposite the door.

The door was opened, and there was a grass-green carpet on the floor, with a mirror set in the wall just opposite. She tried to lift her head, to look at herself in the mirror, as she had always done when she came through this door; but her neck muscles still refused to obey her commands.

She wanted to see her face in the mirror. She was certain that her face was a peculiar sea-green, but she wanted to make sure.

Susan floated down the grass-green carpet to where it came to an end. Beyond that was— What was beyond that? She remembered now. Bluebeard's forbidden room!

The forbidden door opened. She had always wanted to see what was beyond that door. Now her curiosity was satisfied. The first thing she saw was a woman's tiny feet. They were in golden slippers. Beautifully slim and shapely ankles were attached to the tiny feet in the golden slippers.

Susan could see only as far as the knees. There, the slim legs ended in a fringe of gold and red. Susan was sure she saw rubies, as red as blood, sewn into the fringe, and the authentic blue-white flash of diamonds.

But try as she would, Susan could not lift her head to see above the gemmed fringe.

She was sure she smelled incense. Then, far off, came voices. They tinkled, rose and fell. Somehow they had the sound of waterfalls.

Susan wished that she could see the rest of the woman with the beautiful legs.

Another door opened. Beyond was glittering pure whiteness. Even the floor was white. And the room was filled with strange, somehow familiar objects of white enamel. Chairs. Two long white tables. Cases of plate glass with white shelves on which metallic objects glittered.

Susan tried to move her hands. They were without feeling. She tried to move one foot. It would not move. It was as dead as stone.

The floor wheeled and rose toward her. Her brain tingled with a giddy triumph. She knew that she had been seated in a chair. Now she could look at the woman with the beautiful legs. She could not move her head, but she could move her eyes. They slid from side to side until she found the tiny golden sandals.

They traveled up to the fringe again; were again delighted with the rubies and the sparkling diamonds. They went on up to a slim waist, about which a sapphire-blue sash was tied; on up to a neck.

Now Susan could see all of her. Yet she knew that something was wrong. The woman had no hair. Her face, if she had hair, would have been beautiful. It was delicately chiseled and golden in color. It had all the grace and beauty of a golden figurine. It was a young face, and it was a terribly evil face. The eyes were green, and they held the bright, gem-like glitter of a snake's eyes. The eyes were staring at Susan's hair. Susan tried to smile. The woman bared her teeth, and they were the teeth of a bat.

An unaccountable chill stole over Susan. Something was wrong. Something was terribly wrong. But her poor, drugged brain refused to tell her what it was.

A FAMILIAR face floated down and blotted out her view of the beautiful, hairless woman with snake-like eyes. And a familiar voice said:

"Drink this, Susan." She was trying to remember where she had seen the man's face before. It was round and brown and adorned with a black toy mustache.

The man was holding something to her lips—a bright green liquid. Her lips, her tongue, her cheeks were numb. But Susan could feel the cold liquid strike the back of her throat.

Sensation began flowing through her in little waves of fire. She could move her hands, her feet, her head. She clenched her fists, opened them experimentally. Then the fire reached her brain—and the result was chaos. The clearness went in a strange kind of explosion. Things in Susan's brain were topsy-turvy for a number of seconds. Then she shook her head sharply, and realized that the man bending over her was Chong Foo Shommon, the Sultan of Sakala—the man she had foolishly promised to marry.

Her last distinct recollection was of talking to Chong on Hai-Phong Road, in front of the Tiger's Den. Dimly, she recalled the brown powder he had scattered.

Everything since had, then, been a dream: the golden pagoda;

the sounds in the night; the woman with no hair on her head, the gem-bright eyes of a reptile, and the small, sharp, white teeth of a bat.

Susan looked quickly about the room. Instantaneous impressions startled her. This was an operating room! The white tables were operating tables! The glass cases were full of surgical instruments!

Her roving eyes found the girl; leaped from her tiny golden sandals upward to her golden face: her hairless head!

Susan stifled a small scream, and she heard Chong say:

"How do you feel now, Susan?"

Susan cried: "What am I doing here? Where am I? Who is that horrible creature?"

Chong did not immediately answer. While she waited, she heard a familiar throbbing; guessed wildly that she was on the Sapphire; The throbbing meant that it was under way.

The hairless girl now came over and squatted on the white tile floor at Susan's feet, not a yard away, and stared up at her. Her eyes were on Susan's hair. She reached for Susan's left hand; examined it with animal-like curiosity; sniffed at it, then snatched from the engagement finger the sapphire ring which Chong had given her.

Chong looked on with a mysterious smile. He said now: "Susan, this is my wife, Anarra. I am sorry that she speaks no English. You see, she admires your hair. She has no hair of her own. She thinks you have such beautiful hair."

Susan stifled another scream. Anarra arose, and as if she fully understood what Chong had said, ran her long, thin, yellow fingers into Susan's hair. She loosened it at the back and lifted it in her hands, then said a short sentence in Tonkinese to Chong.

"She says," Chong translated, "it is the most beautiful hair, outside of her own, she has ever seen."

"Tell her to keep her hands off me!" Susan cried.

CHONG SPOKE to Anarra; she answered in a shrill staccato of syllables. Chong said, in English: "I am sorry. She says she likes your hair. She wants your hair."

A sense of the horrible possibilities of this situation struck Susan suddenly. Chong went on, in the same calm, almost humorous flavor:

"I will explain what all this means, Susan. You see now, I do not love you. I do not care for you in the least. It was all part of a somewhat elaborate plan. My wife has no hair."

"What has that to do with me?" Susan cried. She was white. Her eyes were terrified.

"I am trying to explain, Susan. Perhaps, under the circumstances, I should say Miss O'Gilvie. I have never loved any woman in the world but Anarra. No request she makes is too great or too trivial for me to grant. When she said she wished to see a woman with hair as beautiful as her own had been, I set out to find such a woman. I searched Shanghai, Yokohama, Singapore—and in Manila I found you. Your hair is truly beautiful—almost as beautiful as Anarra's was.

"I took some pains to arrange that a number of your friends should travel to Hongkong on this yacht. I took some pains that Anarra should have full opportunity to see your hair, and to see if she liked it well enough to have it for her own."

Susan got out in a strangled voice: "What do you mean? How can she have my hair?"

"One moment, Miss O'Gilvie. You asked for a complete explanation. Permit me to continue. It was obviously impossible to detain you on this boat when your friends went ashore. I know that you are a very wealthy American girl. I have no wish to run into difficulties with your government. I could have circulated the report that you had fallen overboard some night. But that would not have looked well."

"But why," Susan burst out hysterically, "did you want me at all? What are you going to do with me? Why am I here?"

Chong said: "One moment. My assistant wishes a sample of your blood."

Susan shrank back. "What for?"

"We wish to ascertain whether or not it matches Anarra's blood."

"But why?" Susan cried.

"I will explain in due course. Will you let my assistant have a sample—or must we hold you?"

The conversation was beginning to have the qualities of a nightmare.

A man in spotless white whom she had seen casually on the trip from Manila and believed to be a deck steward bent over her now. Too shocked to move, she let him puncture her arm with a hollow needle and draw off a sample of her blood. He went away.

In growing terror, Susan looked at Chong. She said desperately: "Chong! What are you going to do to me?"

Anarra, who had been standing beside him, now bent down again and ran her yellow fingers through Susan's hair. They were cold as ice.

"Get away from me!" Susan cried.

Anarra stepped back.

"Chong," Susan wailed, "what are you going to do to me?"

"I will tell you in a moment."

"Are you going to cut off my hair?"

"I will answer no questions until Dr. Ling returns with his report."

Susan was not the fainting kind, but the hideous threat which lurked in Chong's incomplete explanation and in the greedy snake-like eyes of the hairless girl terrified her so that she could not fight off the engulfing blackness. The operating room went gray, then swimmingly black.

CHAPTER X

THE BLOOD RITUAL

SHE RETURNED TO consciousness with the pungent taste of brandy on her tongue. She was still sitting in the chair. A man on each side was holding her up. She recognized one as a dining room steward, the other as a deck steward.

Susan saw Dr. Ling come in from a small room full of shelves which glistened with colored bottles, large and small.

Dr. Ling spoke briefly to Chong in Tonkinese. Susan looked from him to Anarra. Her bat-like teeth were bared in an exultant grimace.

"Miss O'Gilvie," Chong said, "I will tell you now why you are here. About fourteen months ago, Anarra all but died as a result of a jungle fever about which doctors know nothing. One of the after-effects of her illness you can see. She lost her hair—the most beautiful hair in the world. The other after-effect, which is invisible, was an extreme case of pernicious anæmia.

"For a great many months, I have been making experiments with various people in hair grafting. Let me tell you about them."

Susan shrieked, "No! Let me off this ship! Put me ashore! Chong, put me off this ship!"

She knew now where Chong's casual conversation was leading. But the horror, bursting upon her, did not cause her to faint. She wished that she could faint. She wished that she could drop dead. She knew that she was in the hands of an Oriental fiend; a cold-blooded and cold-thinking barbarian from the Cambodian jungles who cunningly concealed his true nature behind a thin veneer of civilization. She struggled against the brown hands holding her in the chair. She was helpless.

Chong went calmly on. He would, she realized, torture her with words first. It would be in harmony with the true nature of the man to do so.

"There have been some amusing experiments," Chong went on. "There was a red-headed Irishman in Singapore, and an Italian from Rangoon with curly black hair. I removed the red hair from the Irishman and grafted it on the head of the Italian, and I gave the Irishman the black hair of the Italian."

Susan let herself go limp. Her heart was thumping laboriously. Perhaps it would stop. If she could only die instantly!

Chong went serenely on: "The operations were a great success. The red hair grew on the black-haired man, and the black hair grew on the red-haired man. I have proved that it can be done. To-night I employed a new technique, but my specimen escaped. You will not escape, Miss O'Gilvie."

Susan was trying not to listen, but the barbarian's voice reached her clearly.

"You will never see civilization again, Miss O'Gilvie. You will not wish to. You are to be Anarra's slave. You are to be Anarra's hair dresser. To-night, I will graft your scalp on Anarra's. When you have both recovered from the operation, you are to supply her with blood whenever she requires it. Dr. Ling says that your blood matches hers perfectly. We will see that you are fed the proper blood-building foods so that, when Anarra needs blood, it will be pumped from your veins into hers. You will not live long, Miss O'Gilvie, but your life will be, for probably the first time, of some real use."

A kindly numbness, a paralysis, was stealing over Susan's mind, shutting out the horror of this brown barbarian's words. Her eyes suddenly stung with tears of self-pity. Her beautiful hair! But she would never live beyond the operation. Certainly, the shock would kill her. She would not live to furnish blood to this bat-woman. It was characteristic of Chong, characteristic of the Oriental irony of the educated savage, that he should make Susan Anarra's slave—should give Susan the task of dressing her own hair on another woman's head!

THE PARALYSIS increased. Dully, she saw a strange-looking man come into the operating room. His face was shiny and purple with paint. There were black splotches of paint where his eyes were. His mouth was vermilion. He wore a black sarong, and carried in one hand a gourd, in the other a pair of bones.

He squatted down on the floor between Susan and the operating table. Anarra promptly squatted down opposite him.

It was fast becoming a nightmare of the deepest Oriental jungle. The bones in his hand looked like human bones. The lumps on the ends might be elbow joints.

He began beating on the drum, and Anarra kept time to him with her uplifted hands. *Tumpa-dum-dum! Tumpa-dum-dum!*

So it was going to be a ritual! With glazing eyes, Susan watched, and with ears slowly going senseless, she listened. She felt her heart keeping time with the drum. Her head pulsed to its rhythmic measure.

She heard Chong say: "I'm going to give you ether, of course. You will kindly lie down on the operating table, Miss O'Gilvie."

Something in Susan let go. She was on her feet, blindly striking at Chong, and screaming. Her screams were louder than the temple gourd. Anarra sprang up and rushed at her with fingers which were suddenly the claws of a tigress.

Some one struck Susan on the head from in back. The blow did not knock her unconscious. It only hurt her. Her head sang and her senses rocked with the blow, but she did not become unconscious.

With a man on each side, she was dragged to the operating table. She saw Dr. Ling bring an ether cone and a can of ether from the laboratory. She freed one hand and struck out at Anarra. The blow caught the golden vampire full in the mouth. Anarra staggered back and fell across the gourd.

Then strong hands forced Susan down on her back on the

table. The cone came down over her face. She could not even twist her head. As she fought for breath against a sudden sweet stifling, she heard Chong say:

"I am giving you ether, Miss O'Gilvie, simply to prevent you from doing injury to your scalp when I remove it. I have no sympathy for you. None in the least. The man or woman who strikes Anarra dies. You can carry this thought into your sleep. To-morrow, I will take all of your blood that Anarra can use. And she can use every drop of blood in your veins."

PETER RAN his thumb along the edge of the knife and knew that it would, if called upon, cleave a head or a hair. It was a *parang*—wickedest knife in the world—with a bone handle which a man could grip firmly, a curving two-edged blade about fourteen inches long ending in a vicious point. The *parang* was a weapon popular with Malays when they ran amuck. Unless Peter was mistaken, he would run amuck to-night.

The light in the sampan's cabin flickered in little golden worms on the keenly whetted blade. Peter, squatting in the stern of the sampan, at the coolie's feet, looked up from the *parang* and said:

"How much wanchee?"

The coolie, not missing a stroke, answered, in a grunt: "Maskee."

Peter said, "Putee book—five dolla'."

"No wanchee," the coolie muttered. *"Parang* b'long my. *Parang* allatime stay mine."

"Ten dolla'."

It was a fabulous price to offer for a *parang*. Both men realized it. Peter suited action to words; drew forth a ten-dollar note on the Bank of Hongkong and said:

"Can do?"

The coolie hesitated; grunted, "Can do." Ten dollars Mex changed ownership.

A black monster loomed up in the thinning fog. A mournful

bellow issued from it. Peter made out, dimly, the name in gilt across a flying bridge: Yokohama Maru.

He asked, "Which side Kowloon?"

"That side."

"I thought so. Hurry up! Chop-chop!"

As he spoke, the gleaming hull of the yacht emerged from the fog—twin necklaces of lights. Moving!

Peter shouted again, "Chop-chop!" But the coolie was doing his utmost at the sweep. The gleaming hull, the twin necklaces of lights, glided slowly past. The Sapphire was under way, picking up speed.

It was a question: was Susan aboard, or had Chong taken her to some retreat of his in Hongkong—Kowloon—Macao—Canton? Every logical reason pointed to the Sapphire.

Peter saw that the companion ladder still hung over the side. A deck hand in soiled white was walking slowly toward it, from aft. He was going to haul the ladder in. Peter gesticulated wildly toward the ladder. The blunt bows of the sampan swung to starboard. Peter tossed a bill to the coolie's feet, not knowing what its denomination was.

The bottom platform of the ladder was at least six feet away when Peter scrambled upon the sampan's flimsy cabin roof. He poised a moment for the leap; gathered himself together, and as an afterthought, gripped the *parang* in his teeth. If he missed the ladder, fell, that two-edged blade would slice his head half off.

He leaped; caught at the lower platform and snatched it with one hand. His legs dangled, trailing in the water.

Peter removed the *parang* from his mouth; laid it on the ladder; pulled himself up; picked up the *parang* and scrambled up the ladder to the deck.

CHAPTER XI

ABOARD THE HORROR YACHT

HE WAS MET there by a brown-faced fury. The deck hand evidently had guessed his designs; had seized from a rack a belaying pin. This crude and burly weapon was swinging up and over when Peter struck down into his mid-section with the knife.

The Tonkinese deck hand collapsed with a bubbling grunt, and the heavy iron pin rolled into the scuppers.

Peter shook blood from the knife and paused for a moment. He did not know the deck plans of the Sapphire, but first he wanted to find the wireless house. As he paused, he heard, vaguely, the beating of the witch drum. *Tumpa-dum-dum!* He thought at first it was in his imagination; then realized that the sound issued from the very interior of the yacht.

He put down the temptation to follow that barbaric sound to its source, espied a stairway and swarmed up it to the next deck. Here were evidently officers' quarters. He strained his eyes into the dimness above, saw a star shining faintly, then others, and found at last that for which he was seeking—the lead-in wires from the yacht's wireless antennæ.

The phosphor-bronze wires came down in a sharp V, terminating at a lead-in insulator of petticoated porcelain above a small, square deck house just forward of the buff-colored funnel.

A light gleamed at a window. Above the measured grinding of the Sapphire's engines, he heard the fine high whine of a dynamo or a motor-generator.

He advanced swiftly to the wireless house door, firmly gripped the brass knob; turned it. The door was locked.

Peter backed across the deck to the white belly of a lifeboat, lowered his left shoulder and charged the door.

It gave with a crash; flew inward in splintering panels and chunks.

A brown-skinned man at the instrument table turned amazed eyes on him. Then he looked at the bloody knife in Peter's hand. From the knife his glance shot back to Peter's eyes. And there he saw, presumably, the look which all southern Orientals hold in the greatest dread—the stark staring look of the man amuck!

He uttered a bleat of terror; sprang up from his chair and executed a neat dive to the deck, via the window abaft the instrument table. It was not a large window, and it happened to be heavily paned; but the Tonkinese wireless man gave no thought to obstructions. He dived cleanly through, carrying shattering glass with him.

Peter stepped outside. He did not intend to stab the terrified man; he wished merely to make sure that the operator did not scream an alarm.

The Tonkinese radio man, misconstruing, seeing only that amok look in the white man's eyes, squealed again, backed rapidly, tripped over the low coaming between two lifeboats— and splashed into Hongkong Harbor.

RETURNING HASTILY to the wireless room, Peter seated himself at the instrument board and glanced at the operator's log. It was fortunately a well kept log. Somewhat unfortunately, the entries were in Tonkinese symbols, a picture language with which Peter was not as familiar as he might have been; yet, studying the neat, five-minute entries, he gathered important conclusions.

He studied the neat lists of call letters which the wireless man had so carefully entered in his log, then grinned rather fiercely and flashed out a call.

It was instantly answered. Peter plied the brass key briskly.

"Where are you? How is the weather out there?"

The answer came singing into the receivers he had clamped over his ears; a position report in terms of latitude and longitude, then: "Fog lifted here. Full moon."

Peter briskly tapped out his urgent message. Then he turned off the generator, picked up his *parang* and returned to the deck.

He could still hear the jungle melody of the witch-drum and he set out now to track it down.

He ran aft to a ladder and slid down it to the promenade deck, landing, surprisingly, athwart the shoulders of a stout man with gold on his cap and gold stripes at his sleeves. The captain, first mate, or chief engineer—whatever his status may have been—went sprawling under Peter's weight.

Peter leaped up, with the red-stained *parang* in his hand, and the officer shrank back against the cabin wall with straining eyes and fully indrawn stomach muscles.

"Where is Chong?" Peter demanded in English.

"I do not know."

Peter pushed the bloody *parang* point toward the officer's stomach.

"Wait!" the man squealed. "I will show you! Come! Follow me!"

Peter, with the point of the knife in the small of the officer's back, followed him. His escort trotted down the deck, the back of his neck glistening with sweat. He threw open a door; stumbled over the rain-check into a saloon of luxurious carved mahogany and grass-green carpet.

"Come," the frightened officer said weakly.

Peter, holding the *parang* in place, followed. The way led down a corridor to a closed door. The officer turned a knob and trotted on into the room. Another luxurious room. Had Susan, Peter wondered, come this way? Yes, assuredly, if Chong were aboard!

Another door. Beyond that was the witch drum. *Tumpa-dum-dum!* Peter was sweating now himself. Sweat was running down his face, into the tight collar of Chester Blunt's uniform coat. His heart was racing with a sick feeling. What would be find beyond that door?

"Don't knock!" Peter snapped. He wanted this to be wholly a surprise attack. "Throw it open!"

"Yes, sair!" the officer hissed. A small round spot of blood had formed on the back of his white coat where the *parang* point had carelessly prodded. That was too bad!

The door opened. The sound of the drum came beating out through the doorway, waves of barbaric sound.

The officer stumbled into the room. The sweet stench of ether stung Peter's nostrils. He observed that a large porthole was open; caught a glimpse of clear moonlit water beyond. The Sapphire was out of the fog! Thank God for that!

An ape-man squatted on the floor beating on a gourd with human bones. *Tumpa-dum-dum!*

Beyond him were two tables—operating tables. Two slim figures were stretched out on these tables, the face of each covered with an ether cone.

The head of the one on Peter's left was bleeding copiously. Beautiful dark hair flowed down from the head of the other.

Which was which? Had the scalping been completed? Was Anarra now wearing Susan's hair—or was the bleeding head that of Anarra, prepared for the transfer?

Chong, in surgeon's white, wearing thin rubber gloves, was holding a scalpel in one hand. Beyond him stood a slender brown-faced man with an instrument tray in his hands.

"STAND ASIDE!" Peter barked at the man who had led him here.

The officer nimbly sidestepped. Peter glanced anxiously through the porthole. Then, before Chong had recovered from his shocked amazement, Peter was within reach of him.

"Drop that scalpel to the floor!"

Chong obeyed him, then abandoned all discretion, uttered a shrill cry and leaped at Peter. Peter, stepping back, brought the *parang* slashing down. It missed its actual goal, which was the Sultan's throat, and its razor edge sliced along Chong's skull bone.

Peter had not intended to scalp him; he had intended that thrust to be a death blow. A patch of hair five inches wide was stricken off and dropped to the floor. Chong sprang back.

Peter knocked the ether cone from the face of the nearest woman. The pale, pinched face of Susan was revealed. Her hair had not yet been touched. She was breathing heavily, stertorously, which was quite natural in a person under ether. But Peter did not know this. He thought Susan was dying. He leaped at Chong again.

Some one enfolded steel arms about his leg. It was the witch doctor.

Chong said: "Moore, you are a fool." His voice was shrill with pain. Blood streamed down his forehead, ran into his eyes. "You will die for this! And how you will die! I will slice you into ribbons! You will suffer as no man on this earth has ever suffered!"

He touched one hand to that bleeding skull of his and danced with agony.

"How," he squealed, "do you expect to leave this ship?" His voice burst into crackling Tonkinese. Peter caught a word now and then, and glanced at the porthole again. Moonlight on gray steel—a beautiful sight.

Chong was telling his first mate to seize and bind this yellow rat of an American. The first mate looked at the bloody *parang* and shuddered. He wanted none of that steel.

"You stand by," Peter growled.

"Yes, sair!"

The ape-man still clutched Peter's leg. Peter lifted his free foot and brought it down in the witch doctor's face.

Chong sagged against a bulkhead and bleated: "Try to escape from me! Try to get off this ship with her! Try!"

Peter noted that Susan was breathing more regularly. He said:

"Chong, I stopped in your wireless room before I came here. I sent a few messages. Look out that porthole."

CHONG LOOKED; gasped. What he saw was a gray lean ship, with moonlight gleaming on her guns. The destroyer was keeping pace with the Sapphire, black banners streaming from her funnels.

"That's an American destroyer, Chong. You see, you're in the midst of the Asiatic squadron. They were making for Hongkong, and I asked them to stand by. They're doing so."

Chong wiped blood from his eyes. The other doctor suddenly burst into excited Tonkinese. He ran around the table and snatched the ether from Anarra's face.

Peter glanced down into the golden face of the famous jungle beauty. But it wasn't gold now. An unforeseen alchemy had changed it to silver. And he knew that she was dead, for the dead have a look of their own, an aura that is unmistakable.

Peter did not linger. He gathered Susan into his arms, jerked his head toward the door, and the first mate scampered out ahead of him.

"Get that launch over the side," he snapped. "Stop your engines."

"Yes, sair!"

Peter carried Susan to the wireless room and arranged her in a chair. Then he seated himself at the instrument table and called the destroyer.

"Everything O.K.," he tapped out. "Miss O'Gilvie and I are leaving in small launch. Many thanks for assistance."

The answer came shrieking back: "What do you mean, 'Everything O.K.'? Commander orders Sapphire stopped for boarding party. If you leave in launch, you are ordered to report to American Consulate for full explanation. Can't you stay aboard?"

Peter flashed back: "Still too risky. Many thanks again. Will be camping on consul's doorstep when he opens office. 30. All through." It wasn't risky now, but Peter hated investigations.

The Sapphire's engines were stopped when Peter, with Susan in his arms, descended to the promenade deck. The ladder was over and the launch was alongside.

THE LAUNCH was humming through Tathong Channel before Susan betrayed signs of returning consciousness. She opened her eyes, looked at Peter, on whose lap she sat, and gasped, "Where's my hair?"

"On your head," Peter answered.

But Susan didn't hear him. The ether had only begun to wear off.

They were passing Sywan Bay when she looked at him again and said: "For crying out loud, Peter, where did you come from?"

"I just got here," Peter replied.

"But I was in a horrible white room on the Sapphire! Chong was going to scalp me!" Her hands leaped to her hair. She sighed with relief.

Peter told her briefly what had happened.

"I've had enough adventure to last me for a long, long time," Susan said finally. Suddenly she shuddered. "And enough of love," she added. "Do you want to know what happened?"

"So much happened," Peter said.

"I wanted you to beg me not to marry Chong. That's what happened. You wouldn't do it. It was all your fault. And I was hunting for a brand new thrill. I found it. Peter, one of these days I'm going to get over thrill hunting. Then you might ask me to marry you, mightn't you, Peter?"

"I might," Peter said thoughtfully.

"But until that time comes, we'll just keep on being good pals. Would you like to make that kind of an arrangement with a girl?"

Peter said he thought that would be a perfect arrangement.

CHINESE FOR RACKET

*Ordered to leave China as a trouble-maker, at
the moment his business mission reaches a crisis,
Peter the Brazen suspects "ways that are dark
and tricks that are vain"—tricks that involve
his too adventurous friend Susan O'Gilvie*

CHAPTER I

AN OFFICIAL ENEMY

FOR PROBABLY THE last time in his life, Peter Moore was watching the sun go down in China. The American consul to Hongkong had just informed him that he was to leave China immediately and to stay out of China indefinitely.

The American consul was a worried-looking man with iron-gray hair and a white spike mustache. He sat stiffly upright in his chair on the other side of the table for two which Peter Moore had reserved for a farewell party in the rooftop restaurant of the Oriental Hotel. Peter's dinner guest hadn't yet arrived. And he hoped that she wouldn't arrive until Amos Brangdon had taken his departure.

"I can't have you deported," the consul was saying, "because you are not, technically, a criminal, and you are not guilty of any actual criminal offense."

"Thank you," Peter said dryly.

"But you are a trouble-maker."

"I am supposed to be a radio research engineer," Peter said, lighting a cigarette and squinting at him over the end of it. "I came to China almost two months ago, as the accredited representative of the General Electric Company, of Schenectady, New York, to track down the rumor that a bright young Chinese scientist had perfected in his Hongkong laboratories a device for eliminating static from radio."

"You should have come directly to me!" Mr. Brangdon snapped.

Halfway across they passed the mandarin's
junk, waiting for its victim

"I don't see why," Peter differed. "I chose to conduct the investigation on a lone-wolf basis."

The American consul laughed hollowly and without mirth. "And what have you accomplished, Mr. Moore? You have interfered repeatedly in the affairs of influential Chinese. I don't mind telling you that powerful interests have requested your immediate departure. It has been brought to my attention that last night you boarded a yacht owned by a native prince of Tonkin—the Sultan of Sakala—and, in a quixotic attempt at rescuing a young American girl on board, enlisted the services of the entire Asiatic squadron. What was the result?"

"The girl got off safely," Peter answered.

"Rubbish! The yacht was boarded. American naval officers found that you had wounded the Sultan—and offended him beyond measure. I will tell you, briefly, what the result was. The Sultan of Sakala is so indignant that he has canceled orders for American power machinery and other kinds of merchandise worth in excess of a half million gold—and given his trade to Germans, Japanese, and English!"

Peter Moore puffed at his cigarette and said nothing. Mr. Brangdon went on:

"Mr. Moore, I have a complete record of what you have been doing in China recently. We won't discuss your previous visits. This is not the first time you have been told to keep out of China. But let's just consider your present visit.

"On the way over you all but caused a mutiny on the Queen of Asia. In Shanghai you precipitated a riot in Native City. Leaving Shanghai, you involved yourself with opium smugglers and pirates—another mutiny. In Hai-Phang, a few weeks ago, you incited a religious uprising among the Ungese, and the country is still very unsettled throughout northern Cambodia. Yet you say you came to China to investigate a static eliminator invented by a Hongkong scientist!"

"Shall I give you my report?" Peter asked quietly.

"Not yet. I am not through. Isn't it true, Mr. Moore, that the real cause, the precipitating cause, of all of these troubles I have enumerated has been, in each case, a young American woman, a Miss Susan O'Gilvie, whom you have, on each occasion, attempted to keep out or get out of mischief?"

"I know a Miss O'Gilvie," Peter said noncommittally.

"Isn't she in Hongkong now?"

"I believe she is."

"Isn't she the young lady who caused all that trouble last night? You needn't answer, Mr. Moore. I know the facts. I have made a thorough investigation. Will you tell me what you have to say for yourself?"

PETER WISHED that the American consul would go away. It was his last chance to see a sunset in China, and he wanted to enjoy it. From where Peter sat, close to the parapet, he could see straight across the misty blue of the harbor to Hongbom Bay. His eyes wandered restlessly among the shipping clustered between North Point and Sulphur Channel: sampans and junks, brown and gold in the growing dusk; rusty-sided little tramp freighters flying among them all the flags of the world; majes-

tic liners which were little more than floating apartment houses
adroitly equipped with just about everything that was modern
and luxurious.

He watched the shadow cast by the peak creep across the
harbor and deepen from cornflower-blue to sapphire-blue. The
streets below him were dark, tortuous channels in which rickshas
and sedan chairs coursed like schools of lazy fish.

A warm puff of breeze carried to his nostrils a mingling
of odors: spice and sandalwood incense and oriental cooking
smells. And from some rooftop near by there floated to him the
soft twanging of a Chinese lute.

He recognized the tune and could have sung the words in the
original Chinese. It was Li Po's "Ode to the Moon." By looking
up and over his right shoulder he could see the moon, a pale
slice of silver sailing in the powder-blue of the late afternoon
sky above Taitam Gap.

Peter said to the consul: "Dr. Fong Toy, the inventor of the
static eliminator, has proved as elusive as a will-o'-the-wisp.
When I reached Hongkong a month ago, I was told he had
gone to Indo-China—Hai-Phang, to be specific—to search
for a particular kind of gum arabic to use in his experiments.
When I reached Hai-Phang he was gone. Back to Hongkong!
I have been here two weeks, trying to see him. So have the
representatives of other large electrical corporations—British,
German, and Japanese. This device, if it works, will mark the
greatest advance in radio engineering since De Forest invented
the audion bulb. It is certainly up to you, Mr. Brangdon, as the
official representative of the United States in Hongkong, to help
me put this matter of business over, not to hamper me."

"You have not asked me for my help," the consul said angrily.
"I would have been delighted to help. My only reason for not
ordering you to leave China sooner is that I wanted America
to have this great invention. But you have had time enough to
negotiate with the inventor. That is my opinion and that is the

opinion of the State Department. You must leave China immediately."

Peter looked at him shrewdly. A corner of his mouth twitched. Then, as if he were deep in thought, his eyes focused dreamily on a liner which lay at her mooring down in the harbor. She was the Mongolia: hull so black that it might have been carved from ebony, upper works of snowy white, twin stacks of buff. Her decks would be swarming with tourists, debutantes, club women, business men, tired of sightseeing, fretful for home— ham and eggs, whole wheat cakes, and Main Street.

The Mongolia was clearing for San Francisco at noon to-morrow.

AT TABLES all about them heads were turning and men were looking up. A girl was coming toward Peter, and at first he did not recognize her. She was lovely in a slim dinner gown of silver net over shining coral silk which gave her a radiance and shimmer all her own. Her sandals were jade-green with diamond-crusted high French heels. They tapped crisply as she came toward the parapet.

Peter knew those heels. She had once admitted indifferently that they were diamonds, not brilliants. Susan O'Gilvie would, of course, wear diamond heels. Why not? She was worth more than ten million dollars, and could afford, if she wished, to throw diamond heels away after wearing them once.

Recognizing her, Peter crushed out his cigarette in an ash tray and stood up. Susan gave him a bright glance from eyes which were not blue but a deep violet, then she looked questioningly at the solemn man across from Peter.

Peter introduced them.

"Miss O'Gilvie, this is Mr. Brangdon, the American consul to Hongkong."

Susan exclaimed: "How thrilling! Shall we all have a cocktail?"

Her voice was of fine quality, like good metal struck upon

sharply; clear and rather sweet and, like the rest of her, curiously suggestive of romance.

Mr. Brangdon did not smile. He acknowledged the introduction with a nod. When Susan was seated he said:

"I have just been talking with Mr. Moore about some of his recent adventures in which, I believe, you figured."

"Weren't you," Susan brightly inquired, "simply spellbound?"

Mr. Brangdon remained standing, and it was now evident that he had no intention of smiling.

"Your recent escapades," he said stiffly, "have caused the consular service and the State Department of your country a great deal of embarrassment, Miss O'Gilvie. You may have the opinion that the Far East is nothing but a large playground for thrill-hunting, wealthy American girls—but you are greatly mistaken."

Susan had stopped smiling. She lifted her chin a little. The American consul went on:

"I had just told Mr. Moore, when you came, that he must leave China immediately."

"How soon," Peter drawled, "is immediately?"

"Within twenty-four hours."

"Regardless of whether I have wound up my affairs here?"

"Those are my orders. There are three ships leaving Hong-kong to-morrow in the late forenoon. I don't care which ship you select."

"But—" Susan began.

"Never mind," Peter stopped her.

Mr. Brangdon addressed himself now to Susan.

"And these same orders," he said, "apply to you, Miss O'Gilvie. You must be out of China within twenty-four hours."

Susan's eyes blazed. Her face was rosy with indignation. Susan was not accustomed to being told what to do. She was as generous as the sun—and as willful as any princess. She flashed an angry, inquiring glance at Peter. To her immense surprise, the lid of his left eye vaguely flickered. It was not a crude wink. It was the merest ghost of a shadow of a wink.

Susan managed a wistful little smile. With resolute chin high, she said:

"Very well, Mr. Brangdon."

It implied that she understood him perfectly—and that he was dismissed.

"No tricks," said Mr. Brangdon sternly. "I am prepared to be exceedingly unpleasant to you two if you disobey my orders. Good evening."

He bowed and withdrew.

Susan fixed round and indignant eyes on Peter.

"HE HASN'T any right to order us out of China!" she flared.

"Look down there," Peter said, indicating the harbor.

"It's beautiful," Susan agreed. "But—"

"See that big black ship with the buff funnels?"

"Yes, Peter."

"See that big white ship with the blue funnels?"

Susan nodded.

"The black one is the Mongolia. The white one is the City of Singapore. The Mongolia sails for the United States to-morrow at noon, via Shanghai, Yokohama, and Honolulu. The white one sails at the same time for Java, via Saigon, Bangkok, and Singapore."

Susan was watching him with parted lips.

Peter removed from an inner pocket a leather billfold the color of seasoned mahogany. He opened it and took out a long printed green slip of paper.

"This is my ticket on the Mongolia," he said.

Susan opened a platinum and sapphire bag. From it she removed a long printed pink slip of paper.

"This is my ticket on the City of Singapore," she said. "Oh, Peter, I know we're both leaving China to-morrow—you for America, I for Java. But that isn't the point. He hadn't any right to talk to me that way, as if I were six years old and had just been caught swiping jam in the pantry. Why were you winking at me?"

Peter smiled. "Did you notice the American consul's eyes?"

"I always notice men's eyes."

"Color?"

"Blue. Why?"

"Did you ever hear of the strange influence the Far East has on white men?"

"Of course! What are you driving at?"

"When I met Mr. Brangdon in the American consulate in Tokyo six years ago his eyes were brown!"

Susan looked at him in puzzlement. Then, "Peter," she drawled, "you wouldn't kid a poor innocent orphan, would you?"

"Couldn't," Peter answered. "Figure it out for yourself."

Her eyes brightened, then crinkled at the corners and narrowed.

"He's a fake!" she cried suddenly. "He isn't the American consul at all! But what's the big idea?"

"Racket," Peter said.

"What kind of racket?"

"Chinese kind of racket."

CHAPTER II

GRAFT

SUSAN NERVOUSLY LIGHTED a cigarette and said to a hovering waiter:

"We want something to drink. What do you want, Peter?"

"Dry Martini."

"Bring us a couple of dry Martinis." Susan's creamy complexion was now pink with excitement. The thrill hunter was on a nice hot new scent. "Let's have some details."

"I don't know what it's all about," Peter confessed. "There is an old and vulgar Chinese saying to the effect that the odor of a dead rat may be more pungent than that of a dead whale and yet be imperceptible to a man's nostrils. I have been trying all day long to make a definite appointment to-night with Fong Toy. For some mysterious reason, he is very evasive."

"I don't see that," Susan interrupted. "You know very well that Hongkong is cluttered with the representatives of other big corporations, all of whom would give their eye teeth to own the patent rights to the static eliminator. Little as I know about radio, I realize what an important invention Fong Toy has. He is simply stalling—playing you off against the others. It's nothing but good business psychology. If he can make you anxious enough, you will offer him more than you intended."

"Does that explain the imitation American consul?"

"Why not? He's part of the picture. If Fong Toy wanted you to become anxious, what better way could he have found? You've got to do business with him inside of twenty-four hours."

Peter was slowly shaking his head. "It isn't as simple as all that. It's a racket, but I smell that rat in another direction. Since breakfast I've been aware that I've been shadowed. It's all very mysterious and suspicious."

"Did you see Fong Toy at all to-day?" Susan asked.

"No. But I spent hours with Wan Sang, his secretary. He will come here—any time now—to let me know definitely whether or not I can see Fong Toy to-night. Fong Toy works, and does business only at night. In the daytime he sleeps. I think he is playing poker—trying to bluff. Wan Sang told me that if I want to show Fong Toy I am really in earnest, I will bring a hundred and fifty thousand dollars with me to-night."

"Mex or gold?"

"Gold."

"Check or cash?"

"Cash."

"What did you say?"

"I said I'd bring it."

"Will you?" she demanded.

"I parked thirty ten-thousand-dollar notes on the Bank of Hongkong—$300,000 Mex or $150,000 in gold—with the manager of this hotel before I came up here."

"Why wouldn't Fong Toy be satisfied with a cashier's check?"

"He's evidently a strange, old-fashioned young Chinese. I've done business with his type before. I know how he feels."

"It sounds phony to me," Susan said. "I think you're right about that rat."

"Nevertheless," Peter answered, "when I sail on the Mongolia to-morrow, the rights to that static eliminator are going to sail with me. Now, if you'll excuse me a moment, I'll do some telephoning and check up on Mr. Brangdon."

Susan, watching him go, had a sense of impending drama. She was sorrier than she would admit that Peter was sailing in one direction to-morrow and she was sailing in another. She was afraid that Siam, French Indo-China, Malaya, and Java would be devoid of thrills without Peter's magical presence.

She was conscious that a number of men were staring at her. Susan was accustomed to that. Idly she stared back. A young Eurasian with paper-white skin and hair as smooth, as black as patent leather, eyed her over the top of a green drink. His eyes were those of a playful python. He fascinated Susan, he reminded her so much of a reptile. As her gaze lengthened, he put his glass down, gave her a silky smile, and started to rise. Susan gave him a look which would have frozen a tropical sunset.

PETER RETURNED, seated himself, and said with a smile:

"The American consul left for Canton this afternoon on the four o'clock boat, to be gone several days."

"Then you won't have to sail to-morrow if you don't want to. Shall we wait another week, Peter?"

"No," he answered firmly. "I was sent out here to do a job— and return."

"With the bacon."

"I'll bring the bacon," Peter said, rather grimly.

Susan laughed. "You look as if you are going to burst into tears."

"Why not?" he answered. "The Chinese have a saying, 'You can hardly make a friend in a year, but you can lose one in an hour.'"

"They have another saying," Susan said: " 'He who falls in love has come to the end of happiness.'"

"The Analects say, 'When the ear will not listen, the heart escapes sorrow.'"

Susan laughed. "Li Po said, 'Never trust a woman, even if she has borne you seven sons.' I'm afraid you don't trust me."

"I don't," Peter said.

"You think I'd try to induce you to go to Siam and Malaya with me."

"You know I'd like to go."

"Then come on! Throw up your silly old job, marry me, and we'll have a grand time. I'll give you a big allowance."

"Every time I think of marrying you, I think of your ten million—and my feet get cold all over!"

"Thank God," said Susan, "we are not in love."

"Yes," he agreed, "thank God for that."

"If we were in love, I think I'd just naturally break down and die to-morrow when your ship goes north and mine goes south."

"It's going to be bad enough," Peter admitted.

"It's going to be terrible," Susan said. "It makes me want to scream. I keep hearing the trade wind in the palm trees, the whisper of waves on golden beaches, the trumpeting of elephants in teak yards, and the silver wind-bells tinkling in the big temples. And I keep seeing the little desert islands in the Malay Archipelago—Wouldn't it be fun to be shipwrecked on one?

"Peter, you're the grandest pal a girl ever had. I'll promise not to get into jams or start trouble if you'll only come along. I'll be so good you won't know me. Think of Java and Singapore! Think of the tropical moon, the palms, the golden pagodas, the lazy blue southern oceans. Think of seeing, hearing and smelling all of those things—with me!"

Peter looked at her murkily.

"Listen, kid," he said, "if you don't cut that out, papa'll spank."

WITH A sigh Susan said: "Perhaps we'd better have another drink. Tell me about this racket. Do you want to know my theory? My theory is that that imitation consul was hired to play his part by one of your powerful competitors, maybe a German. You know how thorough the Germans are."

"No," Peter said. "It's a Chinese racket. The man who had posted our imitation consul must have been Chinese. He knew too much. He knew everything. And the stunt itself was typically oriental."

"But what was the object?"

"I don't know yet."

"What Chinese would want you out of China in twenty-four hours?"

Peter shook his head. "What I want to know is—what's his next move?"

Susan looked at him anxiously and asked, "A knife in the back?"

"The night is young," Peter answered.

The night was, in fact, just newly born. The sapphire-blue of the harbor had vanished before a purple invasion, and this, in turn, had given way to clear blackness through which the lights on ships and the shore lights of Hongbom Bay sparkled like diamonds. Chinese lanterns, electrically lighted, cast a soft romantic glow over the rooftop restaurant, and swayed gently in the warm spiced breeze.

Susan saw a plump Chinese of about forty threading his way among the tables toward them. He wore a suit of tropical white drill, pince-nez glasses behind which shoebutton eyes twinkled merrily, and a pink necktie in which was set a flake of kingfisher jade.

He looked jolly and simple-natured, but Susan, glancing at Peter, saw that his jaw line had hardened.

Peter introduced the Chinese to Susan as Mr. Wan Sang.

"Wan Sang," he added, "is Dr. Fong Toy's secretary. Will you sit down, Wan Sang?"

Susan sensed behind the politeness of his words, and behind Wan Sang's smooth Chinese courtesy, a mutual hostility.

Wan Sang seated himself and beamed at Susan through his thick lenses. He said, in English almost painfully precise:

"Mr. Moore and I are very old friends. We became acquainted five or six years ago, here in Hongkong, when I was *compradore* to Hing Sing Tai Pan, on Ice House Lane."

Susan, resting her chin on her small pink palms, asked Wan Sang what a *compradore* did.

"It is a position requiring the utmost honesty," he answered. "A *compradore* does all of his employer's hiring and firing, and, in some cases, handles practically all of his employer's money. When it is necessary to deal with the natives the *compradore* attends to it. Hing Sing Tai Pan is Chinese for Hannibal and Company, an export and import company. But I find working with Dr. Fong Toy much more interesting. I find science fascinating. And Dr. Fong Toy is a great man with a wonderful mind, although he is only twenty-six years old. He is the greatest scientific genius in China, if not in the entire world."

"I'm taking your word for that," Peter said dryly.

WAN SANG laughed.

"All geniuses are eccentric," he said. "Dr. Fong Toy finds that his brain is more active at night than in the daytime. He works all night and sleeps all day. And he dislikes business dealings of any sort. His mind soars above business—dollars."

"That," Peter said with a wry smile, "is why he insists that I bring a hundred and fifty thousand gold as an earnest of my good faith. How that young man hates money!"

Wan Sang laughed again, politely. "You do Dr. Fong Toy an injustice. I am the one who insisted that you bring the—shall we say, token of your company's good faith? What is a hundred and fifty thousand dollars to the General Electric Company—one of the richest corporations in the world?"

"What time," Peter asked, "is my appointment with Dr. Fong Toy?"

Wan Sang's smile vanished. "Mr. Moore, I have just left Dr. Fong Toy, and I am very much afraid that he cannot see you to-night."

"Why not?"

"He is in the midst of some new experiments. How he hates all these business details! He would so much rather dream and work with his coils and tubes and condensers."

"Have you told him that my company is prepared to offer

him one million dollars gold and a handsome royalty for the use of his invention?"

"I have, indeed, and he was highly flattered and honored."

"Then where's the hitch?"

"It is simply that his mind soars above material considerations."

Susan saw the flicker of fire in Peter's eyes, and wondered what was going on beneath the surface of this polite conversation. But he smiled and said:

"Wan Sang, supposing you and I stop beating about the bush. Wasn't it Confucius who said, 'The arrow is on the string, and it must go'? Let's stop playing poker. I have been in China almost two months trying to put up a very generous business proposition to Dr. Fong Toy. Each time when I am about to corner him, he slips away. You know me. You know my company. You know that G.E. will give him better protection and better terms than he can secure from any of our competitors. I am tired of chasing him. Important work is waiting for me in America. When can I see Dr. Fong Toy?"

Wan Sang lifted his shoulders eloquently. "If I only knew!" he breathed. "I suppose you have the hundred and fifty thousand dollars, gold with which to bind a contract?"

"I have."

"In currency?"

"In notes on the Bank of Hongkong."

"What a pity!" Wan Sang sighed.

Peter leaned toward him and said rapidly: "Wan Sang, wanchee talkee squeeze? How much *cumshaw* wanchee?"

The Chinese, blinking at him, reminded Susan of a frog. What Peter had asked him, in pidgin, was just how much graft he wanted.

"Ten thousand dollars," Wan Sang answered clearly.

"Can do!" Peter said crisply. "I'll pay you ten thousand dollars on completion of my deal with Dr. Fong Toy—and not a dime before. Is that satisfactory?"

Wan Sang arose from the table with the alacrity of a bouncing rubber ball. Susan thought he was insulted by Peter's bluntness, but he said, "Will one o'clock in the morning be suitable?"

"One hour past midnight to-night?"

"Yes, Mr. Moore. I will see to it," Wan Sang said determinedly, "that Dr. Fong Toy drops his work and places himself—"

"And the static eliminator—"

"—And the static eliminator, at your disposal. Perhaps I should warn you that a representative of a large German electrical concern has an appointment with the doctor at two o'clock, and the British and Japanese representatives at three and four o'clock, respectively."

"No one will talk to Dr. Fong Toy before I do?"

"No one! Should I mention that a four-horse chariot cannot overtake the spoken word—not to mention the signed contract?"

Peter smiled and answered: "If two men are of the same mind, their sharpness can divide metal. I'll be there at one. Thank you."

Wan Sang bowed ceremoniously, "It is a distinction to be of service—Ren Beh Tung!"

WHEN HE was gone, Susan asked Peter what Ren Beh Tung meant.

Peter laughed and answered, "Man of Bronze."

"Brass?" Susan suggested. "Meaning nerve—brazen?" When Peter shrugged she asked, "Is it the custom here to name men after metals?"

"Just an old Chinese custom."

"They ought to call you the Chromium Kid," Susan murmured. "They tell me chromium is very hard and tough, and that it yields to practically nothing. All right, Peter the Brazen—what's the lowdown on Wan Sang? Did that ten thousand dollars graft solve the riddle? Was it racket money?"

"Not at all. It was an everyday Chinese business transaction. When a Chinese enables you to complete a business deal, he expects his squeeze. He looks upon his squeeze as money honestly earned. 'You allatime help my; my allatime help you.' There was never any doubt in Wan Sang's mind that I would pay him his squeeze at the proper time."

"Then what's the racket? Why the imitation American consul? Why, by the way, am I to be banished from China within twenty-four hours? Just where do I figure in the racket?"

Peter shook his head. "I can't answer any of those questions. There may be more than one racket in operation. This is evidently the night when Fong Toy's static eliminator is going to be sold to somebody. My hunch, as a research engineer in a small way myself, is that he has been having the usual trouble perfecting his device. After years of trying, he has finally solved his last problem. It is now a case of who is to get it. This is a big night. I am sure that some very mysterious and exciting things will occur before one o'clock."

CHAPTER III

AN ENVOY OF TROUBLE

A WAITER HAD come to the table. Peter said, "Let's order our dinner. I'm starved."

"Are you Mr. Peter Moore?" the waiter asked.

"Yes."

Susan looked behind him and saw a very tall, lank man of about thirty with the gaunt, pallid look of one recently ill. The whites of his eyes were yellowish. His hand, taking a cigarette from his bloodless lips, visibly shook.

The waiter said: "A man is asking for you. He says you do not know him, but that it is very important. His name is Sanderson. He is waiting by the elevators."

The man stepped from behind the waiter and placed his two hands on the edge of the table and stared down at Peter. Susan saw that his fingernails were pale-blue and that his suit of white duck, while freshly laundered, was almost threadbare; that it was frayed at the cuffs and that his white shirt, which was likewise fresh, was also frayed at the cuffs and collarband.

"I was afraid you might not come out," he said in a voice that sounded weak and nervous. "My name is Jim Sanderson, Mr. Moore. I know it's very presumptuous of me to come butting in here like this. I wouldn't have done it if it had not been almost a matter of life and death. I have been very ill. Malaria and some nameless jungle fever. I was discharged from the hospital only this morning."

Susan's quick mind jumped to an obvious conclusion: this was nothing but a touch.

Jim Sanderson was clutching handfuls of the tablecloth, in his nervous eagerness.

"I came to you, Mr. Moore, because I'm certain you're the only man in Hongkong who can help me out. My sister is a prisoner in a dump in Kowloon, and if I can't somehow get her out of there by ten o'clock to-night, they're going to sell her up-country!"

Susan gasped: "You'd better sit down, Mr. Sanderson." But the tall, lanky man remained standing and looking at Peter as if he had not heard her.

Peter was gazing up at him, but he said nothing. And Sanderson went on: "I know you think it's mighty strange of me to bother you like this. In the first place, I'm not certain that she *is* my sister. That's the maddening part of it."

When he hesitated, Susan said clearly, "Sit down, Mr. Sanderson. Tell us about it."

Sanderson looked at Peter, and Peter nodded. "Sit down," he said.

The invalid pulled out the chair and seated himself. He apologized again. "I hate to intrude, but there was no time to lose. I'm absolutely desperate, Mr. Moore. This girl who may be my sister Ellen is in this awful Chink dump over there in Kowloon—the Jade Dragon. I heard definitely this afternoon that she was to be sold to-night into marriage to a mandarin from Hengchowfu. His junk is in the harbor now, all decorated up. Po Tung, who runs the Jade Dragon, is selling this girl to the mandarin for twenty-five hundred Haikwan taels."

Susan asked breathlessly how much a tael was.

"Somewhere around a dollar," Peter answered. And said to Sanderson: "Mr. Sanderson, I don't see why you've come to me. What's the matter with the American consul?"

"I've been to the American consulate," Sanderson panted. "He left for up-river this afternoon, to be gone a week. Besides, it's not a consular matter. They'd say, 'Show us absolute proof that this girl is your sister.' Then, even if I could—which I can't—the whole thing would be bogged down indefinitely in red tape. I came to you because I know your reputation. You know the Chinese, and you're resourceful and absolutely fearless."

Peter asked him bluntly if he wanted to borrow twenty-five hundred Haikwan taels.

"No, no, no!" Sanderson said emphatically.

LOOKING AT Peter, Susan saw his look of skepticism slowly go away.

"Let me tell you the whole thing," Sanderson begged. "Then you'll understand why I'm so desperate. Six years ago, when my sister was just twelve, she ran away from home. We lived in San Francisco. Ellen was simply crazy about Chinatown. Every chance she had, she went down there and prowled. Even when she was a little thing, she insisted that it was her dream to go to China. She was a dreamy, romantic kid. She learned to speak Cantonese from an old cook we had. When she was eleven, she could speak Cantonese as well as a native.

"Our mother thought it was risky for her to prowl around alone in Chinatown. She was afraid Ellen would be kidnaped and held for ransom, because my father was a pretty rich man then. And when Ellen vanished that night, we were all pretty certain that that was what had happened—she had gone down there, as usual, and some one had grabbed her.

"We waited for some kind of notice. My father would have raised a quarter of a million to get her back—was prepared to raise it. But no demand for a ransom ever came. We advertised. We spent a fortune on private detectives. I spent six months hanging around Chinatown, trying to pick up clews. But there wasn't a trace of her. She had simply vanished.

"In that time, my father's health went to pieces. He neglected his business. At the end of six months, he died of a complete nervous and physical breakdown. And when the estate was settled, there was barely enough income for my mother to exist on. She abandoned all hope that Ellen was being held for ransom, and we both accepted the theory that Ellen had run away to go to China and would eventually let us know about it. I was sure that she had come down here to southern China, because Hongkong and Canton had always interested her most.

"When my father died, I made up my mind to come out here and look for her. That was nearly six years ago. My mother and I still believe that she ran away, then became ashamed of what she had done and was afraid to let us know where she was. That is still my belief. Recently, my mother's health has been failing. She has been living all this time with an aunt of mine who has a ranch near San Fernando. She thinks Ellen has fallen into the clutches of some unscrupulous Chinese—and it now seems that her worst fears are correct.

"I have been following one lead after another for these past five and a half years. I've been as far north as Kalgan, and as far south as Amboyna. I've followed false trails over Indo-China and Malaya and even to Borneo. It was in Indo-China that I came down with malaria and whatever this jungle fever is. It nearly killed me. Then, in Pnom-Penh I heard, from an old Chinese woman, of a white girl who had come to Amoy five or six years ago from San Francisco. I had heard the story before. Sometimes it was Shanghai. Sometimes it was Foochow. Each time I lost the trail.

"I was too sick to travel, but I traveled, anyway. Six weeks ago I landed in Hongkong. I took a coastwise steamer up to Amoy. The Chinese women in Pnom-Penh had given me the name of an old chop maker. I looked him up. He said he had heard the story but had never seen the girl. He thought she was in Kowloon.

"By that time I was running such a temperature that I was afraid I'd never get back to Hongkong. But I did. And I collapsed on the dock when I came ashore. Somebody put me into a ricksha and took me to the hospital. I was delirious for a solid week. The only thing that pulled me through was the absolute necessity of following the new trail to Kowloon. A necessity like that will pull a man through anything. I shouldn't have left the hospital this morning, but I did. And I'm glad I did. If I'd waited until to-morrow, it would have been too late."

EXCITEDLY SUSAN asked, "Did you go to Kowloon, Mr. Sanderson?"

He had been looking at Peter while he talked. Now, for the first time, he noticed Susan. His sick, yellowed eyes regarded her. He slowly nodded.

"Yes. I've spent the entire afternoon there. And I'm certain that I'm at last on the right trail."

"Did you see your sister?"

Sanderson shook his head. "No. They wouldn't let me see her. She's a dancing girl there. They call her Plum Blossom. The dancing girls live in a sort of dormitory affair behind the Jade Dragon. They're guarded like trained animals."

"Are they all Chinese?"

"Yes. I made inquiries. There is an Englishman named Chumley in Kowloon who exports camphor and ginger. He goes to the Jade Dragon every night. He told me one of the girls is called Plum Blossom, and that she is white. Certainly, she answers to my sister's description. She has blue eyes, dark hair and a very clear, white complexion."

Peter asked if his sister had any distinguishing marks—birthmarks.

Sanderson shook his head.

"Did you go to the police and ask for aid?"

"Yes. But they would give me no help. They said, if I was certain this girl is my sister, they would bring pressure on Po Tung, the proprietor, to let me talk to her. But Po Tung is powerful—one of the richest men in this part of China. What proof could I give the police?"

Susan sympathetically shook her head and Sanderson went on:

"These dancing girls are so many slaves. When rich mandarins from up-country want to buy a girl, they go to the Jade Dragon and look over Po Tung's assortment."

"Why," Susan indignantly demanded, "don't the British do something about it?"

"Kowloon," Sanderson wearily answered, "is China, not England." He shrugged and said, "I may be wrong. This girl may not be Ellen. Chumley was the one who told me about this mandarin—Yen Chan—who is going to buy the girl they call Plum Blossom. What can I do?" he exclaimed. "Can I go there to-night and declare that this girl is my sister?"

"You'd get a knife in the back," Susan said.

Sanderson said with a hopeless sigh, "I don't know what to do. Even if I were to ask this girl point-blank if she is my sister, she might declare that she is not. She might be too ashamed to admit it. Oh, I know what you are thinking. You are thinking: 'That girl is a bad egg. She has gone the way of all "Melican gals" who come out and go Chinese.' You are saying to yourselves, 'What possible good can come of saving such a girl from the life she has, perhaps, chosen to lead?' That is not the point. If that girl is my sister, she must return to California with me. It's our mother, not she or myself, that counts now. I'd drag her out of the worst dump on the China coast, no matter how low she's sunk!"

Sanderson suddenly clutched the edge of the table. His eyes rolled queerly.

Susan cried, "Peter! He's going to faint!"

Their waiter was hovering near. "Bring some brandy—quick!" Susan ordered.

Sanderson sent her a grateful glance. "Thanks," he said. "This whole thing has upset me terribly."

Susan looked quickly at Peter. "What are we going to do about this?"

And Sanderson put in: "Mr. Moore, please believe me. I would not have dreamed of trying to drag you into this if I had not been desperate. I haven't any strength. I didn't know any one else to turn to. I had to have the help of some one who is capable, who knows how to deal with the Chinese. I had heard about you—of your genius at getting people out of scrapes. Isn't this the young lady you rescued last night from the yacht of a Tonkin Sultan?"

"Where did you hear about that?" Peter asked.

"It's all over Hongkong. I heard you were at this hotel. When I realized I could not carry on single-handed any longer, I came to you. Please don't think I'm yellow or a quitter. If I weren't so damned weak, I wouldn't need help."

The waiter returned and placed a drink of brandy beside him. He gulped it down; turned to Susan and said:

"**YOU AMERICAN** girls have no idea what the life of these dancing girls is like. They have less standing, less of a chance to get a square deal, than a Negro had in the days of slavery. Girls have no standing in China, anyway. Have you heard of the baby towers, where newborn girl babies are dropped into a deep well from a tower—dropped alive into stinking pits? That's characteristic of China's attitude toward women. They aren't wanted. Do you want to hear more?"

"Yes, I certainly do!" Susan said emphatically.

"Men like Po Tung take Chinese girls when they are from ten to twelve years old and have them trained. Women who are experts teach these girls all the arts of lure. They teach them to dance, to sing and to play musical instruments. They make twentieth-century Delilahs of them.

"When these girls are from sixteen to eighteen years old—or salable, or marriageable—they become dancers in places like the Jade Dragon.

"When a wealthy Chinese wants to buy or marry a girl, he visits a place like the Jade Dragon. He sees numbers of these girls dance, sing and so on. He makes his selection. But he does not buy her then. He may come back a half dozen times. The last time, be is entertained at dinner in a private room.

"The girl acts as a hostess to him. He learns then whether or not she is well trained and a good hostess. If the dinner goes off properly—to his satisfaction—he buys her and takes her away.

"Chumley told me that that is what is going to happen to-night. Yen Chan, the mandarin from Hengchowfu, is to be served dinner to-night by this girl they call Plum Blossom. If she is satisfactory, Yen Chan will pay Po Tung twenty-five hundred Haikwan taels for her and carry her off in his junk. If he discovers that she is not a virgin, he can return her and demand his money back—and any court in China will uphold him! That's the law in this benighted land.

"It is a hideous system, and when I think that that girl may be my sister, it makes me want to murder somebody. Mr. Moore, will you help me?"

Susan looked at Peter with sudden determination. If he wouldn't help this pathetic man, she would. She glanced at her diamond and platinum wrist watch. It was almost eight o'clock—and the girl who might prove to be Sanderson's sister would be taken away from the Jade Dragon at ten or earlier.

"Peter, you'll help him, won't you?"

Peter did not seem to hear. His eyes were vague; his thoughts seemed miles away.

"I was hoping," Sanderson anxiously went on, "that you would go over there with me. It isn't that I'm scared. What's my life, anyhow? But I haven't the strength of a half-drowned cat. One punch—and I'd be through. Besides, I cannot talk Cantonese. You can. You could talk to Po Tung. I'm sure you could demand and obtain a talk with this girl. And I'm positive it would not take the two of us long to find out whether or not she's my sister. One glance may be sufficient for me."

"A girl changes more in appearance from twelve to eighteen," Susan pointed out, "than during any other six years of her life."

"I know that, Miss—"

"O'Gilvie," Susan helped him. Her generous heart had gone out to this pathetic man.

He was nodding eagerly. "Yes, Miss O'Gilvie; but one glance

should tell us whether she is white or yellow. Won't you come, Mr. Moore? I don't see why it should be in the least dangerous."

"I'm not thinking of the danger," Peter answered, and hesitated. He was sorry for Sanderson, too; but he was wondering about his appointment with Fong Toy.

AS IF she had read his thoughts, Susan exclaimed, "Peter, it's just eight o'clock! You'll have plenty of time to go to the Jade Dragon with Mr. Sanderson and be back in time for your appointment with Fong Toy!"

"It takes a full hour by sampan," Peter said, "to cross the harbor to Kowloon. The last ferry ran a half hour ago."

"But we can make it. And it won't be dangerous."

Peter smiled. "Any time a white man undertakes to interfere in the private affairs of the Chinese, there's a possibility of trouble. I'm tired of riding tigers."

"But, Peter, think of that girl's poor mother!"

"I'm thinking of her."

"Then why won't you go? If you think it will be dangerous, take a revolver along."

"My pistol was stolen out of my trunk last night. Besides—"

"I'm pretty well heeled, Mr. Moore," Sanderson eagerly put in. "I have two guns right here with me—one on each hip. One for you and one for me!"

Susan said impatiently, "Peter, how can you hesitate? Do you know what I think? I think that poor girl has been kept prisoner from the time they kidnaped her in San Francisco. She hasn't been permitted to communicate with anybody! You know how such things happen! Supposing I was being held prisoner in an awful place like that—and was going to be sold to-night to some Chinese man! You'd tear Kowloon apart with your hands, trying to save me, wouldn't you?"

"This is entirely different."

"Why?"

"I'll tell you why, frankly—with all due apologies to Mr. Sanderson."

"Don't you think he's telling the truth?"

"I don't question him. But, frankly, this is such an old, old story."

Sanderson said stiffly, "I don't think I quite get you, Mr. Moore."

"I'll explain. Whether you know it or not, China is knee-deep in men who are looking for lost or stolen sisters, wives, sweethearts. Like yourself, these poor devils waste their lives and their fortunes following one wild goose after another. Each clew they find, they're sure is the right one. And when they trail it down—they find nothing. Doesn't it occur to you, Sanderson, that your sister may be dead—that she may not have left San Francisco alive?"

"What you mean," Susan said, "is that you're simply scared to death you'll miss your appointment with Fong Toy. I should think you'd rather lose a thousand static eliminators than let one unfortunate girl be sold to some horrible old mandarin."

SANDERSON SAID evenly: "Mr. Moore, I could have lied to you. I could have said I was positive this girl in Kowloon is my sister—and I'm sure you wouldn't have hesitated. But I'm not sure. And it's the uncertainty that is maddening. If I were too late in trying to help her, I could never forgive myself."

"Look here," Peter said sharply. "Give me one piece of proof that this girl is what you think she is. I don't mean that she is your sister; I mean that she is white, not yellow."

"I've already given it," Sanderson answered huskily. "I've mentioned that the price Yen Chan is to pay for her is twenty-five hundred Haikwan taels. That is the current price for white girls. The current price for Chinese girls is one thousand taels."

"There!" Susan cried triumphantly, but Peter still hesitated. She said wildly, "If you don't go, I'm going. I mean it."

"I won't let you go," Peter said.

"I must go," Susan said. "Three are better than two—and a woman might fool two men whereas she couldn't fool another woman. I'm pretty smart, if I must say it myself. Peter, I'm through arguing. I'll help this man find his sister if it takes every dollar I possess!"

She sprang up. "Are you coming?" she cried.

Peter arose with a sigh. "All right," he said wearily. "But it's going to rain. You'll ruin that gown and those slippers."

"I don't care."

As they left the table, Peter observed that several men simultaneously got up from near-by tables—a young Mongolian with a Chicago gunman's haircut; a German with a limp; a Jap with a cherry-lacquer box under one arm; and a Eurasian with eyes as bright and cold as a cobra's.

He was sorry for Sanderson and Sanderson's mother; but he had wanted this last evening alone with Susan. He knew that, after to-morrow, he would probably never see her again. He had wanted to stay here; to eat, drink and dance until it was time to collect his thirty ten-thousand-dollar notes from the hotel manager and go down for that momentous appointment with Fong Toy.

Kowloon and the Jade Dragon spelled trouble. It promised to be an even more eventful evening than he had anticipated. And Peter wished he knew just what the fates were brewing for him.

CHAPTER IV

ORIENTAL NIGHT

WHEN THEY LEFT the hotel, Susan wore a cape over her silver and coral dinner gown, and Peter had on a trench coat over his dinner jacket. His weather prophecy was fulfilled before they reached the sampan jetty. A wind sprang up. A sprinkling of raindrops came on one of the first gusts. Then the wind died down and rain commenced to fall in a steady drizzle.

Peter selected a sampan with a thatched roof which looked more water-tight than the others, and ordered Susan and Sanderson to sit inside, out of the rain. He himself took a position in the stern, facing aft. He was merely curious to see if they would be followed.

He knew that he had been trailed all day long by the Mongolian with the Chicago gunman's haircut, and the Jap with the cherry-lacquer box, and he wondered, as he saw several sampans slipping along astern, just what the German, the Mongolian, the Jap and the Eurasian intended to do.

Sanderson gave him a nickel-plated revolver and Peter, after breaking it to make sure that it was loaded, slipped it into his hip pocket. Its pressure and weight were comforting. He hoped there would be no need for a gun, but he was sure that he had been bullied into an errand which could lead nowhere but into trouble.

Halfway across the harbor, they passed a junk which was gayly festooned with paper flowers, now drab and limp in the rain. Odors of spice and sandalwood incense drifted from it in an invisible smudge. Some one aboard was picking mournful notes from a Chinese guitar.

This was, Sanderson said, Yen Chan's junk.

Kowloon was, when they reached the other side, a sea of mud. They took rickshas to the Jade Dragon. Susan was thrilling to the excitement of the adventure, but Peter felt uneasy. He didn't want trouble. And the least trouble might readily make him too late for that appointment with Fong Toy—an appointment which he had traveled fifteen thousand miles to keep, and for which he had impatiently waited almost two months. Now that it was made, any delay in keeping it would mean that the static eliminator would go to the Germans, the Japanese or the British. If he had been the serious-minded young business man that he swore he wanted to be, Peter would never have left Hongkong to-night on an errand as fraught with menacing possibilities as was this.

AS HE saw the lights of the Jade Dragon through the slanting rain ahead, he asked himself if he were really cut out to be a business man. Sometimes he was afraid he was a hopeless failure.

Peter had never been inside the Jade Dragon, but he was sufficiently familiar with its reputation to know what it would be like. Among men of the sea, it was as notorious as the infamous Number Nine of Yokohama, a spectacular part of the *yoshiwara* which was destroyed by the earthquake.

Chinese music came quivering out of the sprawling black building. It covered an area of at least a square block, additions having been added to additions until it was impossible to say what the original nucleus had been.

Teak doors blackened by age but still stoutly upheld by their massive wrought-iron strap-hinges swung outward like the jaws of some prehistoric monster to engulf them, and they were admitted to an atmosphere of smells, sounds and sights which characterize oriental pleasure resorts: the reek of stale booze, stale cigar, candle and opium smoke; the sustained harsh rattling of voices using a score of tongues, the blare of China's contribution to whoopee music, the clatter of chopsticks on porcelain, the clash of cymbals; the bright silks and satins of oriental women, the familiar blue that is Chinese blue and no other color in the world; all seen, heard and smelled through a fog of smoke so dense that, one felt, it could almost be pushed aside with the hand.

The Jade Dragon made no bows to Western jazz joints as did some of the entertainment halls of Shanghai, Hongkong and Singapore. In them, the East met the West, in decorations, music, food and drink. In the Jade Dragon, China went on as it had been going on for five thousand years—raucous, untamed, unspoiled.

That was Susan's word for it—unspoiled. She liked places unspoiled by the modernizing influence of Europe and America. Here, there was no attempt at cleanliness or catering to Western standards or appetites. If you didn't like the Jade Dragon, you could go elsewhere for your whoopee.

Susan inspected the smoky, gloomy interior with bright, excited eyes. This was China! The walls, whatever their original color may have been, were black with age—a purple-black which only centuries of various kinds of smoke could achieve.

Solemn elderly Chinese men sat openly before tables eight inches from the floor, rolled their pills and smoked opium. At other tables, white men gone Chinese did the same thing. At still other tables, sailors—French, American, British, Australian, Italian—sat drinking sour rice wine or *samshu* or trade gin, or fondling native women they had brought along.

A beautiful, sloe-eyed Eurasian girl whose hair streamed about her face in a thick black cloud glanced up insolently at Susan and stuck out her tongue—a sharp darting little tongue, like the tongue of a serpent.

Susan laughed and exclaimed, "Peter, this is real! This is great!"

But he did not hear her. You had to shriek to be heard. To the clamor of voices was now added the cacophony of the orchestra, playing an encore.

Peter stood beside a thick teak pillar and lazily let his eyes wander about. Automatically, he was acquainting himself with the geography of the Jade Dragon, noting exits, sizing up the crowd.

He came to the conclusion that it wasn't a very good place to wear diamond heels.

Sanderson kept close to his side, and Susan kept close to his other side. Whatever happened now, both seemed to realize, was up to Peter.

He halted a waiter and spoke to him sharply in Cantonese. The waiter jabbered back at him in the same tongue and gesticulated toward the far end of the enormous low room.

"Come on," Peter said, and grasped Susan by the elbow.

As they picked their way along a zigzag aisle, formed by tables almost touching, she peered into booths and glanced eagerly from side to side. The large room opened off at intervals into smaller rooms, alcoves, dim and smoky in candlelight.

They came to the end of the main room and entered a corridor. At the end of the corridor was a heavy slab of wood painted green—a door.

Peter pushed it open, and they entered a smaller room similar in atmosphere to the large one, but with curtained stalls along the sides. The reek of opium became more pronounced.

ON TO the next room. Each room seemed hotter and thicker with smoke than the one before. This one was similar to the last one. Next was a bar, although it bore slight resemblance to any bar Susan had ever seen. One wall was solid with bottles on narrow shelves—bottles of all shapes and colors, but mostly native wines, gins and whiskies from Japan, Java and Malaya. Their colors fascinated Susan. They ranged from palest pink to deepest purple.

A black plank a yard wide and mounted a foot from the floor separated the shelves of bottles from the rest of the room. A tall coolie, horribly scarred, was in charge here.

When Susan, fascinated in her discovery that the tall, scarred man had no ears, stopped and stared, Peter squeezed her elbow and said, "Keep moving, kid."

The next room was, quite obviously, their objective. To the density of tobacco, candle and opium smoke was added the almost sickening flavor of perfume. Along one side of the room a stage ran. It was shallow, as all Chinese stages are, and it had no proscenium arch. There were no backdrops or flats—nothing but a scene painted on the wall: a cherry orchard in blossom. It looked Japanese to Susan. The stage was empty.

Peter led her down the room toward an empty table. She, Peter and Sanderson were, she saw, the only whites in the room. All the others were richly dressed Chinese, and only a few of these wore the clothing of Western civilization. They wore heavy silk and satin robes and little round caps in which beads were set. As far as Susan knew, they might all have been mandarins of remote provinces, *tuchuns, tycoons.*

They gazed at Susan, as one man, with bright, appraising little eyes. Susan did not know that they were not only prospective husbands—and husbands wishing to add to their present store of concubines—but woman dealers; traders come here to look over Po Tung's crop of young and supposedly innocent slaves.

But Susan suspected as much before she had reached the table toward which Peter guided her. She was excited and appalled at the thought.

She said breathlessly, "Peter, they're looking me over, sizing me up, estimating my value. Aren't they?"

Busily sizing up that room from his own point of view, Peter answered with a slight lift of one shoulder.

"Peter, I want you to sit next to me—close to me."

"I intend to. And if the question should arise, you're my wife. Keep that in mind."

Susan didn't mention that she had had it in mind, on and off, for the past two months, since the night she met him.

SHE HAD never been so thrilled. Her eyes were fever-bright, and there were pink spots on her cheek bones.

"Peter, how long has this sort of thing been going on?"

"What sort of thing?"—absently.

"Selling girls like so much merchandise."

"Five thousand years."

"Don't kid me."

"I'm not kidding you. Are you horrified or disgusted?"

"Both. It's shameful."

"The Chinese don't think so. American and European women are shocked and disgusted, but Chinese women aren't. There's always been an oversupply of women in the Orient. What's to become of them all?"

"Peter! Are you arguing for this terrible system?"

"Not at all. I'm merely stating facts. Am I right, Sanderson?"

"Absolutely right, Mr. Moore." Squatting on a cushion across the low table, he had been staring curiously at Susan, Peter's question seemed to startle him a little. He added to his answer: "Chinese women don't mind being concubines. It's better than starving. Chinese wives and concubines are well protected."

"Where are the girls?"

"They'll be along presently," Peter replied.

"Do they all bring about the same—a thousand Haikwan taels?"

"No, Miss O'Gilvie." Sanderson answered the question. "It depends on their age and their looks. The younger and prettier they are, the more they bring. But they must be—innocent."

"How much would I be worth?"

Peter looked around at her angrily. "Don't ask questions like that."

"But I'm serious. I want to know."

Peter's mouth twitched slightly at one corner and a gleam came into his eyes as he looked at Susan's bright, eager face. She was sitting cross-legged on a cushion beside him. He ran his eyes shrewdly down to one slim silken ankle which was visible; paused a moment on one glittering diamond heel.

"Oh—thirty cents," he said.

Susan snorted.

"Five thousand taels," Sanderson said.

Something in his voice caused Peter to look at him sharply, but Sanderson was smiling, too. Susan said anxiously, "No more fooling, please. Would I bring five thousand taels, Haikwan?"

"At least," Sanderson answered. Susan observed that his eyes were glassy, as if with excitement, and that hectic spots burned on his cheek bones.

She turned to Peter and cried, "You see? My value to you is just nuisance value. Other men know how desirable I am. I must be worth almost my weight in gold—to the right man."

"In diamonds!" Sanderson said suddenly.

Peter had been reflecting that those diamond heels might get them all into hot water before the evening ended. He looked quickly at the invalid and asked, "What diamonds?"

"Any diamonds—so long as they are first water and flawless."

Peter decided that he didn't like the way Sanderson had been looking at Susan's ankle.

The door by which they had entered opened again. A man came in, and, by an optical illusion, it looked as if he had come in on a puff of smoke. Peter stiffened a little as he recognized the newcomer as the Eurasian with cobra eyes who had been following him most of the day. The Eurasian sat down three tables away, and elaborately ignored Peter, Susan and Sanderson.

Peter wondered if the painted-paper window above him led onto a street or alley. Unless unforeseen trouble started, Susan was safe. But he wished he hadn't given in. Susan was a thrill hunter. She loved trouble and met it nine-tenths of the way. This situation could readily turn into dynamite, and Susan could be counted on to supply the necessary spark to set off any known explosive.

This wasn't how Peter had wanted to spend his last evening in China, with his hand ready to leap to a gun.

A SMALL door at the end of the room opened, and a half dozen men filed in with musical instruments, fiddles and Chinese guitars. They proceeded to a large grass mat to the left of the stage and promptly began to play.

There was a stirring of expectancy about the room. Susan, glancing at Sanderson, saw that his face had gone paper-white, that his lips were parted, and that his eyes were glittering pinpoints of sharply-focused attention.

They were focused on the little arched doorway which took the place of wings on the right hand side of the stage.

Susan felt her heart begin to thump rapidly. The back of her throat itched, as it always did when she grew excited.

An elderly Chinese man who might have been the last of the Mings, so elegant was his attire, appeared from nowhere and took his stand below the stage, facing the crowded room. His robes were of heavy royal-blue satin heavily embroidered with bright-colored silks and trimmed with gold. A mandarin mustache drooped down about his mouth and gave him a sardonic look.

"Po Tung," Peter said.

"Will they bid for them?" Susan asked.

"No. The Chinese don't do business that way."

Susan was a little disappointed. She was sorry for any girl who was sold into slavery, even if the institution did have the grace of five thousand years behind it; but she wished, as long as they were being sold, that it would be done openly. Seeing girls put on the auction block would be a scene she would never forget.

Susan needn't have worried. She would never forget the scene as long as she lived.

CHAPTER V

PLUM BLOSSOM

SUSAN'S FIRST GLIMPSE of the little Chinese slaves was, in itself, brilliant and unforgettable.

From the arched doorway, they came sedately onto the stage, walking primly, yet with a certain charm and grace. They were like so many bright flowers. All wore jackets and trousers and gay little slippers.

Susan had seen Chinese silks on display in bazaars—the brightest, gayest colors she had ever seen. Now, she saw these colors again—bright greens, blues, pinks, reds, lavenders, until the shallow stage was a giddy explosion of all colors known to artful Chinese dyers.

Small girls and tall ones; slim ones and stout ones. They were restrained, demure, prim; yet there was about them an air of unsuppressible excitement, of expectancy. There were veiled smiles and smiles hastily concealed. And the impression grew on Susan that these girls were not unhappy in their bondage, but were looking upon their sale to unknown men as escape.

So heavily were they powdered and rouged and mascaraed that they all looked, except for their various sizes, as if they had been carefully patterned after the same Chinese doll.

They walked out onto the stage and strolled about; pirouetted and strolled again, gliding about, never colliding, never touching. It was not a dance, because there was no rhythm to it; but it was the most beautiful and barbaric spectacle Susan had so far seen.

They seemed to move about the stage according to a routine—

glide, pirouette, stroll—glide, pirouette, stroll. The orchestra squawked. It wasn't music; it was awful din, and it was as oriental as the Taj Mahal. It got into one's head. It seemed to beat its way into the body through the very pores.

The music suddenly stopped and the girls stood still, frozen in the attitude they had struck when the last note sounded. It was a beautiful tableau.

MEN ALL about the room were rising to their feet. Peter got up and said, "You wait here, Sanderson."

He was the first man to reach Po Tung. Susan watched his rapidly moving lips, his quick, decisive gestures. The proprietor of the Jade Dragon was staring at him, plucking at one end of his mustache. He smiled. He replied, no doubt, in Cantonese, and turned to the stage. Susan heard him jabber a brief sentence. It reminded her of firecrackers.

One of the girls became animate and stepped down from the stage. Peter spoke to her and she shook her head. He spoke again, and she nodded. He looked over at Sanderson and lifted his eyebrows. Susan glanced at Sanderson and was surprised to discover that he wasn't looking at the girl who might prove to be his sister, but at her, with eyes that seemed to swim. Then he jumped up.

"Sit down," Susan said sharply.

He acted like a man suddenly wakened from deep sleep. He took a staggering step, whirled about and sat down so heavily that the floor shook.

"I don't know whether I can live through this," he said. "If it isn't Ellen, I don't want to live any longer."

The girl with Peter had bright, inquisitive eyes. For Susan, one glance was enough. This girl, with her Chinese doll mask, was white, not yellow.

"She's white," Susan said excitedly to herself, "or I'm a full-blooded Senegambian!"

Her eyes had dabs of green in the outer corners. Her eyebrows had been shaved underneath at the outer ends, and these ends inclined upward and fixed with cold cream or grease paint, so that she would have an oriental cast of countenance.

Her jacket was lime-green, her trousers a delicate pastel magenta. She wore small dark-red slippers embroidered with blue, yellow and gold. Her feet, certainly, had not been bound when she was an infant, as some of the other girls' had. They were small, but shapely and normal.

The bright inquisitive eyes rested for a moment on Susan's, then danced on and rested for a longer time on the white, drawn face of Jim Sanderson.

"This young lady," Peter introduced her, "is Plum Blossom. She speaks no English—nothing but Cantonese."

Plum Blossom asked a question in singsong. Peter, with a hard smile, interpreted it.

"Susan, she asks if you're for sale."

"Tell her," Susan answered recklessly, "I am—to the highest bidder!"

Peter translated the answer to Plum Blossom. The girl laughed. It was a silvery, tinkling laugh; then she spoke again.

"She says," Peter told Susan, "that she would bring a higher price in the open market than you would. She says her price is twenty-five hundred Haikwan taels, which puts her at the top of the heap. Now, I'll ask her some questions."

Plum Blossom sat down beside Sanderson; looked at him and quickly averted her face.

PETER BEGAN to question her rapidly. The process was retarded because of the fact that it was necessary to translate each question and answer for Sanderson's benefit.

"What is your province?"

"Canton."

"How old are you?"

"Eighteen."

"How long have you been in Kowloon?"

"A few moons—maybe three, maybe six. I forget. Time passes."

"Will you remove your make-up?"

"No—no!"

"Tell her," Sanderson said grimly, "she must. Tell her we absolutely insist."

"It is very important that you remove your make-up!" Peter told the girl.

"Why?"

"Perhaps you have blemishes. Perhaps you are trying to conceal hideous birthmarks."

"No. My skin is as clear as a flower!"

"A flower is not afraid of the light."

"But it took hours. It took hours and hours." Plum Blossom, it was evident, was on the verge of hysteria.

Peter saw that Po Tung was staring hard at him. This was getting into ticklish territory, perhaps into tabus.

"Make her take that make-up off!" Sanderson panted.

Peter said to the girl: "You must remove your make-up. We must see your skin."

"You are only curious. You don't want to buy me."

"We have asked to see your face."

"Never!"

"Shall I call Po Tung?"

That settled it. Peter provided a large silk handkerchief, Sanderson another; and Susan gave the girl her gold-backed mirror.

Hesitantly, the girl removed the make-up. From time to time she glanced at Sanderson. She seemed terrified. And the feeling grew on Susan that Miss Plum Blossom was no one in the world but Ellen Sanderson. It was the most dramatic moment Susan had ever experienced. To witness the reunion of a brother and sister separated by six tragic years! It was wonderful and beautiful—and terrible!

Breathlessly, Susan watched the girl's natural complexion appear from under the heavy coating of powder and paint.

It was white—as white as Susan's own complexion!

"The eyebrows," Peter said firmly; and Po Tung moved toward the group.

Most reluctantly, the girl removed the paste from the eyebrows. Peter took the handkerchief and straightened the brows. Eyes, moist with tears, reproached him. A rosebud mouth quivered. It was amazing. A young and beautiful white girl had emerged from that mask! Unquestionably white!

CHAPTER VI

CRYPTIC ANSWERS

WHEN PLUM BLOSSOM had removed most of her Chinese make-up Peter said to her sternly, in English:

"Your true name is Ellen Sanderson, isn't it?"

The girl's hand flew to her mouth, and her eyes opened until the whites showed. Then she seemed to gain control of herself. Her face became, with the aid of rigid muscles, quite as much of a mask as it had been before.

"No," she said.

Sanderson broke in: "Then why are you so excited?"

"I am not excited."

"Why didn't you speak to us in English?"

"Because I was spoken to in Cantonese!"

"If you aren't—or weren't—trying to conceal your identity, why did you make up as a Chinese girl?"

"For business purposes!"

"That doesn't go," Peter said curtly. "You know very well that a white girl fetches a much higher price here than a native girl. Your price is twenty-five hundred Haikwan taels because you are a white girl. It is commonly known that you are a white girl. That is why it was so easy to find you. What is your real name?"

"I don't have to say."

Sanderson broke in hysterically, "For God's sake, won't you tell me whether or not you're my sister Ellen? You don't have to be afraid."

124

"Not so loud, please," Susan interjected.

Sanderson lifted clutching hands to her. "You are my sister," he declared hoarsely. "You must be. You're Ellen. You are. Listen! Ellen! Mother is terribly sick. She's dying. Father is dead—he died six months after you ran away. We don't care what you've become. You must come home with me."

"I'm not your sister."

"Listen. Ellen! You needn't be afraid. We won't let them hurt you. This man is a friend. We are both armed. We can get you out of here. Easier than that, we'll pay Po Tung the twenty-five hundred taels. You'll be free. Girl, won't you admit that you're my sister?"

The girl looked at him stonily. "I am not your sister."

"Yes, you are! You're just saying that. You're afraid we'll accuse you and nag at you because of the suffering you caused us. On my word of honor, we won't. You won't have to answer a question. Simply say that you're Ellen. If you only knew how happy mother would be to see you again! Ellen, please—" His voice ended in a husky sob.

"My name is not Ellen. I am not your sister."

Sanderson looked imploringly at Peter. "Moore, talk to her, will you? I can't. My heart is breaking."

"**LET ME** talk to her," Susan interrupted. The girl looked at her with a glint of obstinacy.

"Look here," Susan said gently. "I know that he is telling you the truth. I'm backing up every word he says. I'll personally accompany you back to San Francisco."

"I do not come from San Francisco. I am not this man's sister."

But Susan did not lose heart. "I am asking to be your friend. That is all. I only want to save you hurts and worries. I will take you home. I will furnish the twenty-five hundred taels to buy your freedom, and you will be under obligation to no man—not even your brother."

"But he is not my brother!"

Peter stopped in his fight to aim at
the gleaming yellow chest

Susan began to lose her temper. "Do you think you are giving your mother a square break?" she demanded. "If I were you, I would be damned ashamed of myself."

Peter glanced at his watch. He exclaimed, "Ye gods, it's twenty of twelve! I've only enough time to get back to Hongkong for that appointment."

"What are we going to do?" Susan wailed. "Either this girl is Ellen Sanderson and will never admit it, or she isn't Ellen Sanderson."

Sanderson uttered a deep, heartbroken groan.

Peter said rapidly, in Cantonese, to the girl: "If you are this girl we are discussing, won't you tell me, so that I can tell this man in the morning? I mean, if you are Ellen Sanderson and wish to marry a Chinese, it is certainly none of my business— or even your brother's. You are of age and can marry any man you wish. I won't argue about it. You can go upriver with Yen Chan to-night, as planned, and in the morning I will tell your brother that that was what you wanted to do; that your heart is here and you wish to stay here. The rightness or wrongness of it is none of my business. Whoever you are, if you want to get out of this place, away from China, we will help you, and you will be under no obligations.

"This is true talk, Plum Blossom, and the least you can do, if you are Ellen Sanderson, is to admit it to me, so that your mother will know that you are happy and living the life of your free choice, and not miserable and degraded or lying in an unknown grave. I will give you my word to say nothing until to-morrow morning."

The girl answered, in Cantonese: "It is easier to fill up the bed of a mountain torrent than to satisfy the heart of a man. You are a strange one, my fig tree. If you were not so much in love with this girl here, I might wish that I were being sold to you and not to Yen Chan, although he is a kind and noble man. But the cricket cannot speak of ice, knowing it not; and the well-frog should not talk of heaven."

SANDERSON BROKE in impatiently, "What are you two saying?"

"Just a moment," Peter answered; then, once more, in Cantonese: "What are you trying to say?"

The girl's eyes upon him were murky. "Not to know," she answered mysteriously, "is to be a Buddha. Living, a man knows not his soul; dead, he knows not his corpse. Who am I to say who I am? A flower may be dying for lack of nourishment, yet throw its fragrance onto the air of a desert. You think I am rotten because I choose to live with Chinese. Yes; I am rotten, but I am beautiful. I am the most beautiful girl, yellow or white, in southern China. Listen, my jade tree. Who is this girl to you? Only compare us. Which is the lovelier? I say and you say I am rotten, but is a flower rotten because it grows upon filth? Is the fragrance of a rose any less sweet because of how its roots are fertilized? Then I am rotten—and I am a virgin. Send this man and this girl away and buy me for yourself. If you think my face is beautiful—wait until you have seen my body! Don't speak yet! Wait! A diamond with a flaw is preferable to a common stone with none."

The music started again. The girl's voice was like spiced wine.

Her mouth was shaped like a heart. Her dark, melting eyes would have lured a saint.

"To look at a plum is not to quench one's thirst. My kisses would be the very dew on the blossom."

Peter was tilting his head, as might a man who is listening to the far-away call of seductive music.

The girl's eyes suddenly sharpened, and she said a strange thing.

"Do not dress in leaf-made clothes when going to put out a fire. Go—but come back to me!"

Sanderson broke a spell which was as delicate as a glass bubble by leaping up and shouting: "What the devil are you two saying?"

As if recalled from an opium dream, Peter muttered: "This—this girl is not your sister."

Sanderson cried: "You're lying! She's my sister, and you won't tell me the truth! What have you two been talking about?"

"The rice crop," the girl said, insolently; "plums and passion!"

"She is not your sister," Peter went on evenly.

"You're a damned liar!"

Peter said quietly: "Sanderson, cut that out. Susan, I haven't any more time to lose. Let's get out of here."

Sanderson jumped up, stepped across the table and swung his fist savagely into Peter's face.

PETER WAS unprepared, yet, with the automatic reactions of a trained boxer, he tilted his head so that he received the blow not directly, but glancingly along the line of his jaw.

Even so, the impact sent a flash of fireworks into his skull and threw him sufficiently off balance so that he stumbled aside and fell across the table. His left cheek came down with a crack on the hardwood. And in the moment while he lay there, letting his wits recover themselves, he made the curious discovery that his left eye was within inches of the gold-backed mirror which Susan had propped up for the girl to use.

Certainly, it took no longer than a fifth of a second for his brain to record what his eye clearly saw in the mirror. He saw, all about the room back of him, men rising, and in an open doorway he saw a face that he would not soon forget.

In these bizarre surroundings, it was a distinctive face—that of a young Chinese, sallow, slim and aristocratic. It was a rather scholarly face, made more so by the tortoise-rimmed spectacles its owner was wearing. Below the face was a white shirt and a pale-blue necktie. There was also a suit, unmistakably of fine Shantung silk.

In the fifth of a second while his head lay on the table, ringing with what might have been the music of the spheres, Peter distinctly saw this man—and saw the man vanish as the door closed.

It was like a glimpse into a clairvoyant's crystal, revealing his destiny.

Some one pulled at his shoulders. He heard Susan's voice, as from far away: "Peter! Get up!"

He came groggily to his feet. One hand reached for the revolver in his hip pocket, but before he could reach it, Sanderson sprang at him again. Prepared this time, Peter brought up a short ugly punch to his jaw and saw his eyes snap up as he crumpled.

It seemed to Peter that every man in the room was trying to reach him. He pushed Susan behind him and shouted: "Try to get that gun out of my pocket!"

He felt her fumbling for it; but she did not have time to get it out. The Eurasian was clawing toward him. Peter struck at a face as round, as orange as a ripe pumpkin and saw blood instantly squirt from a little bump of a nose.

The Eurasian reached his side, kicked him on the ankle bone and stretched out clawing hands for Susan. Peter turned on him, seized him by the waist and, lifting him into the air, threw him into the crowd.

The Eurasian sprang up and came at him. Peter, advancing to meet him, had to desert Susan. The Eurasian charged at him with the cold fury of a panther. Peter sent him flying back and down with a blow in the face—and was then hemmed in by moving arms and elbows. A wedge of bodies sent him crashing back against the blackened wall.

Peter was separated by that flying pack from Susan. He saw her head tossing about a dozen feet away, then saw her head and shoulders rise up magically and move swiftly down the room, as a chip is carried by a breaking wave.

Peter tried again to reach for his gun, but his arm was struck down. He began striking out methodically with both fists, making no attempt to cover himself; doing nothing but fighting frantically to reach Susan before she disappeared.

He snatched a bottle from a table and splintered it on a shaved skull. He kicked and clawed and punched; and it seemed miraculous at the time that no knives reached him. And each time he reached for the revolver, he was somehow frustrated.

He broke clear of the pack that held him against the wall, leaped across a table, struck a man down, and raced toward the door through which Susan had disappeared. It was the same door, he recalled later, where the aristocratic young Chinese man in tortoise-rimmed spectacles and Shantung silk suit had been momentarily glimpsed.

AS HE ran toward the door, he managed at last to pull Sanderson's revolver out of his hip pocket. The door opened and a coolie, naked to the waist, came plunging through. There was a long, brass-handled dagger in his hand.

Peter stopped headlong in his flight, aimed at the gleaming yellow chest and fired the revolver. He fired it four times. But the coolie did not collapse. And no bullet holes appeared in his chest, although Peter's aim was excellent and he had fired at very close range.

The coolie now rushed at him, with the long knife-blade held inward, along the arch of his wrist.

Peter stepped aside, as he would have stepped aside to avoid the attack of a charging bull. But his stratagem was not successful.

As he leaped, he slipped in a pool of spilled liquor on the floor. He threw up his hands in a frantic attempt to recover his balance, and exposed his face, his throat and chest to the coolie's knife.

With parted, puffed lips and glinting wild little eyes, the coolie held the knife poised just where it was, as if he were a statue.

He could have plunged the dagger into Peter and plunged it in again in the time that elapsed before Peter could recover his balance. And in the same time, Peter could have been attacked by those behind him.

This was mysterious. In fact, the whole aspect of the fight, from start to finish, struck him as mysterious. He could have been shot, stabbed, had his head smashed in long before this. But he did not stop to reason now. He plunged past the man with the knife and rushed headlong through the doorway.

Distantly, he heard Susan cry out, "Peter!" And he kept on down the murky corridor. He called her name, and she answered again.

"Here I am! Here!"

Her voice came from a doorway a dozen paces beyond. He rushed on and into a room, dark, save for the glimmer of light at one of the familiar ornamental paper-covered windows. A light beyond showed that there were bars on the other side as thick as a man's arm.

He rushed into the room and called her name again. She came to him as the door behind him slammed.

Susan, sobbing, clung to him. She asked him if he were hurt.

"No."

"Peter, what will we do? What will they do to us?"

"I don't know. What happened? Where are they?"

The fight had exhausted him. He was gasping for breath.

Susan said hysterically, "Some man picked me up in his arms and rushed me into this room, then left me. There was only one. Then I heard some one shoot. Was it you?"

"Yes."

"Weren't you hurt?"

"No. Give me a moment to catch my breath. We've got to get out of here."

"Peter, it's my fault. You'll miss your appointment with Fong Toy."

"No," Peter said. "I'm going to keep that appointment."

His eyes were gradually growing used to the dim light which filtered through the paper window pane. His heart was thumping dully with fatigue. His throat was stiff and aching with dryness. He was exhausted, but he had to get them out of this place. He had to return to Hongkong for that appointment.

"Come on," he said.

Susan screamed, "Look!" He felt her body against his stiffen, then begin to tremble.

HE LOOKED. In the blackness of the far corner of the room, a snake of jade-green fire had suddenly come into being. It was as large as a full-grown python. It writhed and convulsed, but without a sound. It advanced toward them with open mouth of green fire and eyes as white, as clear as diamond pebbles.

It was not a python but a dragon—the ghost of a dragon: a luminous, terrifying apparition of green fire.

Susan screamed again as the glowing green monster coiled and leaped toward them.

With hairs bristling on the nape of his neck, Peter watched the specter. The thing was fascinating—hypnotic! Each moment, he was certain it would leap upon them and wrap them in its coils. He reached into his pockets for matches. There were no matches; yet he was sure he had placed a box in one of his pockets.

Susan's teeth were chattering. Peter suddenly cried: "Look out! That thing's meant to distract our attention!"

He wrenched his eyes from the glowing jade monster; looked swiftly behind him. And the dim light filtering through the paper window showed him what the green dragon had intended to distract his attention from.

Susan saw it, too—and screamed once more.

A black slab of metal was slowly descending over the teak door which led into the corridor. The purpose of it was, obviously, to seal them in the room.

Peter said curtly, "Stand back."

"What are you going to do?"

"Smash clown that door, if I can."

The descending slab of bronze was now only five feet from the floor. Peter hastily tried the knob of the teak door. It was locked.

He stepped back and rushed at the door with his shoulder down. A brittle teak panel cracked, but the door held. He stepped back and, with his other shoulder as a battering ram, smashed into the door again. Again the panel splintered, but the door still held stubbornly.

The thick plate of metal which would form an inner door was descending faster now. If Peter could not smash open the teak door with one more try, the iron or bronze slab would cut off their escape; make them prisoners.

Peter ran back and charged the door a third time, putting every ounce of his weight and strength into the attack. It gave way with a splintering crash. He went stumbling out into the corridor, head low, and so into the coolie who had been stationed there.

His head struck the guard in the chest; knocked him back against the wall. Before he could recover, Peter struck him down and wheeled about, shouting mightily for Susan to follow him.

He saw, to his horror, that the metal slab was a foot from the floor and coming down rapidly.

Peter dropped to hands and knees as a white hand appeared.

He grasped it and pulled. Susan, attached to the small, groping hand, came flying out, just as the lower edge of the metal door came down the remaining distance.

It came down with a heavy, grinding crunch on one of Susan's diamond heels, smashing the heel and sending diamonds popping out of their sockets and spinning like globes of liquid fire. The rest of the jade-green slipper was squashed to the floor.

Peter seized her hand and pulled her along the corridor, away from the room in which his encounter with "Plum Blossom" had taken place. He had no idea where he was, and he had still less of an idea in which direction escape lay.

He glanced at his watch as they started down the corridor. It was one minute past midnight. He had fifty-nine minutes in which to return to Hongkong, collect three hundred thousand dollars, Mex, from the hotel manager and keep his appointment with Fong Toy.

Where the corridor bent to the right, he paused a moment and looked back. He saw the coolie on hands and knees picking up one of the diamonds which had been dislodged from the heel of Susan's trapped slipper.

CHAPTER VII

CHAOS

A RAT IMPRISONED in a wire cage must enjoy sensations very similar to those which Peter and Susan underwent in the next few minutes as they raced madly up one corridor and down another, desperately trying to find a door leading to a street.

It was a wild, confused and panicky few minutes. They ran through rooms in which men sprawled asleep; other rooms in which fan-tan was being played; they ran into and down corridors with dead ends.

Susan's impressions were chaotic. Every attempt at escape was frustrated by a blank wall or a locked door. It was like trying to thread your way out of a Chinese labyrinth. It was like a nightmare in which you cannot escape from some nameless, invisible ogre.

At first, there seemed to be no pursuit. Doors opened and closed. Faces peered at them—and withdrew.

Then, suddenly, a bullet sang past and flaked off a lump of aged green plaster from the wall within inches of Peter's head. Peter kicked open a door and pushed Susan ahead of him into a room lighted by a single candle. The air was sour with the fumes of rice whisky. The room was almost filled with small empty kegs, bound with dried grass.

At the far end was a door half closed and hanging on one hinge. As Peter made for it, the door burst open, falling inward and twisting off the hinge. A coolie in wet blue rags shot in, as if he had been propelled by a spring. His momentum carried him well into the middle of the room, and Peter saw a wet, rusty knife in his uplifted hand.

Armed with nothing but a revolver loaded with blanks, Peter had only one recourse. He picked up one of the empty samshu kegs and hurled it at the coolie's head.

The keg squarely struck the target and disintegrated. Staves flew. The coolie dropped his knife and would have fallen on Susan if she had not stepped quickly aside.

Peter shouted, "Through that door!" And Susan ran on.

They found themselves now in a smaller room with doors in three of the walls. The floor was wet. As they hesitated in indecision, the sound of running feet came to them through one of the closed doors. Then they heard men running into the room they had just left.

Susan whimpered, "We're trapped!"

Peter kicked open the other door. It gave upon blackness— and mud. A gust of wind tossed raindrops into his face.

"Give me that slipper!" Peter snapped. But before she could answer or act, he had swooped down and snatched the slipper from her foot. He stuffed it into his pocket. Then he picked up Susan in his arms and ran out into the mud.

A volley of oriental expletives burst out behind them. Peter staggered on. He knew that the chase had only begun. And he had not the slightest idea where they were—north, east, south or west of the Jade Dragon.

Rain pelted his face and hair and ran in cold streams down his neck. He waded through slimy mud almost knee-deep.

Susan struggled and said, "Don't be silly, Peter. Put me down. We can make better time."

Peter said nothing and staggered on. Where was the water front? Which way was Hongbom? Which way was Hongkong?

Scattered yells behind him indicated that the pursuit was deploying.

FAR AHEAD he saw a light. He crashed into the side of a

wooden building and found what must have been intended to be a sidewalk, but its boards were under three inches of mud.

He flattened against the wall as he heard the splashing of feet close behind. An unseen man, puffing and cursing, went floundering past.

The distant street light was blotted out now by a fresh torrent of rain.

Another unseen pursuer went staggering past.

Peter waited a moment longer and started toward where he had seen the light. The muddy sidewalk was slippery. Several times he almost fell.

The light proved to mark a wide, muddy street, with native houses and shops on either side. He did not know Kowloon well; did not recognize the neighborhood. But there were more lights glimmering through the rain in the distance, and he guessed that that was the water front.

Bedraggled and limp, Susan clung to him. At intervals, she insisted that he put her down, but Peter strode on, hopeful only that he would reach the water front before the pursuit closed in.

The torrent ceased. Farther away, he saw more lights rising into the sky; a constellation of faint dancing stars. That would be Hongkong.

Shouts behind him caused him to break into a run.

They reached the water front. Street lights along what passed for the bund threw faint radiance on mud and rain-swept buildings.

Peter whistled. A sampan came fishtailing toward the retaining wall. A coolie with the mushroom hat of an Annamite was at the sweep.

As the sampan came alongside, Peter said, "Wanchee go Hongkong. Five dolla'—can do? Chop-chop—ten dolla'."

Which meant that he would pay five dollars for the trip—ten if the coolie made it in a hurry.

"Can do," the coolie muttered.

Peter helped Susan over the wall and aboard. When he

stepped into the stern, the coolie dropped the sweep and leaped at him. He had been concealing at his side a short, thick club.

He brought this up and over, with the obvious intention of smashing Peter's skull.

Peter ducked; shot his fist into the face of this newest enemy, missed his jaw, and knocked off the mushroom hat.

To his immense surprise, Peter now saw that the Annamite coolie was not an Annamite at all; saw that his hair was slicked back like patent leather; and saw that the man's eyes were the eyes of a cobra or a python. The man was, unquestionably, the Eurasian.

Susan shrieked encouragingly, "Kill him, Peter!"

Peter did not kill him, but he did his best. He knocked the club aside as it came up again, and put all his weight into a blow which crashed into the Eurasian's jaw.

The spurious coolie went overboard with a splash. And as if this were a signal, another man came scrambling out of the dark little cabin. This one Peter recognized as the tall Mongolian who had reminded him of a Chicago gunman.

Peter had a certain advantage, because of the elevation of the stern. The Mongolian was inches taller than he, and he was evidently an experienced fighter.

He quickly eliminated Peter's slight advantage by leaping up onto the stern. Then he put his head down and fought. He backed Peter to the rail with scientific rights and lefts; and Peter ducked, dodged and waited for an opening.

Peter straightened him up with a left uppercut, then put what little remained of his fast oozing strength into a straight punch intended for the jaw. His foot slipped, however, and the punch landed high on the Mongolian's shoulder. But the blow accomplished its desired result, and in a rather curious way.

The Mongolian slipped, or tripped. In endeavoring to regain his lost balance, he shot out his hand for the top of the retaining wall. His push sent the sampan away from the wall. For a precarious moment, he remained there, at a slant, his hands on the wall, his feet hooked onto the stern.

In this moment, while Peter's affairs were in a delicate balance, Peter snatched up the sweep and shoved the outboard end of it against the wall. The Mongolian lost his grip on the edge of the wall, and at the same moment, his feet became dislodged from the slippery stern rail as the sampan moved out into the harbor, and he plunged into the water.

HARDLY HAD this latest antagonist been dispatched, when Peter's attention was captured by another man who came crawling out of the darkness of the thatched cabin. He was a short, wide-shouldered, bow-legged coolie. His eyes were a-glitter with terror. He chattered:

"My allatime allee light!"

And Peter growled, "Oh, you're all right, are you?"

"Yes, masta'!"

"Does this sampan b'long you?"

"Yes, yes! Him b'long my!"

"Tell him to step on it!" Susan wailed. "Look back there, Peter!"

Peter looked back. His pursuers from the Jade Dragon—a knot of six or eight men—had gathered on the wall. A knife flashed. It came, end over end, to thump against the stout teak after wall of the little cabin.

"Chop-chop!" Peter said.

The coolie, having picked up the sweep, began to waggle it with desperate haste.

Peter, looking astern at the dwindling knot of men, saw them suddenly scatter. They began shouting. The distance rendered their words unintelligible, but he gathered that they were shouting for sampans. The chase, then, was to continue!

He squatted down, with his back to the cabin; and Susan huddled down beside him. He said: "An awful lot of people seem to hate the idea of my showing up at Fong Toy's to-night."

He saw two sampans move in to the retaining wall, and start out briskly in pursuit.

Peter glanced at his watch. It took some seconds for the radium dial to become visible.

"It's twelve twenty," he announced. "I've got just forty minutes to collect that money and go to Fong Toy's."

"IT'S MIRACULOUS," Susan breathed, "that we're alive."

"Not so miraculous," Peter grunted; "at least, not the first part."

"What do you mean?"

"Until you lost that diamond heel, we weren't meant to be hurt. After that, it was an open season for our scalps—and the other heel."

"Why weren't we meant to be hurt?"

"Racket. Sanderson—Plum Blossom—the fight—all part of the racket."

"You don't mean it was all a fake!"

"I sure do."

"Sanderson's story about his runaway sister?"

"Yep."

"And that girl was in on it?"

"She was!"

"Do you mean they staged the whole thing as an elaborate scheme to keep you from going to Fong Toy's?"

"I do."

"Is that why they wanted to clamp us in that room, where that horrible green monster was?"

"It is, Susan."

"But—but—I just can't believe it. Sanderson—"

"A smooth liar. Just like our imitation American consul. His story was phony. Sanderson was phony. The girl was phony. The fight was phony. Everything was phony—but that bullet and this chase."

"Why did somebody shoot at you?"

"Kid," Peter answered dryly, "ladies who lose one diamond heel are apt to be chased for the other. The racketeers lost control of the situation when that coolie found your little heels were studded with real diamonds. Ever hear of Frankenstein?"

"Wasn't he the man who created a human monster?"

"Correct! The monster was fine and dandy until he got it into his head that he wanted to run the show. That's what happened back there. The monster our racketeer created got out of hand when he found that the diamonds that came spouting out of your little heel were real. A ten-dollar coolie saw a thousand-dollar opportunity."

SUSAN OBSTINATELY shook her head. Incidentally, she sneezed. They were both soaked to the skin.

"You're too fast for my poor dim old brain," she said. "How do you know it was a racket?"

"I knew it," Peter explained, "when I tried to use the gun Sanderson gave me. I shot a man four times in the chest with it. The customary results didn't follow. The bullets were blanks."

"Who," Susan asked, "is behind the racket?"

"I don't know. But I do know something about him. He is clever, ingenious and imaginative."

"Why?"

"His obvious purpose was to keep me from connecting with Fong Toy. If he had been crude, he would simply have put a knife or a bullet in my back. Certainly, it required an imaginative man to conceive of that fiery green dragon. We are dealing, as I see it, with an imaginative man—and a gentleman. If he were not a gentleman, he would have had us thrown bodily into a room and had us locked in. But his mind doesn't work that way. He must employ fantastic jade dragons, sing-song girls, malarial beach combers, clever impersonators."

Susan murmured, "I can see all that. And I still stick to my original theory. How many competitors have you who would prefer that you didn't see Fong Toy to-night?"

"I know of at least four—Herman Stagle, the German; Narubi Hosakai, the Japanese; Bruce Granville, the Englishman; and Henri Beauclaire, the Frenchman. There may be others."

"It's one of them," Susan said positively. "Any one of them could have afforded to spend thousands to prevent your date with Fong Toy. Didn't Wan Sang say that a German has the appointment with the doctor immediately after yours? Wouldn't it be most to his interest if you missed your appointment? And isn't this whole racket positively Prussian in its thoroughness? I would certainly say that your racketeer is Herr Stagle."

"It still looks Chinese to me," Peter answered. "And I'm wondering what surprises they're going to spring on us when we reach Hongkong—if we reach Hongkong."

He was looking astern at the two pursuing sampans—dim shapes seen now and then through the rain in the light of some anchored ship as they passed. Their coolie was working his sweep with herculean energy, but the distance from their stern to the leading sampan's bow was gradually lessening.

Susan shouted excitedly at the coolie, "Chop-chop!"

He was sweating—a human machine being driven to its peak capacity.

The lights of Hongkong rose, tier upon tier, above them.

"Twelve minutes left," Peter announced.

"I'm going to Fong Toy's with you," Susan said determinedly. "And I'm going to bring along my thirty-two automatic."

"Too risky," Peter said firmly.

"That's why I'm coming along. Isn't it risky to stop at the hotel for that money?"

"Very."

"Don't you think," she asked, "you'd better go there without the money?"

"Going there without the money," Peter answered, "would be

the same as not going there at all. The Chinese have funny ideas. Fong Toy expects me to bring a hundred and fifty thousand American dollars as an earnest of good faith. A check won't do. The Chinese have distrusted American checks since a number of sour ones were circulated here."

"I'm going with you," Susan stated. "I've been looking forward to this for weeks. I must be in on your hour of triumph. I simply can't picture you as a business man, and I want to see you in action. It's only a business adventure, but it's our last adventure together. I know it'll be perfectly fascinating. Please, Peter."

Susan generally got what she wanted.

"All right," Peter said.

There was a faint jar as the sampan grated against the timbers of the Hongkong landing stage.

CHAPTER VIII

ZERO HOUR

PETER PAID OFF the coolie and sprang out warily on the jetty; but no one was in evidence but a tall, red-turbaned Sikh policeman; and the Bund, so far as Peter could see, was deserted.

Susan suggested that they enlist the services of the Sikh in blocking their pursuit, but Peter wanted no police assistance, with its accompaniment of tedious explanations, red tape, delays.

He selected two registered rickshas for the short ride up to the Oriental. They started off as the two sampans were maneuvering alongside the sampan jetty.

The hotel lobby was crowded with a party of tourists who had just come in from a dinner dance at Recourse Bay.

Susan hesitated in the doorway. Her hair was plastered wetly about her face. Her silver net and coral silk evening gown was in a state of bedraggled ruin. She looked as if she had just been dragged out of the sea.

Heads turned. Murmurs arose. Curious eyes stared at her. One young man laughed.

Susan elevated her chin. Very haughtily she strode across the lobby and into a waiting elevator, leaving behind her a track of wet prints from her stockinged feet and a trail of rain water, and the impression somehow that an infuriated princess had passed.

Peter, making his way to the desk, watched her go—head high, eyes blazing, cheeks flaming.

With one eye on the lobby door, he asked for the money he had left in the hotel safe.

Susan returned, wearing a new coat, fresh stockings and dry slippers, before he had finished checking off and receipting for the thick wad of ten-thousand-dollar notes on the Bank of Hongkong. He folded the fortune into a bundle, snapped a rubber band about it, and dropped it carelessly into an inner coat pocket.

"I've got my automatic," Susan said huskily. "Loaded—and three clips of cartridges. And don't forget that I'm a dead shot. I think it's awfully nice of me to come along and help you gloat in your hour of triumph."

He saw that she was much more excited than she pretended to be. Susan was trying to appear casual.

Peter smiled. "The next time you listen to Amos 'n' Andy—without static—maybe you'll appreciate my efforts."

"I appreciate you plenty as it is."

Peter seized her arm and said sharply: "Out the back way, kid. Pronto!"

Susan, glancing over her shoulder, appreciated his roughness and haste. The tall Mongolian and the Eurasian had entered the lobby and were looking about. As they started toward the lobby's rear, their pursuers saw them and hastened after.

Peter pushed Susan ahead of him, down a hall. He opened a door which gave on a lane running behind the hotel between Des Voeux and Queen's Roads. They ran down the lane to Des Voeux, where Peter secured two rickshas. He helped Susan into one, jumped into the other and quickly gave directions.

They were a block away, turning into Jubilee Street, when he saw the two men come rushing out of the lane.

Peter shouted, "Chop-chop—*cumshaw!*" at the coolies, and hoped that they had finally eluded their pursuers. Then he permitted himself a moment of congratulation. It still lacked three minutes of one o'clock. He would be on time for his appointment. He had worked hard to bring this interview about, and he had spent a great deal of his company's money.

THE COMPOUND behind the gray stone building which Dr.

Fong Toy and his assistants occupied was brightly lighted. A flight of stone steps led up to an open door from which golden light streamed. At the top of the stairs was the reception room. Peter knew that room well; had cooled his heels in it for several hours to-day—or yesterday.

Voices issued from the door. Following Susan into the room, Peter looked about him with surprise. He had not expected his competitors to be here now, but he recognized Herman Stagle, Narubi Hosakai, Bruce Granville and Henri Beauclaire. There were two others. All were gathered about Wan Sang.

Peter glanced at his watch. It was just one o'clock.

Wan Sang, talking rapidly, saw Peter. The plump, jolly-looking Chinese stared at him through his *pincenez* glasses, and stopped talking. His mouth remained open, as if with astonishment. His little eyes blinked. Then he smiled and came over.

Peter asked, "Am I late, Wan Sang?"

And the Chinese answered, "What do minutes count in the majestic march of the centuries? What is time but the measuring-rod of the impatient?"

Susan thought that he was more nervous than he looked. Behind his quaint philosophy she sensed a champagne-like bubbling of uneasy excitement.

She was not trying to conceal her eagerness. Peter, glancing at her, was reminded very much of a small girl about to be ushered in to see her first Christmas tree. Her violet eyes were bright, and her cheeks were pink. He had never seen Susan so eager, so excited.

Peter was saying, "Wan Sang, I do not understand this." But he did understand it. He was to have seen Fong Toy first. Herman Stagle was to have come next. It was quite obvious that Wan Sang, or Fong Toy, had decided on a peculiarly un-Chinese method of disposing of the static eliminator. The invention was to be auctioned off!

Wan Sang made the mendacious explanation that Peter had anticipated.

"This unspeakably mean secretary to the eminent doctor humbly begs that you forgive him this quite necessary rearrangement of plans."

"Necessary?" Peter dryly asked.

"Quite," Wan Sang answered. "The doctor is exhausted. He has suffered so much in perfecting his great invention, Mr. Moore. We suddenly decided to beseech all of you gentlemen to inspect the static eliminator at one time."

"And to sell it to the highest bidder?"

Wan Sang blinked. "I assure you, Mr. Moore, that, after you have inspected the static eliminator, you shall have the first interview with the doctor."

"Alone?"

"Quite."

"Will Fong Toy see us now?"

"He is waiting in his laboratory. He is ready."

"Will he object to Miss O'Gilvie's accompanying me?"

For a fraction of a second, Wan Sang hesitated, then he said, "Not at all. And may her visit to this vile and lowly place be smiled upon by heaven! The virtuous man loathes all material considerations—but did you bring the money?"

Peter smiled. "Wan Sang, you are too greedy. Did all of these rivals of mine bring their money?"

"All of them!"

"All seven of us?"

"All seven."

"Then we have among us better than a million dollars in terms of American gold. That is a lot of money to be walking about the streets of Hongkong at this hour."

"Yes. Dr. Fong has quaint notions regarding business. There was no other way."

"But aren't they wasting their time, Wan Sang?"

"Such is my humble opinion, Mr. Moore. There is no question in my mind that you shall secure the rights to the static eliminator. But before I take you to the doctor, may I see the money?"

Peter laughed and said, "Certainly." He took the fat wad of bills from his pocket and unsnapped the rubber band. Wan Sang glanced at the stack of ten-thousand-dollar notes.

"Very well," he said. "Do you wish to give me my *cumshaw* now?"

Peter looked at him with an indulgent smile. "Wan Sang, don't you know me better than that?" He replaced the money in his pocket.

"But I have gone to such pains!"

"The melon seller," Peter said ironically, "always declares his melons sweet. You will receive your *cumshaw* when I have the signed contract in my pocket."

"VERY WELL," Wan Sang said. He now introduced Peter and Susan to the six men. Several of them Peter already knew.

Susan was thrilled. She shook hands with Herman Stagle, the German representative, who she was sure had put on that wild party for her and Peter in Kowloon; Narubi Hosakai, the Japanese; Bruce Granville, the Englishman; Henri Beauclaire, the Frenchman; Pierre Lousac, the Belgian; and Salvatore Biletto, the Italian—and was amused at the stiffness with which they all greeted Peter Moore, the American. He was their most dangerous rival, and they knew it.

Susan's heart was racing, and the back of her mouth was visited by that dry, aching feeling which always came when excitement or trouble was brewing.

Yet, eager as he was, Peter remained cool and somehow detached. A little corner of his brain was sending out uneasy warnings. Nothing to put your finger on. Nothing definite. Nothing specific. It was only that cool million dollars.

Then Wan Sang murmured, "This way, gentlemen—and Miss O'Gilvie—if you please."

Susan strode with head high beside Peter as the plump, jovial Chinese secretary led them across the reception room, out into a hall and up a flight of worn teak steps. In the right-hand pocket of Susan's coat her hand snuggled the little automatic pistol. She had forgotten it was there. Its presence seemed absurd now.

Except for their echoing footfalls, silence accompanied the group up the stairs and along the wide hall on the next floor.

At a closed door painted sea-green, Wan Sang paused and looked back over the group. He seemed to be counting noses. He knocked delicately.

A muffled voice called, "Hai!"

Wan Sang opened the door a crack. And the voice from within, now clear and crisp, said: "Have the gentlemen all arrived?"

"Yes, doctor."

A pause. "Has Mr. Peter Moore arrived?"

"Yes, doctor."

A perceptibly longer pause. "Mr. Moore—is out there?"

"Yes, doctor. With a Miss O'Gilvie, whom he has requested to accompany him."

"And the rest of the gentlemen are all there?"

"Yes, doctor. There are seven gentlemen in all."

"Bring them in, Wan Sang."

Wan Sang opened the door the rest of the way and stood aside with a ceremonious bow. The room beyond was so dimly lighted that Susan could not, for a moment, see what it contained. She caught the gleam of hooded lights on polished nickel, chromium and hard rubber; on coils, cabinets and elaborately complicated switchboards of slate, hard rubber and marble.

Susan glanced excitedly at Peter. His blue eyes were boring into the velvety semi-darkness. He felt the pull of her eyes and looked down. His smile was wan; but he did not seem nervous or excited.

"Peter," she whispered; "at last—here at last!"

"Yes," he said quietly.

They walked into the room whose magic had been whispered in the scientific capitals of the world.

THE CALIFORNIA BROADCAST

SUSAN MARVELED AT his complete self-possession. She was sure that this was, to him, the greatest hour in his life—finally to meet the man who had struck down the last barrier which stood in the way of the triumphal progress of radio telegraphy and telephony.

Static—that mysterious and little-known quality of the ether which often prevented radio communication! It was known to be caused by lightning; but there was static not caused by lightning. Some said this static was caused by unequal electrical pressure in the air about the earth. Others said it emanated from the stars; others, from the moon. Some more imaginative scientists had even claimed that it was the planet Mars trying to send signals to the Earth.

It was, at all events, and had always been the worst enemy of communication by radio. Peter had told Susan of ships which had sunk with all hands because static interfered with the reception of S O S messages. He had told her of men who had died of sicknesses which doctors at distant points might have diagnosed and cured—if the demon of static had not prevented.

The man who eliminated the curse of static would rank in scientific importance with Galileo, Newton, Marconi, Pupin. And Susan, thinking of this, wondered how Peter could be so calm. For he was the man who, if all went well, would introduce this scientific marvel to humanity; to ships at sea, to wireless land stations, and, in time, to the millions of users of the radio broadcast receiving sets.

It was, to Susan, positively fascinating. This hour would make history! And it seemed wonderful to Susan that the inventor of this boon to mankind should have sprung from the ranks of the world's most decadent nation.

It might be tremendously significant, this hour! Why mightn't it be the awakening of China to the new civilization—the hour when she again took her stand among the nations of the world?

Then she forgot Peter in her eagerness to glimpse the man who would, to-morrow morning, be hailed on the front pages of the press of the world as the peer of Edison, Marconi, Einstein.

Wan Sang had softly closed the door behind the delegation. For a few seconds, Susan stood staring about her in the dimness, wondering why the room was not more brightly lighted. It should have been flooded with limelight!

Peter, standing beside her, was making out familiar pieces of radio apparatus: banks of rheostats, condensers, tubes; complex networks of wires in amplifier circuit hook-ups. In one corner of the large room, a rotary converter whined. Waist-high benches all around the walls were stacked with apparatus. In one corner stood the black hulk of a high-voltage transformer with the familiar petticoated white porcelain insulators projecting V-wise from the rounded top. Coils of antenna wire hung on pegs on the wall near by.

A SLIM pale shadow near the transformer said: "Gentlemen, I must apologize for this lighting. But the work I have been doing, night and day, has weakened my eyes so that they cannot tolerate light any stronger than this."

Peter, listening to his voice, was looking at Dr. Fong Toy's feet. They were shod in black shoes. What peculiarly interested Peter was that they stood in small puddles of water.

Why?

Susan was having her own reactions to this celebrated laboratory. Somehow, it reminded her of that room of horror from which Peter had snatched her so recently. She argued that she was silly to feel this way; that her unfamiliarity with such a complex array of electrical equipment naturally made her feel uncomfortable. She looked across the room at a gap between two benches. In this gap was, presumably, a doorway. Just now it was concealed behind a heavy blue curtain embroidered in golden dragons. What lay behind that golden curtain?

Peter had crossed the room to shake Dr. Fong Toy's hand, and he was followed by the other members of this unique international little group. Peter looked at the slim, pale face, with its black glasses, and he wondered why Dr. Fong Toy's shoes were wet.

The Chinese scientist said briskly, "Gentlemen, I must ask your pardon for the long delays I have caused you. I would have sent for you before, but I did not want you to hear the static eliminator in operation until it was absolutely perfect. It has been so hard. As Confucius said, 'A hundred paths present a hundred difficulties.' I was exploring along new roads—blazing new trails. At any fork in the road, I could have made serious mistakes. And in the course of my experiments, I came upon many interesting new things. But I would not let myself be distracted from the road leading on to my goal."

He paused, and there was a general, nervous clearing of throats among the delegation.

"I make only one request—that none of you approach closely or touch with your hands any of my apparatus. You will say that I have a suspicious nature. That is probably true. Yet I have been working so hard—and ideas are so easy to steal. As you all know, I have not yet applied for a patent in any country."

He paused again. His voice had a curious breathless quality, as though he had been running. He went on:

"You will perhaps wonder why I have this transformer here. I installed it to discourage the prying of my Chinese colleagues—and others. This transformer delivers at its terminals exactly one million volts. Look!"

His slim, aristocratic hand reached for a switch on the wall. There was a dull and sinister humming. Almost at once a livid green snake of fire sprang to life between the brass electrodes which projected upward and inward from the transformer's terminals.

It hissed and crackled explosively. The sound was not unlike an intermittent discharge of machine guns.

The delegation had stepped back. But Peter remained where he had been standing. He had conducted some experiments with a million-volt transformer a few months before. Coolly, he watched Dr. Fong Toy, and the black spectacles of the young scientist seemed to glitter personally at him.

Wan Sang had meanwhile been busy arranging chairs in a row facing one of the instrument-laden benches.

Fong Toy now said, "Gentlemen, if you will be seated, I will demonstrate—my static eliminator. I must ask you not to leave your chairs while the demonstration is taking place, but you are, of course, at liberty to ask any questions you wish. I have nothing to conceal but the actual secret of my invention."

When the delegation was seated, with Peter and Susan on the inner end of the row of chairs, the eccentric young scientist went on. Susan, listening to his voice, did not hear his words. The million-volt spark had frightened her. It was uncanny and sinister. The hum and the deafening crackle of the discharge had scared her. She clutched Peter's hand and tried to listen.

"—And the air, fortunately, is full of static to-night, so that I can give you a demonstration under the most trying conditions."

PETER'S EYES, more accustomed to the dimness, were searching the complicated banks of apparatus on the bench before him with shrewd attentiveness. Stretching down from the edge of the bench to the floor was an apron, or panel, of some light-colored wood—sandalwood or sappan.

Fong Toy had walked to a glossy bakelite panel upon which was mounted a complex arrangement of dials, meters and switches.

"We should be able to pick up some of the California broad-casting stations." He threw on several switches; twisted one dial, then another. A bank of large amplifier tubes became darkly red. Another tube, glowing more brightly, sent a faint beam of golden light into Dr. Fong Toy's thin, aristocratic face.

A loud speaker horn began to hum. Gradually, the scratchy sound of static became audible; grew louder.

A man's deep voice came faintly through the static: "— Program of dance music is coming to you from the ballroom of the Hotel St. Francis, in San Francisco. Your announcer is Gerald Keene."

Fong Toy said, "I will bring this station in as clearly as I can— *without* the static eliminator."

He adjusted rheostats and condensers. The static became louder and louder. It did not scratch now; it came in sharp bursts, small explosions, a harsh cacophony of interference through which the dance music being played was only dimly audible.

Peter cried: "Give it more amplification!"

Fong Toy did so; turned a knob, and another. The static now came bursting from the loud speaker with the violence of thunder crashes. But the music remained dim and far away.

Peter looked once again at Fong Toy's feet. Where he was standing, new puddles had formed, faintly discernible in the semi-darkness.

"Now!" Fong Toy cried.

Susan eagerly leaned forward. She saw that every man in the row was bending forward but Peter. And she was suddenly aware that the palm of his hand, which had been warm and dry, was now cold and moist.

Fong Toy's slender, pale hand touched a knife switch, threw it over on its two copper points.

Instantly, the music came clear. It was perfect. Not a scratch, a murmur, a whisper of static!

Susan cried tremulously, "How wonderful!" A man exclaimed, "Bravo!"

Peter said in a low whisper, in Susan's ear, "Got that gun handy?"

"Y-yes!" she stuttered.

"Keep it handy."

"Why?"

"Just a Chinese racket."

CHAPTER X

EXPOSED

FONG TOY SNAPPED off switches. Amplifier tubes became dim, then dark. The music died away. The young scientist rubbed his hands together.

"Gentlemen, have I convinced you?"

There was an excited chorus of affirmations. Fong Toy asked, "Is it necessary to give you more proof that my static eliminator will do what I claim for it?"

Granville, the English representative, said eagerly, "Doctor, I will offer you, without a further demonstration, two hundred thousand dollars and a more generous royalty than—"

Herman Stagle spoke up. "Dr. Fong, speaking for Siemens-Halske, I will bid three hundred thousand—"

"Gentlemen!" the scientist stopped them. "Let us not discuss the material side of my invention—yet. Let me have only your scientific opinions."

These were given him with almost hysterical enthusiasm. Susan whispered, "Peter, what's wrong?"

Fong Toy had turned to him. "Mr. Moore, as you must know, we are all extremely desirous of your opinion. You have said nothing. Have you any questions?"

Peter stood up. He said:

"Why was it, doctor, that, when you increased your amplification, as I requested, that the static became louder—but the music became no louder? If you can explain that to my satisfaction, I'll offer you a million dollars for your static eliminator."

"I can explain it!" Dr. Fong cried.

"One moment," Peter said quietly. "I want to ask another question first. Was this supposed to have been a scientific demonstration—or a spiritualistic demonstration?"

The black lenses seemed to glitter.

"I do not understand, Mr. Moore."

Peter said: "I will explain. The announcement that we heard from the ballroom of the Hotel St. Francis, in San Francisco, was given by Gerald Keene, the announcer. Am I right?"

"Quite right."

"Yet I happen to know that Gerald Keene, the announcer, was killed yesterday morning in an automobile accident on Market Street!"

In the electric silence following that disclosure, Peter took a step toward Fong Toy, He said steadily, "Susan, point your gun at Wan Sang. If he moves, shoot."

Fong Toy was staring at him as Peter ran up to him and snatched off the glasses. He had recognized him when the ray from the tube lighted his face—a scholarly face; sallow, slim and aristocratic. A white shirt and a pale-blue necktie. A suit, unmistakably, of fine Shantung silk.

The wet feet were nicely explained. Fong Toy was the man Peter had seen for a fifth second in Susan's gold-backed mirror when the fight started in the Jade Dragon! He was the man behind the attempt to keep the renowned Peter the Brazen from his demonstration.

Fong Toy had shrunk against the bench and was seemingly undecided what to do.

The foreign representatives had sprung up. Each man was trying to make himself heard. The consensus of opinion was that Peter Moore was crazy, or up to some trick.

Peter anticipated interference by kicking in the wooden panel beneath the bench—and finding there what he had expected to find. There was an elaborate device for playing eighteen-inch phonograph records. He had correctly guessed that Fong Toy had merely made records of American broadcasting programs on a night when there was no static.

Beside the phonograph machine was another elaborate device—a small electric motor geared to a disk of gold leaf which revolved in a porcelain bowl filled with flake graphite. This was the static-making machine. By hooking it up in a circuit with the phonograph, amplifier and loud speaker, the broadcasting program was liberally spiked with static. By cutting out the static-making device, the record of the program came clearly from the loud speaker. Devilishly clever, all of it!

NOW FONG Toy made a decisive motion. He reached behind him. He picked up a wrench and hurled it at Peter. The wrench went wild, striking Narubi Hosakai in the stomach. Peter closed in on the pseudo-scientist; grabbed him by the elbows, lifted him into the air and hurled him into the complex mass of radio apparatus on the table.

There was a very satisfactory crash as Fong Toy, clawing at the air, landed amid his condensers, tubes, transformers and rheostats.

For a moment he could not extricate himself. In the high-voltage silence, Peter addressed the dumfounded representatives of rival companies.

"Gentlemen, I hate to see this dream come to an end as much as any of you do. But it was nothing but a racket. It was all most cleverly engineered by this young man who calls himself Dr. Fong Toy—the whole idea being to whet our curiosity and our greed until we would fall for the proposition of bringing here, each of us, a hundred and fifty thousand dollars—that is, a total of one million. A nice little haul. A nice little racket. Part of this racket was to keep me away from here to-night for fear I might upset the apple cart. But I got here."

Fong Toy had freed himself from the tangle of wreckage. As he scrambled down to the floor, he cried out sharply in Chinese.

It was the simple command, "Come and get them!" The heavy blue-and-gold curtain across the room bellied out. The first man through was the tall Mongolian, and the second, the Eurasian. Behind them came a pack.

Peter acted on pure instinct. All of his training led him to leap toward the high-voltage transformer in the corner. He swiftly unhooked one of the reels of bronze aërial wire, hooked one end over one electrode, and sent the gleaming bronze coil paying out in a squirming bright snake into the midst of the pack. With his other hand, he threw the switch.

The wire, as it had fallen, crossed the Mongolian's throat; lay along one shoulder of the Eurasian and lost itself in intricate loops among the coolies behind them.

Crackling blue fire sprang from the nose, the ears, the very hair ends of the Mongolian. It snapped from the fingertips of the Eurasian. Behind them, coolies blazed into an aurora of dancing blue and green. One million volts!

Men screamed, fell, clawed at the wire, and clawing, had convulsions and the most violent of cramps. Those who survived surged back into the room from which they had come. Their feet thundered on stairs as they hastily retreated from that awful death.

Peter pulled off the switch. The Mongolian, the Eurasian and a dozen others lay in awkward positions, dead or unconscious.

Quietly, Peter said, "Gentlemen, I urge you to go. Fong Toy may have still another ace in the hole. That million makes us a menace to ourselves."

Granville said: "How about this rotten little racketeer?"

"We'll turn him over to the police."

Fong Toy, oriental and artistic to the bitter end, had other plans, however, for his disposal. Before Peter could prevent him, he had run to the transformer, cast off the trailing bronze wire and run to the switch. He threw it on.

The vicious green-blue spark hissed and crackled explosively between the brass electrodes.

Peter guessed his purpose now. But before he could act to stop him, Fong Toy—Chinese racketeer extraordinary—had seized one of the brass electrodes in each hand.

His death must have taken place in a fraction of a second.

PETER SAT at a writing table in the lobby of the Oriental, trying to compose a cablegram which would break the bad news as gently as possible to Bill Corliss. Corliss was Peter's immediate superior in the radio research division of the General Electric Company.

It lacked five minutes of three o'clock.

Peter was firmly convinced that he was the world's most outstanding failure.

Fifteen thousand miles he had traveled on this wild-goose chase! Three months of perfectly good time he had wasted! Thousands of dollars of his company's money had been spent!

He felt sick and sore and disgusted with himself. What a great, big joke he had turned out to be!

His thoughts strayed to Susan. She had, in her regal little way, ordered him to have breakfast with her. Ten o'clock breakfast. It would give them a final hour together before they parted forever.

He decided obstinately that he wouldn't have breakfast with Susan. He didn't want to have breakfast with Susan. He was so ashamed of himself that he didn't want to see her—or anybody else he knew.

As soon as he doped out this damned cablegram to Bill Corliss, he'd pack and slip out to the Mongolia in a sampan and stay in his stateroom until she pulled out. Susan would understand. She would have to understand. He wrote a note, which was much easier to compose than the cablegram:

DEAR SUSAN:
    The breakfast date is off. I'm going aboard the Mongolia and the chances are I'll never see you again. You've been a grand pal. I'll miss you like the devil. Think of me when you hear those temple bells a calling. Bon voyage and good luck, kiddo.
                                                    PETE.

He now addressed himself to the cablegram again, and by four o'clock had composed the following bitter confession:

> Greatly regret that Fong Toy static eliminator was nothing but a Chinese racket designed and built for no other purpose but to defraud seven electrical company representatives of a total of one million bucks. Absolutely phony. The laugh is on me. Am taking first ship for America.

Peter walked down to the cable office and filed this. Then he returned to the hotel and packed.

It was dawn when he came downstairs again. He walked to the sampan jetty, followed by coolies with his baggage, and took a sampan out to the Mongolia.

There was a large brass-bound porthole in the stateroom to which Peter was assigned, and from it he could see a generous slice of the harbor and the city in the first pink glow of sunrise.

And this was his last sunrise in China. Never had Hongkong looked more mysterious, romantic, alluring.

From the porthole he could also see the gleaming white hull and the fat blue funnels of the ship which would carry Susan south. The City of Singapore was like a ship carved from ivory on a sea of kingfisher jade. Saigon—Bangkok—Singapore—Java!

Susan had said: "I keep hearing the trade wind in the palm trees, the whisper of waves on golden beaches, the trumpeting of elephants in the teak yards, and the little silver wind bells tinkling in the big temples.

"Think of Java and Singapore! Think of the tropical moon, the palms, the golden pagodas, the lazy blue southern oceans. Think of seeing, hearing and smelling all those things—with me!"

He couldn't stand thinking about it any longer, so he stretched out on his bunk. And promptly fell asleep.

A SHARP knocking aroused him. He sat up and rubbed his eyes. The bright, nearly vertical sunlight of mid forenoon struck through the porthole in a golden shaft. The pounding occurred again. Peter swung his feet to the floor, walked to the door and opened it. A Chinese room steward had a cablegram for him. It had just come aboard.

Peter tore open the message and stared at it sleepily. He rubbed his eyes, grunted, and read it again.

> RECEIVED YOUR COMPETITORS' REPORTS ON LAST NIGHT'S DOINGS ALONG WITH YOURS AND AM CERTAINLY PROUD OF YOUR GREAT WORK. EXPOSURE OF FONG TOY RACKET WAS SUCH A CLEVER PIECE OF WORK AND SHOWS SUCH THOROUGH KNOWLEDGE OF THE ORIENTAL MIND THAT OUR FOREIGN SALES MANAGER HAS URGENTLY REQUESTED YOUR SERVICES AS TRAVELING FAR EASTERN REPRESENTATIVE. PROCEED TO SAIGON, WHERE DETAILED INSTRUCTIONS FOR SALES CAMPAIGN IN INDO-CHINA WILL BE WAITING. BEST WISHES AND HEARTIEST CONGRATULATIONS.
>
> CORLISS.

The deep bellowing of a steamship whistle jarred Peter out of his grogginess. It was the Mongolia's whistle that had blown. He looked wildly out of the porthole, and saw that the City of Singapore's anchors were still in the mud.

Hooray! He'd have just time enough to transfer his baggage and get aboard. And have a lunch with Susan!

CAVE OF THE BLUE SCORPION

Was he myth or man, this Mr. Lu of the jade brain whose palace Peter the Brazen sought at the bottom of a Chinese mountain lake?

CHAPTER I

A LAKE OF MYSTERY

DAWN, ON A cold, thin little wind, crept into this mountain fastness of Inner China. It lay saffron light on torn and tortured ranges of raw granite. Jagged peaks, silhouetted blackly against the glow, became massive chunks of iron bristling with spikes.

The faint light of approaching day, joining the unfathomable blue of the night sky overhead, sent dark and mysterious flashes into the small egg-shaped lake which, almost a mile below, lay like a puddle of purple water at the bottom of a well.

To the sharp-eyed American girl who had, since the night previous, been climbing up the other side of the mountain, so that she could steal this forbidden glimpse, the little lake was dregs of purple in the bottom of a giant's cup.

The granite walls fell away from where she stood, panting and spent from her night's exertions, as sheerly as the walls of any cup. Her eyes, which were not blue, but a deep and velvety violet, explored the encompassing walls and saw not one meager opportunity for a mountain sheep, let alone a man or a mere woman, to descend or to climb.

She could understand why it was called the Lake of the Flying Dragon. Nothing but a creature with wings could possibly make its way to the lake. Except, of course, by the pass. And the pass was out of the question. A slit in the opposite wall, so narrow that it seemed, at this distance, as if a man must walk sidewise to go through it, the pass was well guarded by the Chinese village perched on the narrow shelf at the lake's edge.

The pass was out of the question: impassable, unless a strong-armed force could push through it and take the village by storm. Yet that village, so the girl had heard, had stood there for upward of four centuries, in the heart of the wildest, most hostile section of interior China, and no enemy, however powerful, had entered that pass and lived to return and tell of his exploit.

The American girl, breathing audibly from her exertions, seated herself on a granite bowlder and removed from their case, which was slung from a shoulder strap, a pair of fine German binoculars.

For upward of fifteen minutes, while the apricot light of dawn brightened to lemon and to silver, she studied the purple lake and the village and the pass.

She saw a punt put off from the village. It did not resemble the sampans of the Treaty ports. It was so long and narrow that the girl wondered if it were not a hollowed log. A man standing in the stern manipulated a sweep. There were two passengers. But the distance was so great that she could not, even with the binoculars, distinguish them.

She saw the punt travel out—a brown splinter—upon the flawless purple surface of the little lake. Reaching the precise middle of the lake, it stopped. The two passengers seemed to be moving about.

Susan had no time to cry out

She saw first one, then the other, slip over the side of the boat and apparently enter the water. Magically, they vanished into the purple mystery of the lake.

The man at the sweep maneuvered the punt about and headed for the village. The girl with violet eyes searched the spot in the lake where the two passengers had vanished.

They were not in the boat. They were not visible in the water. Their departure was attended by not the slightest ripple. It was as if, by some feat of Oriental magic, they had become invisible.

THE GIRL on the bowlder did not move until the punt reached the village. Her heart was pumping with excitement. Her large violet eyes, overshadowing her other features, were dazzled with excitement. There was an eager little smile at her lips.

The rumors, she eagerly told herself, were true!

There was nothing now to wait for. She had found what she had hoped to find. Arduous days of climbing about these craggy mountains were amply repaid. Aching muscles, tired bones, bruised and scratched skin no longer mattered.

She had solved, she delightedly assured herself, the greatest riddle of her life.

With dancing eyes and a high heart, she began the difficult descent of the slope which she had climbed during all of last night.

Her saddle horse and her pack horse were patiently waiting at the bush to which she had tethered them the previous afternoon at dusk. She called to them gayly, affectionately. They gazed at her with pricked ears. The saddle horse whinnied.

Having to bestow her brimming exaltation on some living creature, she enthusiastically kissed the cold shining black nose of her saddle horse. She climbed into the awkward Mongolian saddle.

It was dangerous country here for a girl riding without escort. There were roving bands of bandits. There was the difficulty of finding water in time. There was always the chance of getting lost. But she had conquered fear. And she had surmounted the insurmountable.

Two days later, she reached Chungking, which is a filthy and squalid town marking the northern end of the old caravan route into India. Chung-king, on the Yangtze-kiang, is the most westerly stop of the little river steamers which fight their way up the yellow torrent from tidewater, fifteen hundred miles away.

At Chung-king, the girl with violet eyes boarded a river steamer. She paid no heed to two filthy Chinese coolies on the rotting old teakwood dock who gazed obliquely after her as she went aboard.

Nor would she have attached the slightest significance to the fact that one of these coolies, on parting, handed the other a tiny pyramid of pale-blue chalk. It could not, naturally, have occurred to her that her thirst for excitement had set into motion a chain of grotesque and shocking events.

CHAPTER II

BEHIND THE SCREEN

IT WAS A delightful little dinner party. Wong Poon, the president of the Ta Liang Shan Mining Company, was the host. His guests were Mr. and Mrs. Charlie Sing, of San Francisco, and Peter Moore, of Schenectady, New York.

The dining room of Wong Poon's house was cheerfully aglow with candles, according to the approved Western custom. Mr. Sing and Mrs. Sing were thoroughly Americanized, thoroughly modern, and they made charming dinner table companions.

They had, Peter Moore reflected, assimilated American customs and manners without losing any of the charm or courtesy which he admired so much in the well-born Chinese. Mr. Sing was a silk importer: he owned a chain of silk stores in California. They were in Shanghai on Mr. Sing's annual buying trip. Mr. Wong, their host, had met them on a ship on one of his recent trips to the United States.

Peter Moore was here to-night in his capacity of Asiatic representative of the General Electric Company. He and his host had been negotiating for ten days over portable power plants and electric pumps which he wanted to sell and which Mr. Wong Poon wanted to buy.

They would, Moore believed, reach some agreement on the transaction after dinner to-night, perhaps after Mr. and Mrs. Sing had retired.

The meal was delicious—and entirely American. And it was

served perfectly by three of Mr. Wong's wonderfully trained Chinese servants.

Mrs. Sing, a brisk, merry, outspoken little dumpling of a woman with gray hair and bright, snapping black eyes, was, she declared, tremendously disappointed with the trend of affairs in modern China.

"You young Americans out here," she said to Peter Moore, "are fighting a wonderful fight. But it's an uphill fight. I think China has gone to the dogs. There's no more romance in China. Don't you agree with me, Mr. Wong?"

MR. WONG courteously agreed with her. Peter Moore, looking at Mr. Wong, wondered about him. Mr. Wong, in his immaculate dinner clothes, looked out of place. He didn't look like what he was. He was a hard-headed Chinese business man. But he looked, in spite of dinner jacket, stiff white shirt, fastidious tie, as though he belonged to one of the wild tribes which swarm over the Shan hills.

His skin was deeply bronzed, not yellow. His high cheekbones gave him the look of a roving Tartar. He was certainly more Mongolian than coastal Chinese. His eyes, so black that the pupils were invisible, glowed with smoldering fires. There was fire, too, in his deep voice; the fire and the music of the great black hills and the desert which lay at their feet.

"Don't you think so, Mr. Moore?" Mrs. Sing's eyes were upon him.

He hadn't heard a word she had said. He smiled and said, "I do, indeed, Mrs. Sing."

"Don't you speak with authority?" she asked.

"Do I?" he answered, wondering if he were getting into deep water.

"Aren't you known in China as Peter the Brazen, because of your reckless adventures? I've heard about them," this thoroughly Americanized Chinese lady went on; "but I confess I don't take much stock in things I hear. I know China rather well, although I left here for America when I was sixteen. I'm convinced there has never been any of this deep-dyed mystery which so many romantic young people come here to find."

"You're quite right, Mrs. Sing," Mr. Wong said, with a laugh.

"It's a sordid country," the silk importer added.

"There are no mysteries here," Mrs. Sing said. "There is no romance."

Peter Moore was looking thoughtfully over Mrs. Sing's busy little gray head at a remarkable Chinese screen in a corner of the dining room. Its three panels of deepest blue satin were beautiful samples of native embroidery. The screen was a work of art, a treasure. It really belonged in a museum.

The American, gazing at it idly, was a little shocked when he saw, at one of the cracks between the panels, a spot of glittering light. The spark of light was at about the height of an eye in the head of a man of average size. It was precisely the kind of light which would be reflected from a staring human eye.

It was not, of course, a human eye. It could not be a human eye. Why should a human eye be staring out from behind an antique Chinese screen at Mr. Wong's dinner guests?

"China," Mrs. Sing was saying, "is nothing but a hotbed of revolution."

Peter Moore looked back at the screen. The spot of glittering light was still there. As he looked at it, the light blinked off, as if an eyelid had been lowered, then it glittered again.

"Don't you agree with me, Mr. Moore?"

"Of course I do, Mrs. Sing."

Who, Peter Moore wondered, with rising curiosity, was hiding behind that screen? For what purpose would Mr. Wong have a spy secreted there?

"The only mysterious society in China to-day," Mrs. Sing went on, "is the Beggars' Guild. And that isn't mysterious. It's like our American rackets. It's the oldest racket in the world. It's older than Confucius."

THE SCREEN, with its three panels, formed a sort of alcove in that corner of the room. Was it placed there purely for decoration? It had no legs. The panels ran to the floor, so that, if some one were standing there, the spy's feet would have been invisible.

But was some one standing there? Or was Peter Moore the victim of an optical illusion?

He shifted his eyes quickly to Mr. Wong's bronzed, rather barbaric face. Mr. Wong was gazing at him. His eyes seemed to smolder. What, Peter Moore wondered, was going on here, literally behind the scenes?

As soon as he could politely do so, he would investigate that screen. His opportunity came when dinner was over.

Mrs. Charlie Sing was still scoffing at the romantic traditions of China. "Romance! Mystery! Show me anything here more mysterious than what we have back home, on Market Street or the Embarcadero. Things sinister? Things glamorous? Don't you really agree with me, Mr. Moore?"

"Emphatically," he said, smiling at her vehemence.

Mrs. Sing, briskly arose at Mr. Wong's suggestion that they have coffee in the living room. Her husband followed her out of the room. Mr. Wong waited at the doorway for Peter Moore.

The American went to the screen and said:

"This is a Ming screen, isn't it?"

Before Wong Poon could answer, he had lifted it out of the corner, as though he intended to examine it. As he moved the screen, he exposed a door about five feet in height by three in width, which was ajar. Cool night air drifted in through the opening.

"That's strange," Mr. Wong said in a surprised voice. "That door is never used except in the summer. It's always kept locked. It leads into my garden."

He seemed to be sincere. There was a puzzled look about his eyes. He was frowning.

Mr. Wong reached down to pull the little door shut. But his long, thin, brown hand did not just then touch the latch. Midway it hesitated, stopped. A convulsion seemed to pass through it.

It dropped, very much as a hawk pounces on a chicken, to the floor. It came up from the floor in a doubled fist, but not before Moore had glimpsed what Mr. Wong had snatched off the floor.

The Chinese released one finger from his brown fist, caught it like a hook over the latch, and pulled the little door shut. With the same finger he pushed home the brass bolt. The striking bronze color had ebbed from his face. It was now a sickly lemon-yellow. Small pearls of sweat gleamed on his forehead. His eyes were suddenly like ashes, as if the smoldering fires had been extinguished. They looked dull and lifeless. It was very evident that Mr. Wong was in the clutches of an unexpected, a mysterious and a very actual horror.

Peter Moore was not greatly puzzled at these evidences of alarm. It was some years since he had seen one of the tiny blue chalk pyramids such as Wong Poon had snatched off the floor. They always spelled trouble, and often spelled death.

Moore did not have to be told what that innocent-looking pyramid of blue chalk meant. He was pale and alarmed himself. But precisely what, he anxiously wanted to know, did the tiny blue pyramid portend?

Mr. Wong quickly, quite miraculously, recovered his composure. He was once again the courteous, the perfect Chinese host.

He said what the American expected him to say. "The screen is yours, my friend."

Peter Moore politely declined the gift. That, too, was expected. These courtesies, required by Chinese custom, attended to, the two men joined the Sings in the living room.

The American was very anxious to know what would happen next.

CHAPTER III

WARNED IN BLOOD

SEATED IN MR. Wong's luxurious study before a crackling grate fire, Peter Moore and Wong Poon got down to business. Charlie Sing and his wife had retired to their room for the night.

This transaction between Moore and Wong concerned a certain lot of slightly used mining machinery which the American had taken off the hands of a defunct mining concern near Nanking. There were two portable gasoline-driven generators of fifty-kilowatt capacity, two electrical suction pumps designed for use in deep mines, a number of drums of power wire insulated for use under water, and an assortment of odds and ends.

In the present state of the Chinese mining industry the lot was worth, at the most, $15,000, American gold. But the glimpse of that glittering eye behind the Ming screen, and his subsequent glimpse of that tiny blue pyramid, had given the American a hunch. He was now quite certain that Wong Poon was not at all what he claimed to be.

So he said, carelessly:

"I'm asking thirty thousand, gold, for the lot."

That his guess had been quite correct was proved by Mr. Wong's attitude. It was quite evident, now that they bad passed the stage of polite negotiation, that he wanted the machinery more than Moore wanted to sell it, and Moore would have sold it to the first man who offered him $10,000, gold; might, indeed, have taken as little as $7,500.

When the deal was closed, as it was very quickly, at $25,000, the American was sure that Wong Poon was either in a tremendous hurry for that particular machinery, or was holding back something.

And this latter surmise proved to be correct.

"Where," Moore asked, "shall I have it shipped?"

"Hankow."

"Strongly crated?"

"Very strongly crated."

That meant, of course, that the machinery was going well up the Yangtze. Chung-king? Where beyond?

Wong lighted a cigarette. His eyes were clearer. He seemed to have himself better in hand.

"I will be perfectly frank, Mr. Moore. This machinery is not destined for either of our mines in South China."

The American, knowing that it was not, looked innocently interested. He knew something more. He knew that the Ta Liang Shan Mining, Company, of which Mr. Wong was president, was a defunct organization; and he had presumed all along that Mr. Wong had revitalized it with his own personal capital. Mr. Wong's rating at the Shanghai banks was excellent, his credit was good. And Peter Moore, with that tiny blue chalk pyramid in mind, knew precisely why.

"The truth of the matter is," Mr. Wong was saying, "that I am opening up new properties in the hills above Chung-king. I know I can take you safely into my confidence."

PETER MOORE, knowing just what the truth was, suppressed a smile.

"We have discovered very rich deposits of copper in the Shan hills," Wong Poon went on. "This particular consignment of machinery is intended for our first development. It should be," he said significantly, "the first of many orders for electrical mining machinery. I hope I can count on your full coöperation."

The American, murmuring his assent, wondered what was coming next.

"I would like very much, Mr. Moore, to have you accompany this consignment of machinery up the river and to the new properties, and to see that it is properly installed. I know that you are one of the cleverest young electrical engineers in China."

Peter Moore, who was not so much an electrical engineer as an authority on wireless telegraphy, let this pass.

"I am willing to pay you very generously," Wong said. "It will take you better than two months to make this trip, but I assure you it will be well worth your time. Aside from the fact that it will lead to large orders for electrical machinery, I am willing to pay you, say, five hundred a week, gold, from the time you leave Shanghai until you return."

The American, fully aware of what was transpiring behind the scenes, pretended to think it over. But he did not have to think it over. He knew that, through Mr. Wong, he was being offered an opportunity to secure probably one of the largest orders for electrical equipment ever placed in China. And not only that, but Mr. Wong was holding open the door to him for an amazing but safe adventure. All of this he had deduced from his glimpse of the little blue chalk pyramid.

He pretended to be reluctant only because it was a good policy not to be too eager. It took Mr. Wong an hour of persuasion to convince Peter Moore that accompanying that consignment of mining machinery to Chung-king and beyond would be a profitable step for him to take.

Mr. Wong mentioned, among other things, that two or three first-rate American mechanics would be waiting at Hankow to go up the river.

"The very best men I can find. They are going up-river with certain other machinery. A gasoline tractor, for example."

Moore, wondering, finally gave in.

"Very well," he said, "I'll do it. It will take me about a week to get my affairs in order. I'll ship this machinery to Hankow by boat, and follow by train as soon as I am able."

Mr. Wong seemed tremendously relieved. His eyes shone. He

smiled. He said a check for the machinery would be delivered to Peter Moore's office, on the Bund, in the morning.

"If I do not see you before," Mr. Wong said, "I will meet you in Kung Yang, which is the nearest village to the new properties."

They said good night, and Peter Moore returned in a ricksha to the bungalow he had rented on Bubbling Wells Road.

Lying awake, some hours later, he wondered if he would be permitted to see the fabulous hall of rose quartz, or the room paneled with mother-o'-pearl. He again congratulated himself on this opportunity for amazing but discreet adventure, and for an opportunity to secure a stupendous order for electrical apparatus.

IN A genial state of mind, he fell asleep. He was awakened sharply by a sound. He could have been asleep no longer than an hour. The rays of the early spring moon, shining through his open window, were striking the floor at only a slightly different angle. Listening, he heard the sound again. Far away, across the sleeping city, came the faint wailing of a Chinese lute. But closer, somewhere within the house, occurred a groan. It was the groan of some one in mortal agony or mortal terror.

Moore switched on the lamp beside his bed; sat up. As he did so, the bedroom door opened and a man in a suit that had once been white staggered in.

The American, with a gasp of horror, sprang to his feet and stared. Only with the greatest difficulty did he recognize in this terrible apparition his houseboy, Wan Lee. The once white suit was streaked and spattered with blood. The man's ears were gone. Blood was spilling in great thick bubbles from his mouth. His right hand had been severed at the wrist. He had somehow bound a tourniquet, a length of rag, about the stump; but blood, in spite of it, came pulsing out.

When Wan Lee, staggering toward the American, tried to speak, only thick, bubbling sounds came from his mouth. His tongue had been torn out or cut out.

Peter Moore, knowing that Wan Lee was the most peaceable

of Chinese, stared at him with utter horror. Wan Lee had been an honest and devoted servant. What had happened? Moore was certain he would never know. He was certain that Wan Lee was dying, and he wondered how Wan Lee, with those horrible injuries, could stand, could walk.

Wan Lee took another step and pitched headlong to the floor. But even in his failing strength he grasped the stump of his wrist. On his side, he looked up, with glazing eyes, into the American's face. He was trying to speak. He could not speak. Moore saw, in those glazing eyes, a desperate anxiety to convey some message.

The bleeding stump was moving in grotesque jerks over the mat on the floor, leaving its trail of blood. The American snatched a sheet off the bed and began tearing it into strips for bandages. But when he bent down over Wan Lee he knew it was too late.

His sickened eyes stared at the crazy pattern which the moving stump of Wan Lee's wrist had traced on the mat. It was, at first, obscure; but as Peter Moore stared, the widening lines suddenly acquired a significance. There, in letters of crimson, was the word *scorpion!*

Even as the American stared, blood gushed from the stump and obliterated the writing.

But Wan Lee had lived long enough to deliver his message.

CHAPTER IV

FRIENDLY ENEMIES

A MESSENGER CAME to Peter Moore's office early the following morning with a certified check on the Eastern and Oriental Bank of Shanghai for $25,000, gold. On receipt of it, Moore gave orders to have the mining machinery in his godown strongly crated and shipped, via river steamer, to Hankow to await his orders.

The following afternoon he attended Wan Lee's funeral, in Native City, a funeral that befitted a mandarin and that Peter Moore paid for, down to the last firecracker, the last bowl of coolie rice, out of his own pocket. He was still sick over the death of that devoted servant, still hotly resentful over the fact that Wan Lee's horrible mutilation, his hideous death, had been merely a caprice on the part of the powerful, sinister figure who stood behind Mr. Wong like a black and forbidding shadow.

It took the spice, the thrill, out of the forthcoming adventure; but it had not changed his mind. His job, after all, was to sell electrical equipment. He would go to Hankow, to Chung-king, and on to Kung Yang.

He was meanwhile putting his affairs in order; notifying the head of the foreign sales department, in Schenectady, of his projected long absence from the coast; notifying his agents scattered up and down the Asiatic seaboard.

One morning, a day before his planned departure for Hankow, he heard his Eurasian stenographer in the outer office utter a cry of astonishment. His door flew open. He received a bewildering impression of deep violet eyes in a tanned face. A girl's hat flew into the air. Her hair tumbled down. There was a yell of delight, and next moment Susan O'Gilvie was in his arms, kissing him, crying, laughing, knocking objects off his desk, whirling him into the middle of the room, and creating, generally, approximately the confusion of an unexpected intense Chinese revolution.

She held him off at arm's length, cocking her head from one side to the other.

"Darling, I'm so glad to see you! Tell me you're just as glad to see me!"

He was, indeed. He had missed Susan, in the four months which had followed their last quarrel, tremendously. And he had supposed that she had passed entirely from his life.

The quarrel had occurred at a birthday party—his birthday. Susan gave the party, a very elaborate and costly celebration for two in the dining room of the Astor House Hotel. She had, at its conclusion, given him his birthday present. This took the form of a jade Buddha. Peter Moore, who had a weakness for good jade, took one look at the birthday present and blew up. He knew that Buddha. It came from the Jade Garden Shop on Foo-chow Road. It was the finest specimen of jade in the Garden Shop's rare collection. It was worth seventy-five thousand dollars, gold.

He indignantly refused it.

Susan had been furious—outraged. After all, why not?

"I won't accept a gift as expensive as that from you. Take it back and buy me a necktie."

She had called him, among other items, a great hulking mule. After all, why not? Wasn't he the only man she had ever cared a damn about? Wasn't he the only living creature she cared a damn about? Upon whom was she to spend her money, if not upon him?

Susan had, she declared, received advices from the executives of her father's estate, to which she was the sole heir, that her fortune had been doubled by judicious short selling in the bear market.

"What am I to do with all my money, pray?"

Peter didn't know; didn't care. The bear operations of the executors had placed her, as far as he was concerned, just twice as far away as she had been before. She had been one of the wealthiest young women in America, anyway. This made it twice as bad.

IT WAS an old, old dispute. They threshed it over again. Should she give her fortune away, just to please his vanity?

"You'd marry me, Peter, if you were as rich as I am."

"Yes."

"Well, what I have is yours. We'll split it fifty-fifty."

His angry spurning of this proposal always infuriated her. But his spurning of the jade Buddha, which she had selected with such thought for him, was the last straw.

"I'll never see you again as long as I live. I hate you. I loathe you. Oh, how I detest you!"

And she had at least gone through the motions of making that threat good. She had packed up and walked out of his life. Rather, she had, in a steamboat, steamed out of his life.

And now she was back, as slim, as lovely, as exciting as ever. She had been, she said, just bumming around. A while in Peking. Then an airplane trip to Tokio.

"I've forgiven you," she announced magnanimously. "Are you still sore at me, darling?"

"Only a confirmed dyspeptic," he said, "could stay sore at you."

"Do you kind of like me a little bit?" Her large violet eyes were searching his face. She was bewitching. There was something about Susan that set her apart from all women. Over-romantic, over-adventurous, with an inexhaustible capacity for dangerous experiment, she was—well, she was just Susan.

"What are you up to, Pete?"

He told her. He told her of his deal with Mr. Wong. Of the

death of poor Wan Lee. She asked him what the tiny blue chalk pyramid stood for.

"The Blue Scorpion!" he said dramatically. "He's a kind of ogre, a myth, a legend of interior China, Certainly, the most powerful, most dangerous man in Asia. When you speak of the Shadow Over Asia, you're speaking of Mr. Lu."

"Who?"

"The Blue Scorpion. The man with the jade brain."

"What?" Susan squealed.

"It's the legend. Three hundred years ago, when he was a young man, he fell down the face of a cliff. He was picked up at the bottom, nothing more than a pulp. But a pulsing pulp. His face had been wiped off on the rocks. Most of his bones were broken. They say even his brains were oozing out."

"You wouldn't kid a girl, would you, Peter?" Susan said. "Did you say—three hundred years ago?"

"I did!"

"This Mr. Lu, alias the Blue Scorpion, alias the man with the jade brain, is three hundred years old?"

"So they say. They say witch doctors gave him, in place of his brain, a brain of imperial, sanctified jade. There was upon him the sign of everlasting immortality. The jade brain possesses a quality of thinking that no human brain can possess. I know only a few authentic things about him. One is that he lives in a stupendous, magnificent, incredible marble cave in the bottom of a lake in the Shan Mountains—a palace of unbelievable glory in a lake bottom—"

"A dry lake bottom?"

"No. A wet lake bottom."

"Under the water?"

"Under the water. I know that's true, and I also know that he is something of a genius. He has had men of various nationalities captured and brought to him, so that he could master all the tongues spoken. And I know that none of these men ever returned. There seems to be truth in the rumor that no man who looks upon the Blue Scorpion ever returns."

THE GIRL was looking at Peter with clear violet eyes.

"Do you think this is true?"

"Some of it must be true, on the principle that, where there's smoke, there must be fire."

"But just where do you come in?" Susan demanded.

"What else," Peter answered, "does he want pumps for, but to keep his under water palace pumped dry? The Blue Scorpion is going modern. He will, I have a hunch, want his cave wired for electric lights and power machinery. Why not? A man of his age is entitled to *some* comforts."

"I'm afraid," Susan said. "I'm afraid you'll be like those other men—never come back."

Peter laughed. It was the light-hearted laugh of a young man who loved adventure.

"It sounds," she argued, "a little mysterious. Why was Mr. Wong so scared when he found that blue pyramid? Why was Wan Lee murdered so atrociously?"

"Simply," Peter reassured her, "to let me know that I was in the shadow of the Blue Scorpion. Wong, of course, is Mr. Lu's agent. One of his thousands of agents. In deathly fear of his master. The spy behind that screen was simply to let Wong know his master was keeping, literally, an eye on the proceedings. The horrible mutilation of Wan Lee was merely to let me know that Mr. Lu can do dangerous and dreadful things—to give me the proper respect for him."

Susan was pale, the pallor showed even under her bright tan. "You must be careful, Peter."

Looking at her, he smiled. "That doesn't sound like you."

"I'm footloose and fancy free," Susan said promptly. "I'm going along."

Thus began one of their long and heated debates. Any one hearing them would have assumed that two lifelong enemies were at death grips. At the end of an hour, neither had progressed an inch.

"All right, you big hulking mule," Susan said finally. "I'll go anyway. You'll have to take one of the regular river boats. I can buy a passage on it. I won't be a member of your exclusive party, but you can't keep me off that boat."

He begged her to be reasonable, logical, sensible.

Those things, Susan retorted, with flashings of her large, lovely eyes, weren't in her blood.

When Peter started for Hankow, two days later, Susan was on the same train, although not of his party. They weren't speaking.

CHAPTER V

HEADED FOR—WHAT?

SEDATE AND ORDINARY steamers can traverse the Yang-tze-kiang, at some seasons of the year, as far up as Hankow. But beyond Hankow, a unique and marvelous type of river boat must be employed. It is of shallow draft, and it is driven by engines as powerful as those in a modern destroyer.

The Soochow transported Peter Moore, Susan O'Gilvie, three red-haired mechanics and a large assortment of crated machinery up the great yellow river, with its dangerous shoals, its furious rapids, to Chung-king.

Peter, meeting the mechanics, estimated them with the accuracy of a man who has had many dealings with their kind. Three amiable, rollicking, skylarking red-heads, they would have been termed, a little farther south, T.T.T.'s—typical tropical tramps.

One of them, their leader, Bill Jacobs, was a deserter from an American destroyer. The other two, Hank Roberts and Tom Dove, were simply gentlemen of the open road—excellent mechanics, ready for mischief at any hour of the day or night, but preferably the night; as quick with laughter as with fists. Three hard-boiled, red-headed devils.

The three red-heads spent most of their waking hours on the after deck of the Soochow, shooting craps. When they were not there, they might be in the smoke room, drinking beer, or in the engine room or boiler room, annoying engineers or firemen. When they tired of doing nothing, they went into the boiler room and shoveled coal into the insatiable maws of the furnaces.

They introduced themselves to Peter, on leaving Hankow, with the respect and deference of adventurers meeting, say, the crown prince of their order. All had heard of Peter Moore, of his exploits up and down the coast of China and elsewhere. The legends about him, the audacity of some of his adventurous feats made him, in their eyes, a demigod.

Yet this deference, this respect, did not account for their attitude toward him as time wore on, as the Soochow, with grinding engines, churned its way up between red and yellow banks, fighting the great yellow torrent, toward Chung-king. It was a secretive attitude. It was mystifying. They would fall silent when he approached. They would watch him warily. It was not so much respect as it was caution.

But their attitude toward Susan was another matter entirely. They accepted her heartily and boisterously. They had heard of Susan, too, and of Susan's capacity for getting people into the most amazing kinds of trouble. She was a girl after their adventurous hearts: carefree, fun-loving, valiant, dauntless.

And there were other, unseen, activities aboard the Soochow. There were Chinese, invisible by day, who prowled at night, who poked about among the crates in the hold, who slipped ashore when the ship tied up, and were replaced by other men who prowled and spied. But Peter was unaware of them. His thoughts were chiefly on Susan.

For several days after the Soochow left Hankow, Susan and Peter maintained their hostile attitude. Peter was cold and aloof. Susan was haughty.

A LARGE golden Chinese moon effected, one night, a reconciliation. The moon paved a path of cloth-of-gold down the river to the cleaving bows of the little steel steamer. There were scents of spring in the mild night breeze.

Peter was standing in the bows, enjoying all this, and thinking over some of his experiences with Susan. The wild, storm-tossed night they had met on a steamer crossing the Pacific. Her escapade in Shanghai in connection with a priceless jade scepter. Her impulse, which Peter nipped in the bud, to acquire the opium habit. Her fantastic theft, in Indo-China, of the black, withered hand of a native god. Her reckless and insincere infatuation, with a Cambodian sultan.

Looking at the mellow spring moon and the cloth-of-gold it lay on the river, he reflected that Susan must have been born under a star called Danger. She loved trouble as most people love peace. Adventure ran like liquid fire in her veins. Yet she could, on occasion, be as discreet, as tender, as gentle as a mid-Victorian debutante.

She reminded Peter of the girl in the nursery rime, who was either very good or very horrid. When she was gratifying her thirst for excitement, she would have tried the patience of a saint.

The girl who came quietly up behind him this evening was on her very best behavior—the gentle, the sweet Susan, the tender Susan. She was, in these moments, delightful. At these moments, he could have tossed his heart at her small feet. But these moments were so rare, so fleeting, that they were gone before you became aware that they were here.

She dropped her elbows to the worn leak wood rail beside his. Her soft shoulder touched his arm.

"Still sore?" she asked in her sweet, clear voice which always reminded him of good metal struck upon softly but sharply and which was, like the rest of her, curiously suggestive of romance. They were the first words she had deigned to address to him in almost a week.

He looked down into her upturned face, which was small and white and childlike in the moonlight. He smiled.

"Nope."

Susan, snuggling her arm into his, sighed and whispered, "Well, neither am I, darling. I don't suppose you have a kiss to spare for a heartbroken girl."

Peter did, it chanced, have a kiss to spare for a heartbroken girl. He delivered it with enthusiasm. Susan returned it with even greater enthusiasm. Her slim arms, which were so much stronger than they looked, remained fastened about his neck. She clung to him, weeping.

She was crying, she said, because she was so happy. Happy because he had forgiven her for being such a hateful brat. Happy because this was such a wonderful trip, and because they weren't mad at each other any more.

"I like you, Peter," she said, sniffling, "because you're so darned good to a poor, lonesome orphan. Do you realize that this is our thirty-eighth quarrel, by actual count?"

Peter was thankful that peace was restored again, that the quarrel was over. There would, he knew, be other quarrels. He hoped they would all end as satisfactorily as had this one.

CHAPTER VI

MR. WONG UNMASKS

CHUNG-KING. FILTHY AND indescribably squalid. Half-naked, half-starved coolies on the rotting teakwood dock, staring with hopeless eyes at the little steamer, at the white faces on her single deck. Slatternly dwellings of bamboo. Streets of raw red mud. The stench of a Chinese river town. Camels with their cargoes from India. A thousand and one depressing, romantic, wretched, glamorous impressions. For this was the fabled heart of China, unchanged over four thousand years.

With Peter Moore as overseer, the three red-heads as gang bosses, the crated cargo was transferred from the Soochow's holds to the old teakwood dock. Yelping coolies, with stout bamboo shoulder poles, transported the crates through the muddy streets to the caravansary compound.

Bill Jacobs, leader of the red-heads, indicated one mound of massive packing boxes and said, "How about that tractor?"

"You'd better assemble it," Peter answered. "We can use it hauling the trailers and getting carts out of the mud."

"Okay, chief." To the very end, the bitter end, that would be the redheads' customary way of accepting an order from him. "Okay, chief."

There were four commodious four-wheel trailers, intended for transporting countless drums of gasoline and lubricating oil.

While the three mechanics set to work piecing together the tractor, Peter devoted himself to a spirited bargaining with owners of camels, mules, oxen and heavy carts with heavy wooden wheels.

One of the red-heads, gazing at one of these carts, observed, "There goes the original disk wheel. And we thought we had somethin' new when we put 'em on automobiles!"

All that night, in his room in the inn that adjoined the compound, Peter heard the rattle of hammers and the clank of wrenches as the three redheads, working in the light of gasoline torches, cursing, as mechanics have cursed over their labors since there were mechanics, assembled the tractor.

And when he descended, early in the morning, to the compound, an astonishing spectacle greeted him. It was made of steel. It bristled with bolts and rivets. What he saw, glistening in the dawn, was a war tank.

The three red-heads were seated side by side on the caterpillar tread on the side nearest him, smeared with black grease, streaked with sweat. They were smoking cigarettes.

"Where," Peter asked, "did that thing come from?"

"This," Bill Jacobs answered, "is the tractor."

Peter said dryly, "That's strange. It looks like a tank to me."

"Chief," Jacobs said, "your eyes are okay. It is a tank. Mr. Wong told me to buy a big tractor. I couldn't find a tractor, so I bought this tank from the Nationalists. It's the same as a tractor. It'll do the same work as a tractor. But it's better in case it rains."

"Rains what?" Peter asked.

"Rain."

The three red-heads were looking at him with innocent round eyes. But Peter was suspicious.

"Not bullets?" he asked.

"I ask you," Jacobs said, "now, where could it rain bullets?"

"That's what I want to know."

But the three skylarking mechanics remained innocent. What, after all, was a tank but an armored tractor?

Susan, arriving in the compound from her room, greeted the

tank with cries of enthusiasm. She wanted to go for a ride in it before breakfast.

"We ain't tuned it up yet, Miss O'Gilvie," Tom Dove said. "But you'll have a chance to take plenty piggy-back rides on this baby."

SUSAN WAS dressed for the expedition. She was trim and she looked efficient in whipcord riding breeches, laced boots, a deep-blue silk bandanna about her hair, a fuzzy blue sweater with pockets stuffed with cigarettes and matches. Peter, looking at her, decided that she was exceptional indeed. Few women would look as feminine as Susan did in that masculine outfit. A binocular case was slung by a strap from her shoulder. And at one hip was a holster containing an automatic pistol.

"I'm anxious," she said, "to meet Mr. Wong Poon."

"He'll be waiting in Kung Yang," Peter told her.

"How far is Kung Yang?"

"Two days."

She watched him with wistful eyes, sometimes with a secret look of anxiety, as he made arrangements for the caravan. Whenever he caught her eyes, she gave him a quick smile. Susan, he realized, was brooding about something. He had seen that look before. It generally spelled trouble.

The strangest caravan ever to set out over the old Merchants' Trail left Chung-king at dawn next morning. The tank, rumbling and clanking and snorting like some steel-clad prehistoric monster, was terrifying alike to horses, camels and oxen. It led the long procession of carts, groaning under their heavy loads. There was, approximately, one cart to one crate, or box. The caravan was a quarter of a mile long.

Susan and Peter, on horses, rode ahead, to escape the dust. It was all, Susan declared, perfectly fascinating. And she said that Peter was perfectly fascinating. He looked like a bridge builder or something, so she said—very dashing in cordovan and olive drab, with a Stetson set rakishly over one eye, a pistol slung at his hip.

The day was clear; perfect. On their right, for the first few miles, the Yangtze swept by in a tumbling, raging torrent. And on their left were the raw granite hills, reduced to deceiving purple softness by distance. From the trail to the mountains was a sweep of golden sand which flashed and glittered. Even the air, washed by recent rains, seemed to flash and glitter. A brilliant blue sky arched overhead. And there was, in the air, the crisp smell of the wilderness.

But Susan did not seem as fascinated as she said. She was acting, Peter thought, queerly subdued. They rode along in silence disturbed by the muffled roaring of the tank, the creaking of leather, the squealing of unoiled axles, the shouting of men.

Peter asked her, after one of her long brooding silences, what was on her mind.

Susan withdrew her eyes from the distant purple mountains and looked at him sharply.

"Nothing in particular. Why?"

"You seem absent-minded."

"I'm just impressed by the magnificence of all this."

"You don't seem happy."

"I'm perfectly happy."

Her eyes went back to the purple mountains and she became silent again. Her vivacity seemed to have deserted her. The feeling grew upon Peter that trouble was brewing, but from what quarter it would come he couldn't imagine. It wasn't like Susan to be so quiet. She was, normally, a little chatterbox, with an inexhaustible capacity for enthusiasm. She would, ordinarily, have been exclaiming over everything they saw; pointing out to him strange or unusual things, joking.

THEY MADE camp that night on a site which had been used as a caravan encampment for more than three thousand years. It was a wide sandy space beside a roaring tributary to the great yellow river.

The sun, vanishing, left a bloody gleam in the sky. This deepened to purple, then to black and the sky was, suddenly, clustered with bright stars. A night wind sprang up from the great desert to the north, a hot dry wind at first, scented with the very spice of romance. Then, abruptly, the wind turned cold, and a camp fire was welcome.

Lounging on blankets before a fire of faggots which snapped and crackled and sent sparks leaping into the billowing smoke, Peter comfortably smoked his pipe and wondered how large an order for electrical equipment he would secure from that mythological monster who lived in a water-tight castle in the bottom of a lake—the man with a brain of jade! He wondered if he would be permitted to see that fabulous palace built under the waters of a lake.

Susan, near by, hugging her knees under her chin, stared at him. Firelight sparkled in her eyes, and gave her face a rosy glow. There was an elfin look about her.

"Peter," she said, "has any man ever seen Mr. Lu?"

"I never heard of one."

"But it seems so preposterous. I mean, these things we hear. Three hundred years old!"

"Methuselah lived to almost a thousand," Peter dryly mentioned.

"You honestly don't believe Mr. Lu is as old as the legends say."

"The secret of Mr. Lu's power, or part of the secret," the tall, lean young man beside her answered, "is that nobody actually knows. Perhaps he is the descendent of the original Mr. Lu. Perhaps he really is three hundred years old. It's never been disproved."

"And no one knows what he looks like?"

"All I've heard is that he is hideously malformed."

Susan shivered. "He sounds like a monster. Aren't you worried?"

Peter looked at her and smiled. "Nope."

She looked back at the fire, then flashed an oblique look at him from troubled eyes which gleamed with firelight.

"Are you sure it's safe?"

He nodded firmly. "Yes. Mr. Lu can be just as powerful a friend as an enemy."

Once, some years ago, Peter had had just cause to be afraid of the mysterious and malignant Mr. Lu, but he was not afraid now. He saw Mr. Lu, regardless of physical appearance, as a man fabulously rich, a man who had heard of the wonders of electricity and would pay handsomely for them. And Peter was perfectly willing to sell him all the equipment he required.

He was smiling at Susan, but she did not smile. She was looking past him; past the fire, toward the invisible mountains. There was a misty, brooding look in her eyes.

Across the encampment, with its glowing fires, its soft murmur of native voices, he heard the twanging of a lute. He recognized, in the eerie strain, a Chinese love song, a fragment from the Lute of Jade, and he said, "Susan, if I land the order I expect to from Mr. Lu—"

A STRANGE sound caused him to pause. It was, at first, like distant thunder—a sustained rumbling. It rapidly came closer; grew louder and louder until it was like the muffled beating of a thousand snare drums.

He sprang up. So did Susan. Men all about the encampment were awaking to activity. There were shouts and answers. Above the drumming, now almost deafening, Peter heard wild shrieks. He saw the three red-headed mechanics crawl on hands and knees toward the tank.

Susan was close beside him. "What is it—a raid?"

"We'll know in a moment."

Then, with thundering hoofs, a cavalcade of shrieking men swept into the encampment.

A great black horse, a Mongolian stallion, with trappings that glittered and twinkled with silver and precious stones, came pounding up to where Peter and Susan stood. Its eyes flashed wildly. It snorted and stamped. Foam from its mouth was streaked down its mighty chest.

A bronzed barbarian sat in the saddle; a man who was tall and straight and striking. A strip of gold cloth, studded with gems, was bound about his forehead. His jacket was blood-red, worked with gold, with diamonds and emeralds. Black buckskin breeches tightly fitted his legs.

This was no ordinary bandit chief.

The black stallion reared, snorted. Susan ran aside to escape its pawing hoofs. The man swung himself out of the saddle. He came toward Peter with clinking spurs. Diamonds twinkled in them, too. There was a black revolver in his hand.

"Put that revolver away, Mr. Moore," he said, in a deep, rich voice.

"Wong!" Peter gasped.

The revolver in Mr. Wong's hand was aimed definitely at Peter's heart.

"A case of mistaken identity," Mr. Wong said pleasantly. "I am Prince Took Shan. These nine hundred men are my warriors. I regret that I must disarm you, Mr. Moore. You are my prisoner."

"You big brute!" Susan said in a thin, husky little voice.

Prince Took Shan bowed extravagantly, but he did not forget the revolver in his hand.

"A thousand apologies, Miss O'Gilvie. But a sable robe cannot be eked out with dog's tails."

Peter, sharply looking at Susan, saw that her face was crimson; her eyes were glaring; her fists were clenched. Still too astonished to think clearly, he perceived that Susan was, somehow, at the bottom of this.

She shrank back against Peter as Prince Took Shan uttered a deafening shriek. It was answered by a dozen shrieks. His men were working rapidly, applying the knout.

"**WE ARE** pushing on at once," the Tartar chieftain said. "We should reach the Lake of the Flying Dragon by mid forenoon."

Peter said angrily, "This was not necessary. Mr. Lu did not have to send you out to capture me. I was going to him in a perfectly friendly spirit."

Prince Took Shan's white teeth flashed in a smile.

"You misunderstand, Mr. Moore. I do not represent Mr. Lu. I am his ancestral enemy. Mr. Lu possesses the treasure of the Shan Tartars. The men of my family have been trying for two hundred and eighty years to regain our rightful property. My ancestors failed because Mr. Lu was too clever for them. But I will not fail."

His eyes, in the firelight, had a fanatical gleam. His laugh was harsh, metallic.

"It will be so simple, Mr. Moore. We will storm the pass and set up your machinery. We will pump that lake dry with it. Cut off from water and food, Mr. Lu won't be long surrendering."

Peter stared at him incredulously. His fury was forgotten in his amazement at Mr. Wong's—or Prince Took Shan's—optimism.

"You know better than that," he said. "Mr. Lu knows you're planning this. What doesn't he know in China? His men outnumber yours fifty—a hundred—to one! You'll be wiped out, as those other expeditions were wiped out."

"I have no time to argue," Prince Took said curtly. "I know your reputation, Mr. Moore. You will understand why I am placing you under guard. I have no intention of harming you or Miss O'Gilvie unless you attempt to escape."

"Let her go back to Chung-king," Peter said quickly.

The Tartar chieftain laughed again. "Why should she be cheated of an opportunity for which she has paid so dearly? No! She has made this expedition financially possible. She must accompany us. She must see with her own eyes the treasure of my ancestors. Perhaps I will even give her the great Tartar Diamond."

"You can't," Peter said firmly, "get through that pass."

Prince Took Shan swung himself into the saddle and looked down at Peter with the contempt of the superior man for his inferior.

"There is a religious festival in Ling-Fo, beginning to-night. Mr. Lu's village will be deserted. There will be only a handful of old men and bid women. We will get through the pass. And we will see to it that no one escapes."

The barbarian prince uttered a shriek. His men shrieked in answer. He and his warriors were so many madmen. They had whipped themselves into a state of frenzy. But they would not get through that pass.

The encampment was suddenly uproarious with the noises of departure. Prince Took Shan's men were freely wielding their knouts. Men yelled and hurried. Provisions were packed. Tents were struck and loaded. The night was full of yellow- and brown-skinned gnomes, laboring in the light of the dying camp fires.

Peter heard the muffled roaring of the tank's exhaust. He was quite sure that the three red-headed mechanics were part of this elaborate, astounding conspiracy. Many small mysteries were now explained. Susan was weeping like a heartbroken child. He could guess at her part in this tremendous, tragic mistake. She would talk later. Oh, she would talk so volubly in explanation of it all!

Peter, trying to think clearly, saw nothing but a horrible ending to this piece of magnificent folly.

CHAPTER VII

A MADMAN'S PRISONERS

SIX TALL AND warlike guards rode, three on a side, and kept vigilant eyes on Peter Moore. Fresh horses had been saddled for him and Susan. Her fury at Prince Took Shan found an outlet in stormy tears. She said nothing until the encampment was far behind them, a faint rosy glow in the night. Sobs became fewer and farther spaced. Sniffles subsided.

"I did it all for you," she declared indignantly. "I wanted you to be rich. You said you wouldn't marry me until you were as rich as I am. I was going to let you capture the old treasure of the Shan Tartars from Mr. Lu."

Peter had suspected it.

"I met Prince Took in Peking," she went on. "He told me all about the treasure. He said you were just the man. He said if I would finance the whole expedition, you could have half the treasure. He said he had thousands of warriors who would spring to arms at a word from him."

"They sprang," Peter said dryly.

"So," she went on, "we organized the Ta Liang Shan Mining Company. I put up all the money for that. I put up all the money for buying the tank and for arms and ammunition for his men."

"How much?" Peter asked.

Susan told him passionately that he must not use that tone. "I'm hysterical enough now. I did it all for you. You are so stubborn. What does it matter how much it cost?"

"A quarter of a million, gold?"

"I don't know. More than that. What difference does it make? That is not the point. I trusted Prince Took. I didn't dream he'd double cross me. He was so pathetic and so anxious to be helpful. Damn him!" Susan cried. She was silent a few seconds. Then she burst out angrily:

"Well, I've done it again. I've gone and got you into more trouble. We're going to get killed. The whole scheme is preposterous. How can we possibly match ourselves against anybody as clever, as ruthless as Mr. Lu?"

Peter had no answer to that. He wished he had. He had been, since the beginning of all this, in the malignant shadow that reached over Asia—the shadow of the most powerful, most sinister man, perhaps, in the entire world. What chance, indeed, had they to cope with this monstrous power, this evil genius who dwelt, like a horrible fish, in the bottom of that land-locked lake? The Blue Scorpion!

He was sorry for Susan. He did not see, at this dark hour, any hope of saving her or himself from this mad plan of Prince Took Shan's, or from the cold, spider-like wrath of Mr. Lu. An opportunity might present itself, but he saw no hope for them now.

A moon appeared presently, a wasted fraction of the moon past the third quarter, to shed unhappy magic on the caravan. It looked formidable enough in this half-light. In the lead, the tank sent blue-red flame from its exhaust. The tank might get through the pass. But what then?

The night passed. There was no pause for food. Whipped on by the fanatical Tartar chieftain, by his nine hundred blood-mad warriors, it progressed through the night and on into the new day. A purple mountain ahead was their objective. The pass was still invisible.

The purple of distance turned to blue, then to the cold raw gray of the granite itself. And Peter presently saw that slit through the mountain which they must traverse. His eyes, lifting, saw dots moving about up there. They would be, of course, Mr. Lu's guard. A religious festival might be taking place, which had drawn the bulk of the people from the shore of the Lake of the Flying Dragon, but Prince Took Shan was a fool indeed to suppose that Mr. Lu would leave the entrance to his lake unguarded.

WORD CAME presently that Peter and Susan were to go to the end of the line. They must not be exposed to danger. Yet, at the end of the line, there was no chance for them to escape. Their six guards, ranged three on a side, kept watchful eyes on them.

Above the shouts of men, the rattling of harness, the squealing of unoiled axles, Peter suddenly heard the rapid, savage detonations of machine gun fire. The tank, in the vanguard, was opening the attack. And then he was a witness to one of the most amazing and horrible spectacles in his experience.

Prince Took Shan's men were swarming up the rocky face of the mountain, firing, using their swords, as they advanced. He saw them, in ones and twos, come to grips with the defenders; saw men, slaughtered, go rolling headless down the rocks; saw their heads go tumbling after them.

It was evident that Prince Took meant to make this a complete massacre. Not one life would be spared to take out word that the village was captured.

For it was evident, too, that Prince Took Shan's men, principally because of the tank, would take that village. He learned, when he and Susan were eventually taken through the pass, that the tank had performed as a juggernaut, crushing out the lives of Lu's men who opposed it, grinding them down, driving them back and back.

It emerged triumphantly from the narrow slit in the rock, and poured its hail of steel upon surprised and helpless villagers. No one was to escape. Not one man, woman or child was to be spared.

Peter was thankful that he and Susan escaped seeing that. But they did see something of the horrible destruction, by the Tartars, of the men who defended the pass.

It was over in less than an hour. The Tartars finished with

the sword what they had started with the rifle. Not one life was spared. Upward of five hundred men, women and children were slaughtered by Prince Took Shan's men.

Yet one gray shadow in the hills did manage to escape. Unseen by the Tartars, this shadow slipped from rock to rock; and so Prince Took Shan's very comprehensive massacre was, in the end, defeated of one purpose.

Peter and Susan were, late in the afternoon, conducted into a village the streets of which quite literally ran blood. It ran in thick streams through the gutters and out into the lake, until the lake was red with blood. The village stank of blood.

Susan, terrified and sick, stayed close to Peter. She was hysterical. It was all her fault. She had precipitated this.

With the exception of Peter and the three red-heads, every man in the caravan, every one of the Tartar warriors, was set to work carrying the dead out of the pass, burying them in the sand on the other side of the mountain, in a deep trench.

PETER TRIED to comfort Susan. It wasn't, he said, her fault. Prince Took would have found some other means of executing this scheme if he hadn't succeeded in tricking her. He was a fanatic, and fanatics always found ways.

At least they were, for the time being, safe. Prince Took Shan declared to Peter, a little later, that they were more than merely safe.

"We are victorious! For the first time in centuries, in history, this pass has been penetrated by the Shan Tartars. I am proud. I am triumphant. I can think of my father and my grandfather and all the others who tried and failed, and without shame I can say, 'My genius has done this!'"

Boasting, Peter thought, was a little premature. He was watching the three red-headed mechanics and a score of native helpers feverishly at work setting up the power plants on the edge of the lake; assembling the great pumps.

"It will take you weeks, months," he said to Prince Took Shan, "to pump the water out of this lake. What will Mr. Lu's men be doing?"

"What if it should take years?" the Tartar chief countered. "We hold the pass now. We can hold it as Lu's men held it. No one can get through."

Peter looked up at the sheer granite walls of the mountains which surrounded the lake. He saw what Susan had seen from a distant mountain top months before—the utter impossibility of a force of men ascending or descending those steep walls.

"He can besiege you," Peter pointed out. "His men, blocking the pass, can prevent you from bringing in supplies. You'll run out of food. This supply of gasoline and oil won't last more than a couple of weeks."

The fanatical light was shining in Prince Took Shan's black eyes. "Ah! But you don't know my plans, Mr. Moore. By the time our supplies are exhausted, Mr. Lu will have surrendered."

He looked out over the lake with flashing eyes.

"Can you imagine his feelings," he excitedly demanded, "when he learns that this pass has been taken? Can you imagine his state of frenzy when he learns that powerful pumps are draining the water from this lake? He will be frantic! He will gladly surrender!"

"Provided," Peter said, "he hasn't made his escape with your ancestral treasure through some underground passage."

"No!" the barbarian cried. "Because there is no underground passage!"

"Then how does he ventilate his palace? From all accounts, it's of tremendous size. There must be some means of ventilation. If you want my opinion—"

"I don't want your opinion!" the Tartar prince cried.

Peter's opinion, denied expression, was that the wisest move Prince Took Shan could make was to move himself and his warriors out of here as quickly as possible. He was sure that the prince was destined to a disastrous disappointment, and that they were all exposed to a sudden and complete annihilation.

Peter had the utmost respect for the man who dwelt in the bottom of that lake. He knew that his power was mighty, that it reached out into the farthest corners of Asia. He did not believe that, merely because this village had been captured, Mr. Lu was trapped. He would strike back. And when he struck, Peter hoped that he and Susan would be far away.

But there was no opportunity for them to escape. They were under the constant watch of guards. Wherever they went they were followed, and they were not allowed near the pass.

CHAPTER VIII

MR. LU STRIKES BACK

THE FANTASTIC PREPARATIONS for the final blow at Mr. Lu were meanwhile being carried forward with zeal and enthusiasm.

The three red-headed mechanics were the most zealous, the most enthusiastic of all. Peter, watching them, could not help marveling at their energy and their ingenuity. They had discovered that the lake level was higher than the land on the other side of the pass. They had decided to siphon off the lake!

With hundreds of sweating men working at this task, pipe lines were stretched from the lake to the slope outside the pass. The pumps were rigged up. The gasoline motor-driven dynamos were assembled on the edge of the lake. And by dawn of the next morning the dynamos were whining and the pumps were working.

Then the three tireless red-heads lost interest in pumps and syphons. They fell to work on a scheme of their own. They were erecting a power plant on a barge. Bill Jacobs, hollow-eyed from lack of sleep, explained to Peter what his plan was. It was, to say the least, an amazing plan.

They were going to drive the Blue Scorpion out of his cave with heat! They were going to boil him out!

They had, during the previous night, gone out in a small boat to investigate the strange contrivance they had heard about. The stories, Jacobs told Peter, were absolutely true!

"Dove took his clothes off and dived down and found this big bronze tube sticking up from below."

Through this great bronze tube Mr. Lu's visitors came and went. When not being used, it was kept under water. Some cumbersome machine raised and lowered it. If Mr. Lu wanted to admit anybody to his underwater palace, the tube was raised to the surface, like the periscope tube of a submarine. There was a hatch at the top, a watertight hatch. The hatch was opened and the visitor went down a stairway or a ladder inside the tube. Then the hatch cover, or lid, was closed, and the tube was pulled down under water.

Bill Dove, swimming around down there, had found the tube and the hatch.

Peter, listening to this exciting account, did not mention that he knew of the existence, from authentic hearsay, of a knob on the hatch cover which, if pressed, caused all this to happen.

"I'll tell you somethin', chief," Bill Jacobs went on. "We keep thinkin' these Chinks are behind the times. That tube isn't all."

He now described a remarkable system of upright spears which protected the tube from approach. They were in concentric circles, sticking up from the bottom to within an inch of the surface, like so many bayonets. When the tube came up, Bill Jacobs had heard, these spears went down; and when the tube went down, the spears came up again, so that no craft could approach within a hundred feet of the tube.

"That tube," the red-head declared, "and those circles of spears are a wonderful piece of engineering. We damned near sunk our boat last night on them spears. But we've got him licked! We're going out there to-night in this barge and send all the current we have through the water by the tube. You know what happens to water when you send electricity through it."

Peter knew. The powerful current would heat the water. It would heat the bronze tube.

"Ain't that a great idea, chief?"

"I don't see it," Peter answered. "You can't heat up enough water to make him feel uncomfortable."

"We can give him one hell of a surprise, can't we? He'll think we're a flock of magicians, won't he? He'll wonder how we're makin' the water boil and turn his palace into a Turkish bath, won't he? He don't know anything about electricity. He'll think, sure as hell, it's white magic. You know how these natives are."

To Peter, the scheme was so fantastic, so madly impossible, that he laughed. Bill Jacobs gave him a hurt look.

"What's wrong with the gag, chief?"

"Mr. Lu isn't a superstitious native. You're forgetting what feats of engineering he must have accomplished to build that palace under water."

"But white magic is different, chief. We'll scare his pants off!"

PETER DIDN'T think Mr. Lu would be greatly alarmed by electrically boiled water. And he didn't think that Mr. Lu was greatly alarmed by the capture of the pass and the village. The greatest mistake any man could make was underestimating the genius of the Blue Scorpion.

Both pumps and two siphons were working. They had been working almost twenty-four hours, and the water in the lake had not yet receded a fraction of an inch. The lake was more than a half mile long and perhaps a quarter mile in width. To pump and siphon that lake away was quite as preposterous as the red-heads' scheme to frighten Mr. Lu with "white magic."

Peter was convinced, as he had been at the outset, that the safest and wisest plan was to escape before Mr. Lu struck. But there was nothing to be gained by arguing with these fanatical enthusiasts. They were within days, perhaps hours, of seizing that fabulous treasure. Even Susan had caught the infection. Still horrified by the scenes she had witnessed on entering the village, she was beginning, however, to believe that Prince Took Shan's scheme, by its very audacity, might succeed. And she was thrilled at the thought of those chests upon chests of precious stones— perhaps the greatest store of precious stones in existence!

Prince Took Shan was beginning to talk of using dynamite. He would drop sticks of dynamite on the underwater palace. Then he argued that, if he used dynamite, the palace would be ruined and the treasure probably lost forever. And Peter wondered if Mr. Lu had not thought of explosives when he had built the palace under water.

The approach of their second night in the village found Peter decidedly uneasy. Some years ago, thousands of miles from here, he had had an encounter with Mr. Lu's men, and he had learned how thorough, how clever, how ruthless Mr. Lu was. The Blue Scorpion was not merely a legend. He was an actuality—a man it paid to leave strictly alone.

Toward nightfall, an incident occurred which, while Susan and Prince Took Shan accepted it lightly, confirmed his fears. From somewhere above them—and no one knew where—tiny pyramids of blue chalk began to fall. They might have been lumps of the very afternoon sky. Perhaps a hundred of them fell into the village.

But nothing more happened. Mr. Lu had sent his respects! How had he sent the tiny chalk pyramids? Just what did they portend?

But Prince Took Shan was not dismayed. Mr. Lu was trying to scare him. But Mr. Lu was whipped. He was using his famous little chalk pyramids as a last resort. But they didn't work. Not with Prince Took Shan!

The three red-heads accepted the chalk pyramids as a challenge. They'd show that yellow devil! The barge on which the gasoline-driven dynamo was mounted was pushed out into the lake. It made its clumsy way to the exact middle of the lake.

Darkness settled before it reached there. But Peter heard the whining of its dynamo, the soft mutter of the gasoline motor's exhaust. It was, Peter thought, the final incongruous touch—this strange attempt at steaming out the Blue Scorpion!

THE SKY was overcast, and there would be no moon to-night. Thunder grumbled ominously off to the north. The dynamo whined like a hysterical mosquito. The pumps chugged. Men's voices, speaking river Chinese, speaking the thin, cricket-like tongue of the Tartars were raised with excitement. All of them were talking about that treasure, for Prince Took Shan had promised each man a share.

He said to Peter, "I know you can think of much better schemes than we have devised. If you will help us, if you will give us the benefit of your genius, you will be one of the richest young men in the world. Why won't you give us your advice?"

"I've given it," Peter said. "My advice is, clear out of here as fast as you can get these men and this equipment moving. Or— never mind the equipment."

"You credit Mr. Lu with supernatural powers," the barbarian accused him. "You believe all these legends. You refuse to realize that I have got him trapped at last."

"I only give Mr. Lu credit for having too much intelligence to let himself be trapped so easily. I know that he is the most powerful man in China. I know that his men are in all parts of the Far East."

He moved away from the Tartar chieftain and walked toward the pass. Somehow, he must get Susan out of here. He observed that the lights of the village were growing misty, and he wondered why. There were never fogs in this desert country. Where was this fog originating? Then it occurred to him that the fog was electrical. It was being caused by the electrically-heated water in the middle of the lake—vapor rising, covering the surface of the lake until it invaded the village in the form of a fog. Steam from a devil's caldron!

Then, suddenly, Peter became aware that the dynamo was no longer whining. Far out in the lake, he saw, through the mist, a ghostly white glow, and he wondered what was happening out there. Had the gasoline motor broken down? Had the dynamo burned out?

He walked slowly toward the lake. Mist in thin, tenuous wisps floated past his face—warm clots of dampness in the chill mountain air. He paused at Susan's tent and called. There was no answer. A light gleamed at the flap. He called again, then pulled the flap back.

The tent was deserted. A candle: burned on an empty crate near the head of the cot. A rifle and Susan's automatic pistol, easily identified by the mother-o'-pearl handle and the gold-mounted barrel, lay on the cot with an opened and nearly full package of pistol cartridges.

His own pistol had been taken away from him. He had instructed Susan never to leave her tent after dark. He called again.

Shrill native voices rose up all about him. Men grinned and gibbered over blazing camp fires. The Tartar treasure! They talked of nothing else.

"Susan!"

No answer. Anxiously, he ran down to the lake, calling her. The mist was like a veil. Somehow, he associated this mysterious fog with Mr. Lu, as if the Blue Scorpion were somehow magically creating it as a screen which would hide his actions.

At the edge of the lake, staring at the ghostly spot of light where the barge was, he stopped. The dynamo and the gasoline motor were still silent. The dynamo farther down the shore was silent, and so was the pump which it drove. The dynamo's gasoline motor had probably run out of gasoline. With the red-heads away, there was no one to attend to it.

Peter listened. The fog rolling in from the lake seemed to grow more dense. He was certain he heard, not far from shore, the scuffing of wood against wood, then the sounds of a struggle, quickly subdued.

"Susan!" he shouted.

This time she answered. Or did she answer? He heard, or thought he heard, a muffled scream, out there in the mist. He called again. His forehead was suddenly wet. He felt cold and sick all over. There was no question in his mind that Mr. Lu's men, under the very eyes of the Shan Tartars, had captured Susan.

BENEATH THE LAKE

SUSAN HAD BEEN sitting on her cot, cleaning and loading her pistol, when the three men came in. They surprised her so completely that she had not time even to draw her breath and scream. She saw three yellow faces; three pairs of cool black eyes. One of the men had something pale-blue in his hands, like a wad of cloth. Before she could move or cry out, this cloth spun out about her. It seemed to infold her, as she struggled, as, perhaps, the strands of a web infold and tangle an insect.

Nothing was said. There was not even a whisper, but one of her captors must have struck her on the head, because, although she was frightened, she seldom fainted; and the world-engulfing blackness that suddenly blotted out all impressions must have been the unconsciousness resulting from a sharp and savage blow.

With legs, hands and face securely enwrapped in the blue cloth, she found herself, when the blackness went away, lying helpless on her side, with some sharp object prodding her just above the hip bone. She heard splashing water, but no other sounds save the babble of men's voices ashore, until her name was shouted. And it was Peter's voice.

Susan tried then to answer. The beginning of a scream left her lips, then a wet hand came smothering down on her mouth. A finger and thumb pinched her nose, so that her breath was entirely shut off. She struggled to free her face of the imprisoning hand. She was suffocating. Rage and helpless terror swept her. Her heart was hammering madly in her ears.

And when the hand was taken away, she was too spent to utter a sound. Wood rubbed against wood. She heard the gurgling of water running along the sides of the boat. She could do nothing for a time but gasp for air. Something touched her face. The hand, again. And she knew that the instant she tried to cry out, the hand would clamp down and smother her again.

It was Susan's first taste of Mr. Lu's methods. For she knew that these could be no other than Mr. Lu's men. Merciless. Ruthless. As cold, as horrible, as that hand poised there, ready to clamp off her breath if she made a sound.

A gleam in the night drew nearer. She found, by twisting her head a little, she could look over the side. The worn flanks of a familiar object came into sight. It was the barge on which she had watched the three red-haired men embark upon their amazing adventure some hours ago.

Her breath caught in her throat, as sharply as a thorn, as the flat planking of the deck became visible. A large electric tubular flash light, the kind that contains dry cells, was lying on the deck, sending its white beam across the planking. The barge appeared to be deserted. All she could see was the formless bulk of the machinery looming against the glow.

Then she saw the blood. There were pools of it on the planks, and these pools were running off into the water in little streams. She heard the dripping of blood as it ran into the lake.

The air here—though this may have been in her imagination—was clammily warm. It must be due to the electrically heated water. Where, she frantically wondered, were Bill Jacobs, Hank Roberts, and Tom Dove, those three happy-go-lucky trouble hunters?

The cold wet hand dropped over her eyes. She was lifted up. Then a breath of sweetened air swam up about her. In it she detected the odor of sandalwood incense and the perfume of freshly cut jasmine, a sweetness that was almost sickening. These odors came rushing up about her in a strong draft. Her hand touched hot metal.

THEN SHE stopped descending, but she could not see, for the hand was still clamped over her eyes. There was no doubt where she was being taken. She was, there could be no question now, in the underwater palace of the Blue Scorpion. Icy tingles of fear danced over her flesh. So great was her terror that she had the sensation of her flesh pulling away from her bones; of actual iciness attacking her spine.

She was carried a long way. Once, through a crack between her captor's fingers, she caught a glimpse of a flesh-pink wall, which gleamed like the scales of a freshly caught fish. The sensation of dampness, which she had first experienced, was absent now. The smell of incense and of fresh jasmine grew stronger. It was sickening. It was overpowering.

Susan knew she was on the verge of fainting from sheer terror. Terror of the unknown. Terror of the thousand and one horrible legends she had heard of this human monster who lived under the Lake of the Flying Dragon.

Then, suddenly, the clammy hand was taken away. With a whisk, the blue shroud was removed from her, and she was standing alone at the end of a room as blue as any cavern, any grotto, under the sea. It was a dazzling, sapphire blue, and it was in the shape of a thin, long triangle, or wedge. She stood in the center of the wide end of the wedge, looking down the room toward the apex. Looking into a glaring spot of brilliant, intense, sapphire-blue light.

This dazzling blue light hissed softly as it burned. Above the glare of it Susan, staring with utter terror, could see fumes rising—rising and vanishing, as fumes from an incense pot vanish upward into the stark blackness of a pagan temple.

Below the glare of flaming sapphire Susan saw, or believed that she saw, the black form of a man. But she could not be sure, until a voice spoke—a soft, thin, whispering voice, so cold that it sent chills through her and caused her legs to go weak and tremulous.

Yet it seemed an age before that shapeless black bulk below the glaring sapphire incandescence uttered these words.

In English, the soft, thin, whispering voice said, "Yes. You will do." Then there was a phrase in Chinese.

She did not have the strength to cry out. Her throat was parched. Her lips felt stiff. Every nerve in her body was shrieking a protest against this, against some hideous, inevitable fate.

HANDS SEIZED her, and her flesh seemed to shrink from them. She was propelled forcibly from the horrible blue grotto, with its staring sapphire light, and the formless bulk of the whisperer beneath it. Who but Mr. Lu? Who, indeed, but the Blue Scorpion—the man with the brain of jade? Oh, she could believe these fantasies now. For this was Susan's moment of extremity, when fear and dread and hopeless horror had her for their own.

The hands propelled her from the wedge-shaped blue grotto. She was pushed across a corridor. Not in the hands of men now. She was the prisoner of a dozen—two dozen—silent, cold-eyed women. They pushed her down a corridor whose walls were of a gleaming snowy whiteness. A door swung open. A stronger breath of jasmine and incense assailed her.

This room, into which she was pushed, was of a pale and miraculous green. It was the green of a freshly cleaved glacier, of the chill Arctic seas. Green walls. Green ceiling. Green rugs of tremendous area and the familiar dragon design.

Mr. Lu's tastes evidently ran to vivid color effects. Even the benches were of pale green lacquer.

Susan was pushed and pulled, with no gentleness, into this room and down the length of it. She was roughly spun about. And she found herself staring, with transfixed eyes, at a white woman, dressed as she had been dressed; in laced boots, whipcord breeches, fuzzy blue sweater—a white woman with staring eyes and a face as white as chalk, with blue lips. A ghastly face. Her own face.

It was a silver mirror—a slab of silver polished to the brightness of plate glass. How wild her hair was!

She saw the native women as blue-clad ghosts, with light from invisible sources glittering on their varnished black hair. She shrank, whimpered, when she saw a knife gleam in the hand of one of them. A young woman with slit-like black eyes, high cheekbones, thin lips, pinched nose.

One of the other women snatched the knife from this one's hand and lifted it above Susan's head. Powerless, robbed of all hope, Susan closed her eyes for the gleaming blade to strike. She felt the sweater come away.

The woman was slicing off her clothes. Swaying with faintness, Susan tried to master her nerves. She felt the last of her clothing snatched from her body. Swimming eyes glimpsed, in the silver mirror, a slim, ivory body that certainly could not be her own.

One of the women forced her to her knees. Another fetched a green-lacquered tray containing numberless pots and jars from which arose a sickening perfume. Undiluted attar of roses.

They did her hair, coiling it down, flattening it, drenching it with sickeningly sweet stuff. They brought garments—a scarlet jacket, with tiny pockets, sapphire-blue satin trousers, small sapphire-blue slippers.

In the mirror, Susan saw her slim white nudeness vanish into these scented garments. She saw the slit-eyed girl snatch up the knife from the floor where the older woman had laid it. She saw the yellow girl's lips part and reveal white, fine teeth.

And the knife, gripped firmly in the small yellow hand, flashed downward and sidewise at Susan.

ACTING ON the certainty that Susan had been taken prisoner by Mr. Lu's men, Peter wasted no time on inquiries. He ran back to Susan's tent, snatched up her pistol and the box of cartridges and stowed them in the side pockets of his coat. He ran back to the lake front, searched desperately for a boat of any description, and at length found a long narrow one—the very craft, it may have been, which Susan had glimpsed through her binoculars from the mountain top at dawn some months ago.

He found a crude and heavy sweep in the bottom. With this he maneuvered the craft away from shore and pushed on out into deep water, toward the ghostly glow where the barge lay. He was certain that any attempt at rescuing Susan was utterly hopeless—quite as hopeless, quite as fantastically hopeless, as the sundry schemes of Prince Took Shan for acquiring that fabulous treasure.

The Blue Scorpion had struck. It was an oblique stroke, such as might have been expected. And it gave Peter no choice between life and death. He would join Susan in the Blue Scorpion's palace—and that would be the end of them both.

Peter reached the barge, saw the pools of blood, and drew obvious conclusions. Then the moving prow of his boat collided with some object close under the surface, and nearly capsized. Peter's hand, fumbling in the warm water, encountered the point of one of the bronze spikes. Six inches to the right and six inches to the left, he found others.

He removed pistol and cartridges from his pockets, maneuvered alongside the barge and secured the flash light. This he added to the little collection in the bottom of the boat. He removed coat, boots and shirt, and lowered himself into the water. By bracing his feet against the spikes, he hauled the boat up and over their points. Then he pushed the boat again to the next ring of bronze spears. There were, in all, four concentric circles.

His frenzied efforts were quickly exhausting him. He reached and pulled the boat over the inner circle of the giant spikes, then dived down for the bronze shaft. He did not find it until his sixth dive. Then, groping about the hatch cover, he fumbled until he had found the small square knob which had, long ago, been described to him. He felt the shaft begin to rise. It came slowly out of the lake until it was, perhaps, a foot out of water. The lid, worked by the same mysterious mechanism, slowly lifted.

A blast of scented air struck his face. He gathered up the pistol, cartridges and flash light and stowed them about him.

The shaft was in complete darkness. The fingering light of the flash light showed him rungs down which he went into dank darkness. Halls gave off from an octagonal cubicle in eight directions. Light glowed dimly down them all. He assumed now that the bottom of the lake was honeycombed with such passages off which, no doubt, rooms gave.

Any attempt at a search for Susan in this labyrinth would have been hopeless if he had not, fortunately, seen two imprints of a small heel, spaced at least twenty feet apart in the green mold which carpeted one of the tunnels. Susan, he presumed, had been carried, but her heel had touched the floor twice.

He ran down that corridor. The dampness came to an end. The walls and ceiling were cobalt blue. How these passages were lighted mystified him. It was as if the walls, the ceilings, had a luminance all their own.

He came to a cross corridor; glanced into a room of deepest crimson. Yet he saw no one, and he heard no sound, until, standing there, straining his senses, he heard a woman's faint cry. It might be Susan. It might be any one. She was lost. He was lost. They would never, he was certain, live to see the light of another day. His only hope was that they might die together.

He plunged on down another cross corridor in the direction from which that cry had come. It was faintly repeated. He passed a room of alabaster white, with walls inlaid with mother-o'-pearl. It, too, was empty. So far he had seen no living creature. Yet he sensed that he was spied on, that his every movement was under observation.

He came to another cubicle which was like the hub of a wheel. Halls radiated out from it in ten directions. He was lost again. He was hopelessly lost.

CHAPTER X

THE WORLD'S TREASURE HOUSE

SUSAN MIGHT HAVE been the statue of a girl clad in the barbaric garments of a sing-song girl of the Chinese rivers. She could not move. She could, if she had not been so terrified, have stepped aside or leaped back, to save herself from the girl with the jade-handled knife. But Susan had lost all power of action.

Women seized the girl, and Susan faintly screamed. The girl struggled, scratched and kicked. She broke away, still with that terrifying knife in her hand. And still Susan could not move, but she could, and did, scream again, this time at the top of her lungs. All of the terror of this last hour was expended upon that ear-splitting scream.

The yellow girl threw herself at her, and the gleaming knife, striking into Susan's arm, opened the flesh to the bone. Then the women fell upon the panting yellow girl and dragged her away. A door opened and Susan saw Peter, bare-footed, stripped to the waist, paused an instant on the threshold. He came running down the room, shouting, "Susan!"

The women fled, silently vanished. And he was binding up the bleeding slash in her arm with strips of orchid silk from the pile of clothing that had been slashed and ripped from her. In her relief at seeing him, Susan was crying. She didn't mind the slash in her arm, though it was beginning to throb. Clinging to him, she asked him what they were going to do.

"Get out of here—if we can find the way."

"We can never find the way."

Peter went to a door and flung it open. Susan saw him stagger back a step; saw ghastly green light in his face, light as vividly green as kingfisher jade.

"Here it is!" he said excitedly. "We'll never live to tell about it, but—here it is."

There, indeed, it was. The fabulous treasure of the Blue Scorpion. The large room, with its walls of glittering jade, was full of chests, true to those traditions.

Chests of brass. Chests of teak, of sandalwood, of ebony; brass bound and brass studded.

They were not locked. In the dazzling splendor of their discovery, the man and the girl momentarily forgot their danger, forgot the shadow of the Blue Scorpion. The chests lined the walls of the great jade room.

Susan knelt at the nearest. It flamed and glittered with diamonds and emeralds. It was a solid mass of diamonds, unmounted; of emeralds of all sizes. It was like a dream of impossible riches. Here was the treasure house of the world. Chests of raw gems, some cut, some uncut. Chests of sapphires, of rubies, of diamonds. One chest alone was brimming with carved jade, Buddhas, amulets, beads, pendants. That chest must have been worth millions in itself.

IT WAS a cruel, a maddening vista. Wherever they looked were greater, richer treasures. There were chests of the rarest rose quartz, chests of amethysts, of pearls. Pearls the size of marbles. Strings of pearls. There was a rug of pearls which filled one chest; which Susan seized and lifted out, forgetting once again the throbbing wound in her arm. The rug was, roughly, six feet square, of pearls bound together by slender gold wire—a treasure in itself richer than any undiscovered treasure in the world.

Susan was making soft whimpering sounds. She may have been one of the richest girls in America, yet her riches, compared only to that rug of pearls, were those of a pauper.

It made Peter's eyes go dull. It made him poorer than the most ragged beggar in the streets of the poorest village in Asia.

It was indeed the gruelest kind of torture. Mr. Lu, with his ingenuity as a torturer, could have planned nothing more diabolical than this. It was showing—and withholding—a drink of sparkling cold spring water to a man dying of thirst, with swollen black tongue and bulging eyes. It was displaying a feast to a man dying of starvation.

Here was the treasure of all his dreams, yet he could have none of it. Susan, with a cry of actual pain, had opened a chest of blazing blue sapphires. Sapphires were her favorite stones.

She could not resist the human impulse to stuff the little pockets of her jacket full of sapphires.

"It's useless," Peter said.

"I don't care," she cried. "It's cruel. It's torture."

"We must try to get out of here."

"Is there any use? Here it is, Peter. Here's what I brought you here to have. It's all yours. You're richer than Midas, darling. You're the richest man alive. Here's your fortune. Compared to you, I'm but a penniless pauper."

A door across the room opened. A yellow face was suspended there. Peter fired. The face vanished. Peter seized Susan's hand and pulled her down the room.

He pulled her through a doorway into an arched black corridor. He did not know where they were in relation to the bronze tube. And this was the beginning of a mad, a hopeless search for an escape from the fabulous palace of Mr. Lu.

They raced down corridors which were parts of the elaborate underwater labyrinth. They ran into and out of empty rooms. Hopelessly lost, they were, Peter knew, being subjected to another cruel jest on the part of Mr. Lu.

It occurred to him presently to follow to its source the breath of fresh air which he frequently detected. This search led them eventually into a low arched tunnel which was cool with a strong current of the night air. The tunnel climbed up and up. The current of air grew fresher, stronger as they advanced.

The tunnel ended finally and forever in bronze bars as thick as a man's arm, set less than an inch apart into the solid masonry of ceiling and floor. Beyond was darkness. He used the flash light. Beyond were other bars; still other barriers of bronze bars. They were like reflections in two mirrors placed squarely opposite each other, so that what you saw was repeated and reflected infinitely.

He said, in a thick, exhausted voice: "We've got to turn back. Look!"

Behind them, down the long tunnel, were a sea of yellow faces, turned toward them. By magic they had appeared.

Slowly these yellow faces advanced on them.

PETER BEGAN firing. Slowly, systematically, he fired. He saw bodies fall, wilting before the fire. Then suddenly the tunnel was plunged in darkness.

Susan frantically seized his arm.

"Take this flash light," he said.

She took it and played its wavering beam down the tunnel.

It was empty again! By some trick of mirrors, some legerdemain of Oriental mechanism, where there had been a swarm of yellow faces, of living yellow men, there was now emptiness.

The man and the girl, with hands touching, raced down the tunnel. The flash light was snatched from Susan by an unseen hand. Other hands snatched the pistol from Peter. Half-naked bodies brushed lightly against them.

Susan clung to his arm. A bony hand had clutched at her throat; relaxing, had let her go. There was no sensation in her body. They came to the end of the tunnel. Mysteriously, the lights came on again. But where were these mysterious lights? Peter would never know.

Hand in hand they passed an open doorway. Susan uttered a dry, pinched little scream. Sapphire blue light glared into their faces. And against the pure white wall beside them there fell the shadow, perhaps, of Mr. Lu—the shadow of the fabulous, the monstrous man known throughout Asia as the Blue Scorpion.

No half-crazed artist could have conceived of a figure of such hideous design as was cast by that black shadow. It was human, yet it was inhuman. Remotely, but only remotely, it suggested the spider-like form of a scorpion, with its scaly legs, its shiny black body, the poisonous, articulated tail. Only a horribly misshapen man, a human monstrosity, could have thrown such a grotesque and hideous shadow.

Shrinking from it, Susan recalled, as in a drugged dream, the tale of Mr. Lu's fall down a cliff; of his losing his entire face; of men finding his body a pulsing pulp at the cliff bottom. She could understand, in this monstrous shadow, that legend.

Momentarily frozen there, Peter dragged her on. He had smelled dampness. He would trace that smell of dampness. It took them down other corridors. It took them presently, to Susan's utter hysterical relief, to the octagonal cubicle from which rose the great bronze tube.

Neither she nor Peter was surprised when that tube, as they started climbing, began to rise. They were accustomed now to the dark magic of their Oriental host.

The little boat was floating where Peter had left it. Peter helped Susan aboard and followed her. He picked up the paddle and pushed off.

In the faint amber gleam of dawn he saw the bronze tube disappear, but knew that he was safely away from the concentric circles of spears. Susan was in the bow, crouched down, sobbing from sheer nervous relief. But Peter was certain that they had not yet enjoyed the last of their thrills at the hands of Mr. Lu. What, he anxiously wondered, would happen next? And while he was wondering, Mr. Lu struck.

CHAPTER XI

"OUR ONLY CHANCE!"

DAWN HAD COME swiftly, changing from amber to the palest rose-gold, then to glowing ivory. Silver clouds floated luminously in the purple-blue of the night sky. On the shore there were signs of fierce activity.

Men were racing about. Horses were plunging. It reminded Peter of hasty retreats he had witnessed on battlefields. Shouts, shrieks, the brisk detonations of rifle fire reached him.

Mr. Lu was striking. And it was evident that Prince Took Shan and his men were running for the pass. Standing in the stern of the little boat, he saw the barbarian chieftain vanish into the hatch of the tank. And he saw the tank stagger off toward the pass. He saw, too, that the mountain on the right hand, the northern side of the pass, was dark with swarming men. Mr. Lu's warriors. There were thousands of them. They were swarming down the hill. They were hurling rocks. Prince Took Shan's men, and the men of the caravan, had evidently, in their dreams of fabulous treasure, been taken completely by surprise.

Peter did not know just what had happened. And he would never know. He reached shore as the war tank, rattling and clanking, started through the pass, climbing over the bodies of dead and dying, climbing over the bodies of horses and mules and oxen; smashing down carts.

He saw bowlders go sliding and leaping down the steep side of the pass; saw them bound from the steel turtle-back of the tank. A bowlder larger than the tank, somehow set free from above, came plunging down. It blocked the tank's path. The caterpillar treads ground hopelessly against it. More bowlders came down. With them a hail of smaller stones, some the size of a man's head, others no larger than a fist.

They came down by the thousands. By the ton. They rose about the tank until only its top was visible. Then, in a deluge of rocks, it became invisible.

Peter waited to see no more. He had witnessed, he felt sure, the sealing of Prince Took Shan's tomb. The last fantastic attempt on the part of the Shan Tartars to recover their fabulous treasure had failed as had all the previous ones.

Hordes of men in blue were sweeping down the hill, leaping with remarkable precision from niche to niche. Some stumbled. Some fell headlong to their doom.

Peter succeeded in reaching Prince Took Shan's tent. He found a submachine rifle, a half dozen disks loaded. He gave Susan the disks and told her to follow him. He took his stand behind the pump which had pumped its last futile stroke. But its steel bulk would turn aside bullets and rocks alike.

When a spearhead of men, fifteen or twenty in number, came charging across the opening from the base of the mountain, he fired into them until the last man stumbled and dropped. One disk of ammunition was gone. He ran, with Susan beside him, clutching at his arm, to the nearest of the great bowlders which Mr. Lu's men had dislodged and sent crashing down. There he withstood another charge.

The next sprint would take Susan and him into the pass. But did they dare enter the pass? It was, it seemed to him at the time, a miracle that they had been saved thus far. Rocks were still plunging down on the remnants of Prince Took Shan's men, and on the remnants of the caravan. It was quite evident that Mr. Lu's warriors intended to do quite as thorough a job as had Prince Took.

Peter, crouched behind the rock, emptying the submachine gun into bodies of the blue-clad warriors as they came endlessly down the steep slope, became certain that he and Susan would not escape. He saw Prince Took Shan's men put to the sword, mercilessly decapitated.

The stench of blood and the odor of hot flint filled the pass. Pulverized rock formed a dust cloud as dense as the thickest fog. Through that cloud, Peter and Susan might escape. Yet he was sure that Mr. Lu had willed that they must not escape.

He said finally, "It's our only chance—before this dust settles."

THEY RACED toward the pass. Through the fog of dust they saw phantom forms—specters. They climbed over dead bodies. They slipped in pools of blood. The rain of rocks had ceased.

Holding the gun in readiness, with Susan following him, Peter made his way into the pass. He exhausted another disk of ammunition before they had progressed a hundred feet. The dust became thicker. Here, the pass was its narrowest, hardly twenty feet from wall to wall, and filled now with large and small fragments of rock. These fragments, many of them larger than coffins, gave him a new conception of the ruthless fury of that human monster who lived in his incredible under-water palace. Mr. Lu had given the order that the invaders be wiped out. And his men had responded accordingly.

The invaders had been wiped out. Yet, by one of the miracles of that dreadful night, Peter and Susan were spared. His rifle was jammed; useless. They were unarmed, subject to destruction at any instant.

Perhaps it was the fog of dust that saved them.

Suddenly, they were beyond the pass. The yielding golden sand of the desert was under their feet. Yet they could not see. For the dust cloud, pouring from the pass, was a billow of fog.

In this lesser fog they saw no living thing. The horrible scenes in the village, in the pass, were definitely behind them.

Peter threw away the rifle. He and Susan started trudging in the direction toward which he believed the old Merchant's Trail lay. Yet he did not take hope until they gradually left the dust cloud behind them. The mid morning sun blazed down on them from a sky as blue as sapphire.

Peter, taking stock, did not believe that they could reach the Merchant's Trail. His lungs and throat were parched from the fine, cutting dust. He was bleeding from an unaccountable gash in his left cheek. And Susan was utterly spent. Now that they seemed safe, for the first time in hours, she was on the verge of complete physical collapse. The wound in her arm hurt her terribly. Her legs, she said, were giving out.

"Darling, I can't go any farther. What are we going to do? I've got to rest."

They sat down on a dune. Susan's head drooped to Peter's shoulder. She was either instantly asleep or instantly unconscious. Perhaps it was a combination of the two. But there was nothing Peter could do about it. There was no water within a day's travel. And the sun was rising, growing hotter. Without a hat, without clothing to his waist, Peter wondered how he could withstand sunstroke.

A MOCKING answer to his problem was provided, as he sat and wondered, by that most perverse, most provocative of all living creatures, a mule. It was a pack mule, a stray survivor of the caravan. It came strolling out of the dust cloud to the east. Its bone pack-saddle was laden with food. Skins of water hung on either side of the cantle.

Peter, deserting Susan, walked toward the mule. It eyed him warily. He whistled. It cocked its ears. He walked toward it with the outstretched hand of friendship. It backed away. He ran. The mule trotted. It stopped and gazed at him with wide, curious eyes. He called to it, in English, in Chinese, in one of the few phrases of Tartar at his command.

But the mule declined his friendship. It was content to stay near, but it would not let him approach. It narrowed simply to this: Peter had to have those skins of water. He would prefer to have the mule, but he must have the water for Susan. Quite obviously, he could not secure the mule without securing the water.

The mule would permit him to approach almost within grasping distance of the water, then it would shy away. Peter, so exhausted he could hardly stand, let alone walk, forced himself to run.

This cruel game went on, Peter supposed, for hours, at least until the desert sun was high overhead. Then without reason, without cause whatsoever, the mule capitulated. It lost interest in the game and permitted him to seize its horsehair lead-rope.

Grasping that rope firmly, Peter led the mule back to where he had left Susan. He poured water into her mouth and over her face from the skin. She was alive. But she was unconscious. He discarded such items from the mule's load as were least useful, and loaded Susan into the saddle. He found a blouse of coarse blue cloth strapped under one of the water skins. This he slipped on over his head. The situation, he congratulated himself, was at last in hand.

But he wondered if Mr. Lu, in his underwater cave, was through toying with him.

Late in the afternoon, with the round blood-red sun of the desert poised for its plunge into the west, the three survivors of Mr. Lu's ruthless attack entered the encampment of a tea caravan. The amiable tea trader, a fat and jolly Chinese, took them in; gave them thick green tea to drink and roasted goat meat to eat. He was going on to India. He took Peter's *chit*—or Chinese I.O.U.—for a pair of fresh horses. And next morning, refreshed and once again optimistic, Peter and Susan set forth down the trail from Chung-king.

Susan was quiet and thoughtful at the beginning of that morning. The wound in her arm ached. But as the day advanced, her spirits arose, and it wasn't long before she had decided that the adventure they had been through had been, by long odds, the most exciting, the most thrilling adventure she had ever had. It had been, she decided, perfectly fascinating.

It seemed like a dream, she declared. Would he ever forget

the horrible hopeless feeling as they had run here and there in the labyrinth which was Mr. Lu's palace?

"Never," Peter, said, with feeling.

Susan uttered a little cry.

"I'd forgotten the sapphires!" she cried. She plunged both hands into the little pockets of her Chinese jacket. Her face suddenly lost its eagerness. Her mouth and her eyes became round.

"Peter!" she whispered. She looked down at her hands. He looked, too.

In the palm of each hand lay, not sapphires, but a cluster of tiny blue chalk pyramids!

MR. LU'S LITTLE JOKE

CHUNG-KING AGAIN. BUT no longer a filthy, squalid Chinese village of the third order. It was civilization. Here, one could step aboard a stout little steel steamer and be spirited away from terrifying shadows and Oriental ogres.

There was a steamer in four days. Peter secured the money he had left with the innkeeper, and paid for their tickets to Hankow.

The steamer started down river at dusk. Peter and Susan were standing on the after deck when it got under way. Chung-king vanished into the blue mists of evening. A coolie approached Peter. He carried on his upturned palms a rectangular box painted a vivid sapphire blue.

Chinese characters on the box spelled Ren Beh Tung—literally, Man of Bronze. Peter had earned that picturesque name six years before. It was the Chinese equivalent of Peter the Brazen. Without opening that box, he guessed that its contents would prove to be ironical. A tiny pale blue square, in the lower left-hand corner of the lid, gave him this hunch. He was being presented, he suspected, with a parting gift from the Man with the Jade Brain.

He hesitated to open it. It might contain some Oriental surprise that would kill him. Susan was—being Susan—tremendously curious. But Peter was wary. He would not, he declared, let her see what was in the mysterious box until he had himself examined its contents.

The lid was nailed down. He borrowed a screwdriver from

the polite Chinese chief steward and took box and screwdriver to his stateroom and locked the door.

There, alone and unobserved, he pried off the lid. It came off quite easily. Peter, with a gasp, dropped the box to the floor.

Within the neat sapphire box, side by side, were the embalmed heads of Bill Jacobs, Hank Roberts and Tom Dove. But that was not all. There were also the hands of the three red-headed mechanics. And they were arranged in a very familiar, conventional Chinese manner. The hands of Bill Jacobs were nailed down with bronze spikes to his eyes. The hands of Hank Roberts were nailed down with bronze spikes to his ears. And the hands of Tom Dove were nailed down with bronze spikes to his mouth.

It was quite like Mr. Lu to send him this grisly souvenir, this favorite symbol of the three great Chinese virtues:

Hear no evil—see no evil—speak no evil!

A hint worthy of Mr. Lu.

And it was fortunate that there was an open porthole in Peter's stateroom.

He returned to the after deck when he had himself in hand, and lying freely, told Susan the sapphire box had contained probably one thousand tiny pyramids of blue chalk.

It occurred to him, as Susan slipped her soft, warm little hand into his and snuggled against him, that he was on the verge of making the same vows that he had made some half dozen times previously. But this time he meant them. Susan—the lovely, the alluring, the adorable Susan—had once again pushed him just a little too close to the brink of disaster. She would, in a very little time, be plotting ingenious new ways to satisfy her thirst for excitement. That horrible experience above and under the Lake of the Flying Dragon was already, to her, a glamorous adventure.

No. She would never satisfy her thirst for excitement. But he had had his fill. He loved her. He would probably always love her more than any girl he would ever know. But Susan was, decidedly, not for him. What he wanted was peace.

"I hoped," she said wistfully, looking up at him with her big violet eyes, "that you would get that treasure. But I'll have other ideas."

Peter shivered slightly. He hoped he wouldn't be within reach when she had them.

PETER WAS back at work, in Shanghai, trying to sell electrical equipment. Susan was preparing to run down to Hongkong to visit friends. It chanced that, at their farewell dinner, Mr. and Mrs. Charlie Sing, of San Francisco, espied Peter.

They paused at Peter's table and he introduced them to Susan.

"You've been away on a business trip," Mrs. Sing accused him. "I'm sure it was successful. Do you remember that talk we had at Mr. Wong's?"

Peter, recalling also the eye that had stared at him from the priceless Ming screen, said that he remembered it very clearly.

"I'm never coming back to China if I can help it," Mrs. Sing said. "It's grown too sordid. We've been here almost three months. I've been bored every minute. China is spoiled and dull. Where is there any romance? Any adventure?"

"The future of this country," Mr. Sing said, "is up to hard-headed, practical young American business men like you."

"I hope," Mrs. Sing added, "you're selling lots of machinery."

Peter thanked them. They went on, across the hotel dining room, to their table.

"I love that," Susan said. "No romance! No adventure!"

She laughed. But Peter didn't laugh.

"I think," he said slowly, "that this is one adventure neither you nor I will ever mention to any one." The memory of the three red-heads was strong in his mind. "Mr. Lu has his own special treatment for people who know too much about him and are indiscreet. So, as far as you and I are concerned, Miss O'Gilvie, the adventure in the Cave of the Blue Scorpion never happened."

ABOUT THE AUTHOR

THE DECISION TO become a writer of fiction was made for me by fate. In 1914, in Panama, where I spent a week when I was a wireless operator on a little steamer that creaked up and down the Central American coast, I met an author who painted the joys of free-lancing so vividly that I could not resist the call. We were drunk. I was twenty. Since then, I have been trying to catch up with all of those joys he mentioned.

Starting to write stories in 1914 and, four years later selling my first one, marks up, I suppose, a very poor batting average. But in those years I was getting experience, seeing the world, and acquiring knowledge. I "punched brass" as a wireless operator all over the Pacific. I entered Columbia University in 1915, and one year later left because I didn't believe in higher learning. I still don't believe in it. I became a newspaper reporter, later a magazine editor.

Then came the war, which I won practically single-handed by writing high-pressure publicity to induce patriotic Americans to send books to Washington for camp libraries for soldiers and gobs. Books came by the carload, by the ton: McGuffy's readers, old almanacs, spellers, arithmetics, out-dated novels and just trash. The soldiers and sailors who read those books soon hated the war so bitterly, that they promptly got busy and ended it. That's how I won the war.

After the war, I wanted another look at China, and was sent

to the Far East by *Collier's* to write articles on China, the Philippines, India
and Malaya.

The first story I sold was written
while I was editing a motion picture
trade paper. It was bought by the
Argosy, and it was about a wolf named
Murg. Don't ask me why. In the inter-
vening years I have written millions of
words. Perhaps it is Murg who sits so
patiently at my door!

*George F.
Worts*

I started writing fiction under the
pen name of Loring Brent, because it would have annoyed the
owner of the motion picture magazine to learn that I was writing fiction out of hours. He thought I fell asleep at my desk
because I was working so hard for him! When my income from
fiction exceeded my salary, I quit the job. Since then I have been
free-lancing exclusively, except for a two-year period when I
lived in a Florida swamp town and added to my writing the
duties of postmaster, game warden and deputy sheriff. Out of
that experience came a long series of stories about a Florida
town I called Vingo.

I have enjoyed most writing stories about certain established
characters. Apparently the most popular of these have been the
Peter the Brazen, the Vingo and the Gillian Hazeltine stories. I
stopped writing about Peter the Brazen (a swashbuckling wireless operator on ships in the China run) about ten years ago.
He was, incidentally, the subject of the only novel I have had
published in America. I am now starting a new series about him.

When I am not traveling I live in Westport, Connecticut. My
interests are horses, sailing and flying. I took up flying about a
year ago to write some articles on how it feels to learn to fly, and
was badly bitten by the bug. I can make a three-point landing
about five times out of ten.

I like New York, but would prefer to live in Honolulu. I smoke sixty cigarettes a day. I like murder trials. I have never mastered the noble game of poker, although I once wrote a book about it. In my spare time I study law and medicine. I have two young sons and a still younger daughter; an able crew for my sailboat—except that there is usually mutiny aboard the lugger!

www.ingramcontent.com/pod-product-compliance
Lightning Source LLC
Chambersburg PA
CBHW030537030726
47495CB00004B/1031